Doggone It!

June Whyte

A Gumshoe Chicks Mystery
Book 3

White City
Press

Books by June Whyte

Sex on Tuesdays

THE GUMSHOE CHICK MYSTERY SERIES
Gone to the Dogs
For the Love of Dogs
Doggone It!

VETS 2U MYSTERY SERIES
Murder at Kangaroo Downs
Death at Dingo Creek
Homicide at Emu Lodge

KAT MCKINLEY GREYHOUND MYSTERIES
Chasing Can Be Murder
Muzzled
Hounded
Leashed

CHIANA RYAN CHILDREN'S MYSTERIES
The Case of the Disappearing Corpse
The Case of the Missing Dinosaur Egg

www.amazon.com/author/junewhytebooks

Doggone It!

✦✦✦✦✦✦✦✦✦✦✦✦✦✦✦✦✦✦✦✦✦✦✦✦✦✦

June Whyte

This edition published by White City Press
An imprint of Misti Media LLC
https://www.mistimedia.com
Available in both Paperback and eBook Editions
1 2 3 4 5 6 7 8 9 10
Text Copyright © June Whyte 2021
Paperback ISBN: 9781963479201
eBook ISBN: 9781963479096

'Doggone It!' is dedicated to YOLO, the sweetest greyhound in the world. We miss you more every day.

Acknowledgements

I'd like to acknowledge and thank those who have helped me on my writing journey. My beta readers, Nancy and Bev – couldn't do without you. You're my backbone, my flag wavers. Robyn, Wendy and June K – always there for me. I can whip off an email with a writing question and the answer will ping back with a smile. Cover artist, Annie Moril, who produced my latest amazing cover when only a week out of hospital. K.D. and Jay of *Untreed Reads* who've been with me since the start. And Traci Andrighetti, USA bestselling author of the *Franki Amato mysteries,* my inspirational guru.

1

As much as I loved my life, sometimes it felt like a car crash waiting to happen. So much to do and so little time…

Meat defrosting for tonight's barbecue? Check.

Kayla's fairy wand glued back together and drying on kitchen table? Check.

Advertisement sent to all new hydro-bath clients offering a free nail clip? Check.

My two 'Gumshoe Chick' besties babysitting Kayla the Cute and Jake the Joker so I can handle Penelope in the show ring? Check.

I let out a sigh and scratched behind my ever-patient greyhound, Penelope's right ear while watching the effervescent teenage-handler of a Bedlington terrier, young, carefree, so unaware of what hurdles lay ahead in life, set off around the show ring.

Today's dog show was our biggest event of the year. Being an active member of the Ladies Kennel Club, I'd spent the morning setting up show rings and organising coffee and sandwiches for the judges before actively taking part in the show itself.

Intent on presenting Penelope to her best advantage, I glanced down to make sure her back legs were exactly square, just as a flashy silver-backed dog brush skimmed my head and landed with a thud on the manicured grass, right under Penelope's nose.

I let out a startled gasp. Penelope didn't bat an eyelid. My unflappable black-and-white greyhound continued to stand proud, neck arched, body centred evenly over four strong legs. Miss Cool Calm and Collected, showing off her Best-in-Group assets in the line-up for Best in Show.

The irate, arm-waving men arguing on the other side of the show-ring fence directly behind me, however, were not so cool. In fact, the two poodle breeders, Stephen Channing, a bombastic bully, bedecked as always in gold chains and multi-coloured satins, and Chi, his normally sweet-natured partner, were becoming more and more heated by the second.

Hmm... trouble in Paradise?

While the winner of the Non-Sporting group, a twinkly eyed brown and white bulldog, huffed and puffed his way around the ring, I peeped over my shoulder, loath to miss a second of round two in the fight of the century.

Chi, angrier than I'd ever seen him, stabbed at the air with one finger. "And what about *my* feelings, Stephen?" Another poke. "It's *always* about *you*."

"For the last time, Chi, you're delusional. I did *not* wink at the guy with the cute beagle." Stephen, his face fire engine red, stamped one knee-high booted foot. "And stop *throwing* things. You almost hit me on the *nose* with that brush, and you know how *easily* I bruise."

"In that case, I'll try harder not to miss next time," snapped Chi, hands braced on hips as he glared up at his flamboyant lover.

I couldn't supress my grin. Go Chi! About time he stopped taking Stephen's poisonous gaff.

Eyes widening in feigned disbelief, Stephen took a step back and shook his head which set off an overload of clinking gold rings in nose, lips and ears. "My, oh my! What's got into *your* boxer shorts today?"

"Your temper-tantrums and your cruel insensitivity. *That's* what's got into my boxer shorts today." A sharp right cross came out of nowhere, luckily only glancing off Stephen's satin-clad arm. Chi winced, rubbed his fist and sniffed. "Sometimes you make me *so* mad,

I could…I could *kill* you." Shoulders slumped, Chi stomped off toward the brightly colored converted bus that transported their prize-winning poodles to the shows, week after week. "And I-I just can't take it anymore."

"Well, go live somewhere else, then!" sniped Stephen, throwing his arms around and crashing into a passing competitor, Corey Black, a meek little man in his mid-forties whose black miniature poodle rarely won a ribbon due to poor grooming – and the fact that the dog sometimes lay down and refused to move when asked by the judge to show his gaits. An occurrence that always sent Stephen Channing into a noisy and vicious bout of jeers and ridicule.

Corey, still off-balance from the unexpected collision, staggered head-first into one of the steel poles supporting the viewing platform. Blood oozed from a cut on his forehead. He clutched at the pole, swaying and blinking up at Stephen, who refused to even give him a sideways glance. Instead, the overbearing poodle breeder pouted, wriggled his booty and flounced along behind Chi, the clunky gold chains around his neck swinging with each step.

Chi spun around. "Why would *I* leave? It's *my* money that bought our property."

"Yes, but you put *Windswept Kennels* in *my* name…"

"Competitor number 38. Did you hear me?" The show judge, a tall thin bearded man in his mid-thirties, cleared his throat. He pointed at Penelope with a nod of his head, bringing me back to the task in hand. "Once more around the ring, please."

"Um…yes, of course."

Dodging Chi's sparkly dog brush, I set off, Penelope striding out beside me, my aim to show off her anatomically correct body and smooth gait to the bearded judge and thereby win the coveted and final event of the day – *Best in Show*.

Not only was Penelope the gentlest, most loving greyhound in the world, she also knew her job in the show ring. She powered along beside me, neck stretched, muscles moving smoothly, each toe pointed before touching down on the grass.

All I had to do was keep up with her.

As we rounded the corner near the kennelling area and began heading back toward the other six Best-in-Group finalists, I encountered distraction number two. Yikes! In one of the kennels, my adventurous twenty-month-old son, Jake, was attempting to fit his head inside the mouth of a large German Shephard – *Champion Grimshaw I'm the King of the Forest* to be precise.

Oh. My. God. Where were my friends, Abi and Molly? They were supposed to be babysitting Jake.

I slid to a halt – as did my heartbeat.

One – the dog didn't know my son from a bar of soap.

Two –a bowl of fresh kibble had been placed under the German Shepherd's nose by his owner, who'd walked away, oblivious to what was happening.

And three – was that dog eying Jake like a juicy steak, tossing up whether the delicacy on all fours currently kissing him on the nose might prove tastier than the dry kibble in his bowl?

Just as I was deliberating between whipping through the gate or taking a shortcut over the fence, Abi and Molly, all arms and legs and yelps and white horrified faces, appeared one each side of Jake. Ignoring his highly vocal opposition, they snatched him up in the air and transported him bodily away from the dog's gleaming teeth and into his stroller.

"Sorry, Dana," mouthed Abi pulling an apologetic face at me as Molly attempted to strap Jake into his stroller while dodging flailing arms and legs and resisting his roof-raising vexed howls of protest.

My two best friends, Abi Truelove, who owned an upmarket canine boutique called, *The Pampered Pooch* and Molly Gibson, a best-selling author of rather raunchy romance novels, may have been successful in business but not having any offspring of their own, hadn't realized exactly how slippery a determined twenty-month-old boy-child could be.

Why had Peter, my husband, who was supposed to look after Kayla and Jake on show day – at home – away from danger – forgotten it was his day for child minding and put his hand up to work this Saturday? He knew how wired I got when I had to not only handle Penelope in the show ring, but also keep tabs on our two munchkins under the age of four. Last time this happened, Jake and Kayla had somehow smuggled a prize-winning Shih Tzu into the back of our car and the irate owner came close to having me arrested for theft. I refused to let Peter near me for three weeks after that little debacle.

But some men were slow to learn.

I looked down at Penelope. Penelope looked up at me. And I swear she rolled her eyes before trotting me proudly back to the other six dogs in the Best-in-Show line-up.

"Everything okay?" The judge, a twinkle in his eyes, stood waiting for me.

"You got kids?"

The upturned lips transformed into a wide-open I-know-where-you're-coming-from grin. "Five."

I rolled my eyes. "You have my sympathy."

With a laugh, he turned away and moved slowly along the line of dogs until standing in front of a beautifully turned-out white Maltese terrier, complete with dark eyelashes and a pretty pink bow. The judge shook hands with the dog's owner. "Congratulations. Your dog is the best-coated Maltese I've seen in quite a while." And with that he accepted a tri-colored *Best in Show* sash from a nearby attendant and handed the ribbon to the dog's owner.

Immediately the runner-up in the toy group, a rat-sized smooth-coated chihuahua, entered the ring attached to his owner, a flamboyantly dressed senior citizen sporting a scarlet beret and matching scarf. They affixed themselves to the end of the line-up ready to show off their wares to the judge.

The bearded judge studied the newcomer, asked the senior citizen to trot her dog around the ring once then moved back down the line, pausing firstly at the wide chested bulldog and then the lamb-like Bedlington Terrier until finally coming to a halt in front of Penelope. I tensed, moved her right back leg a miniscule to the left and chucked her under the chin hoping she'd flaunt her beautifully arched neck. Statue-still, Penelope radiated class and good breeding.

Finally, the judge turned to the attendant tagging him and asked for the blue and white satin ribbon with *Runner up in Show* printed in gold lettering across the front. With a smile, he handed the ribbon to me. "Your greyhound bitch is a lovely correct specimen of the breed and has a temperament to match. Congratulations."

Unable to control my delight, I gave a whoop, waved the sash in the air and grinned at my support team, Molly and Abi, who were yelling themselves hoarse, Kayla, one fairy wing drooping as she leaned over the fence waving and calling out, and Jake, who'd been coerced out of his tears with a bar of chocolate. When he saw me waving, he giggled and hurled Doggo, his much-loved stuffed toy, over the fence into the show ring.

"Best in Show is Mr. Graham Smith's Maltese terrier, *Australian Champion Austral Friendly Fire* and Runner up is Ms. Dana Fox's greyhound, *Australian Champion Twinkletoes of Pettigrew*."

While Penelope cavorted along beside me, enjoying her moment of glory, I took off behind the ribbon-bedecked white Maltese terrier, for one final euphoric circuit of the show ring.

This was a first for Penelope and me and I intended to milk it to the max. Award-winning moments like this were what brought dog owners to shows week after week. Encouraged us to rise in the dark, get a load of washing on the line before daybreak, grumpy kids fed, even grumpier husbands out of bed, groom dogs until they shone and arrive at whatever showground was the pick of the week, just as the sun was stretching its golden rays.

I puffed out my chest, let off another whoop and threw my arms around my oh-so-adorable greyhound's neck. She was the star of the show, the Queen. I was merely her lady-in-waiting.

As I kissed Penelope on the nose and ruffled her soft ears for the umpteenth time, out of the corner of my eye I spotted Stephen Channing again. His pink satin shirt, tight-fitting white satin pants, glitter be-speckled boots and jewellery shop of clunky gold chains was hard not to miss. What was he up to now? One arm around the good-looking guy with the cute beagle, he leaned closer, laughing affectedly at something the other man was saying before taking a coy glance over his shoulder.

I looked around for Chi but couldn't see him at first. All I could see were tired competitors packing up after a long day at the show, eager to get home.

My eyes drifted across to the big rainbow-colored bus with *Windswept Kennels* emblazoned across both sides. And that's when I spotted Chi. The little poodle breeder was sitting hunched on a metal dog crate, shoulders slumped, hands dangling between his knees, a picture of misery.

He was watching Stephen laugh pretentiously at something his new friend said. And if looks could kill, both Stephen and Cute Beagle Guy would have been incinerated on the spot.

2

Show ring equipment is much easier to erect than it is to take down, reorganise, and pack away neatly.

"No, Jake." My voice cracked as I strained to keep my mummy-voice cool, calm and friendly, advice strongly advocated in, *'Rear Your Child Like a Hot-House Flower'*, the child-rearing bible all the Yummy Mummies at the local day care centre spouted reverently as though authored by God himself. And Tweeted, Facebooked, Instagramed and probably Tik-Toked. "Please don't put that steel peg in your mouth, darling, it could be sharp and cut your tongue off."

Where the freakin' heck was Peter?

He'd promised to pick up Jake and Kayla from the show as soon as he'd finished the meeting with his client. Supposedly, two hours ago. I ground my teeth together while imagining sinking them into my husband's right ear.

"Mummy, Jakey's done a poo." My three-and-a-half-year-old fairy, one wing wilting, long socks scrunched down around her ankles, came dancing across the grass, flapping her arms. "An' its running down his legs."

Ugh...

I packed the last of the steel post pegs back into their box before scooping up my stinky baby boy and heading for the bathroom. "Hey, Moll, keep an eye on Kayla, will you? I won't be more than five minutes."

"Luv Mumma." Jake's sloppy kisses wet my cheek as I shouldered the bathroom door open.

My heart melted. "How much?" I nosed him in the chest, making him laugh out loud.

"Thicks."

"Six? Wow! That's lots and lots."

His grip around my neck tightened as an even sloppier kiss landed on my nose.

Although promising to be the next intrepid Steve Irwin and giving me a near-heart attack at least three times a day, Jake was a cuddler. A cuddler whose big blue eyes got him out of at least ten scrapes a day.

After a nappy-change and a quick face-wipe to clean off the smeared chocolate decorating his face, it was back to work. Not only were rings to be dismantled but kennels disinfected for the following week's dog show. And where were all the Ladies Kennel Club members when there was work to be done? Already home with their feet up if my guess was correct. Many enjoyed the status of being a member when there were free drinks and food on offer, but when it came to actual manual labour, enthusiasm faded like a stunted squib on fireworks night.

A heap of show-competitor numbers spilling every which way had been dumped haphazardly, much like the fish John West rejects, into the middle of Ring 2. Next job on our list – sort and bag. After we'd arranged the numbers into four piles of thirty, Molly held the corners of the first bag open while I tossed numbers 1-30 into its depths and was tying twine around the top of the bag when Cute Beagle guy, toting a navy-blue gym bag, hair tousled sexily, a frown marring his perfectly chiselled Chris Hemsworth look-alike face – right down to the cultivated unruly lock of hair that tumbled onto his forehead – rocked up beside us.

Being a huge fan of Thor, I couldn't help checking out the guy's assets. With assets like his, who wouldn't? He was relatively new to the show scene, having started up *Starling Beagle Kennels* a little over three months ago. His dogs were doing okay at the shows – as was he with his love life. That's if you could believe the gossip of the female competitors who flirted outrageously and hung on his every word.

"Hi, ladies. Anyone seen Stephen Channing?"

Molly shook her head while I gave a loud sniff in the negative. Why was God's Gift to Women hanging around with bolshie Stephen Channing?

He ran a hand through his hair then did several knuckle cracks, making sure the muscles in his arms rippled with each crack. "I had an appointment with him half an hour ago, but he didn't show up."

Abi, who'd been wiping kennels down nearby, spasmodically assisted by Kayla and Jake, dropped her sanitised cloth and scooted across the ring to join us. She passed a smoothing hand over her hair, straightened her top and grinned up at Cute Beagle guy, all big eyes and sparkling teeth. "Hey, Rick, thought you'd have gone home by now."

"Been hanging around waiting for Stephen Channing," he said, swinging his gym bag with *Shape Up Fitness Center* emblazoned across the front, over his shoulder. "You know, the poodle breeder. Said he had a proposition for me."

Abi dimpled and raised that one eyebrow that she does she well. "Proposition?"

Rick – aka Cute Beagle guy – aka Thor – chuckled. "Steve has this amazing website advertising his kennels, you know, all bells and whistles, and I learned today that he set it up himself. Anyway, I asked if he could create a website for my kennels and he said we'd talk it over after the show." He shrugged one shoulder. "Must have forgotten, because he was a no show."

I passed Kayla, who'd followed Abi, two packets of juice from my bag, indicating one was for her brother, then turned back to Rick, resisting the urge to scrunch up a little of his well-fitting navy tee-shirt and check out the muscles residing beneath. You know, to see if they were anywhere near as good as Thor's. "Have you tried their bus? Steve's probably with Chi helping to load the dogs and all their gear. If the bus has gone, so has Stephen."

"Already done that. Bus is still there but neither Steve nor Chi are nearby." He shrugged one powerful shoulder, did a couple of neck crunches. "Guess I'll leave it for now. I can always ring him tomorrow and make another appointment." He winked at Abi who acknowledged the wink with a grin that almost burst off her face. "I'm off home now. See ya later, girls."

Swinging his hips, he jogged off, all man.

After ogling his cute backside until he was completely out of sight, Molly and I both turned to Abi.

"What was that all about?" I asked. "He *winked* at you."

"And you know each other's names," added Molly, eyebrows shooting up towards her fringe. "What about Nathan?"

Abi rolled her eyes. "I met the guy a couple of years ago at a birthday party for one of my ex's friends, okay? And hey, just because I'm in a relationship with Nathan, doesn't mean I can't *look* at cute guys. You'd have to be blind not to look at that one."

I thought of the aristocratic nose, the thick tousled hair, the cheeky wink, the well-toned muscles, the come-hither grin and nodded. "Or dead."

Another half hour passed. A long half hour. In between packing up competitor's numbers, sweeping the three show rings and rescuing Jake from nose-diving off a platform, I kept scowling down at my watch.

Where the heck was Peter?

"Daddy! Daddy!" I spun around to see Kayla, squealing and flapping her arms as she dashed across the tarmac towards her father.

My husband, Peter, the man who was destined to sleep on the couch tonight, had finally arrived.

He swung Kayla up in his arms before turning to me. "Sorry, darling, when my client left, I got caught up with some guys at the Hilton and it would have been rude not to have joined them. They were past clients and it's always good business to keep all avenues open."

Geez, you'd have thought Peter was a high-profile lawyer instead of a car salesman.

Instead of answering, I thrust Kayla's backpack at him, and almost took out his left foot with Jake's pusher.

He looped the backpack over the handles of the pusher, wriggled Kayla into a more comfortable position and reached for me, planting a kiss on my nose. "And I love you too."

"You were due here two hours ago."

"I know and I said I'm sorry." He lifted my chin with one finger, and kissed me again. "I'll make it up to you, babe. I promise."

I looked into those big blue eyes, so like his beguiling son's, and sighed.

Why is it that men still believe their life is more important than a woman's? Surely, we've progressed further than aspiring to be a man's arm ornament; our job to look attractive, take care of the kids and house, and to be seen and not heard – or was that last one related to children?

Whatever. I sighed again. Well, not this woman.

"Jake will be ready for a nap when you get home and I'll probably be another hour. Still a bit to finish up here yet."

Turning my back on those persuasively charming big blues, I grabbed the four bags of competitors' numbers and stomped my way across to the secretary's office. If Peter didn't start pulling his weight more around the house, he'd find his pillow, his pyjamas and a blanket with his name on it permanently decorating the couch.

As I pushed the door of the secretary's office open, I spotted two other Ladies Kennel Club members, both poodle breeders, in a heated discussion. One was filing today's judges' cards away, the other sweeping the floor.

"No good trying to dissuade me, Debra, first thing in the morning, I intend to file a complaint against that man with the South Australian Canine Association. He's a disgrace to the breed and if he gets disbarred and can't show his dogs, I certainly won't lose any sleep over it." Bec Middleton, a long-time member of the Club, her dark hair now peppered with gray, looked ready to set a bomb off first and ask questions later.

The other woman, sweet face, late-fifties, slightly stooped shoulders, stopped sweeping the floor and leant on her broom. "But what about Chi?" she asked, her voice soft. "He's a doll. Only last week, when I had trouble whelping in the middle of the night and couldn't get hold of the vet, I rang Chi and he came straight over. I'd have lost at least two of my puppies if it hadn't been for him. Just because his partner is so rude and arrogant, it's not fair to penalise Chi too."

"Chi can still show the dogs."

"But he's not the handler, is he? You know what Chi's like, too shy to handle dogs in the ring. Stephen is the showman."

"Well, I can't help that. Channing needs to be taught a lesson. Did you hear him screaming at the judge in my Puppy class this morning? He was throwing his weight around and demanding to know how she could possibly justify putting a badly conformed specimen like mine over his flawlessly correct entrant? The man's out of control."

The other woman shrugged.

"He spoke so loudly the competitors in the ring on the other side of the grounds would have heard him. Made me feel two inches tall." She peered across at me, still standing by the door. "What about you, Dana? Did you hear Stephen Channing having a meltdown in the Standard Poodle Puppy class earlier today?"

Reluctant to get involved, I shook my head. Stephen Channing was always in the middle of a meltdown. In fact, he'd turned meltdowns into an extreme sport worthy of entry in the Olympics. "No, sorry." I held the bag up. "The competitors' numbers? Where would you like me to put them?"

"Oh, thank you, dear," said Debra with a sweet smile. "That's kind of you to bring the numbers back. Just leave the bag on the table by the door. When I've finished sweeping, I'll sort through them before storing the bag in the cupboard ready for next week."

Leaving the two women to continue their debate, I closed the office door behind me and scanned the eerily silent, almost empty showgrounds – so different to the excitement and the buzz and energy of only half an hour ago. Competitors had packed up and gone home leaving less than a dozen members, like us, to help clean up ready for next week's show.

I peered across to where the *Windswept Kennels* bus normally parked. The colorful vehicle was still there but neither owner was in sight. Which was strange. They rarely left their valuable dogs unattended at a show. Even stranger, the crated dogs were still sitting outside the bus along with grooming tables and other equipment. Stephen and Chi hadn't started to pack up yet.

Which made me think. How far had their relationship deteriorated since their very public quarrel this morning? Were they off somewhere throwing more heated words and sparkly brushes at each other? Or had they made up and gone off for a quick cuppa before starting the backbreaking job of loading the crates full of dogs back up into the bus?

I'd known Stephen Channing for a year and a half now and he hadn't always been quite so foul-mouthed and offensive, hurting people with his barbed comments – even likening a rather plain woman to having a face like a lump of dough. Okay, he'd always been a little prickly, but his personality took a drastic nosedive around the beginning of this year, suddenly, when, for no apparent reason, he became not only rude and arrogant, but quite cruel in the way he belittled people, not caring a jot for the other person's feelings. Like, a few months back, when we *Chicks* were investigating a fellow show competitor's murder, we even had him down as a suspect because he'd called her a bitch, a conniving little tart, and threatened her.

All this made me wonder what had happened to change him so drastically. It couldn't be his love life, because Chi – although I couldn't fathom out why – seemed just as besotted as the first day they met, which, I guess, was a testimonial to the saying, 'love is blind'. A tragedy? Drugs? A medical problem? Whatever, the man was a pain in the backside and although successful in his quest to breed exquisite poodles was a dismal failure as a human being.

Curious as to why the *Windswept* dogs were still sitting outside in their crates instead of inside their transport, I wandered across the tarmac toward the agitated poodles. Maybe Stephen had stormed off in another snit and Chi was seeking help to lift the crated dogs up into the converted bus.

Nah. Something was off about the scene. Neither of these guys would neglect their dogs. No matter what. A band of maggoty zombies could swarm the showgrounds, arms outstretched and teeth bloody, but rescuing their dogs would still be their first priority. Chi even baked illegal marihuana cookies and distributed them to their senior dogs in a quest to alleviate arthritic pain and make the retirees happier and more comfortable.

In a crate parked closest to the vehicle, *Windswept Fly-By-Me*, a distinguished show winner and prolific producing stud dog, emitted a high-pitched bark when he saw me approaching. Upping the level of his barking and whining, he began digging up the paper in his crate, his eyes never leaving the bus. I frowned. The apricot poodle was normally a model of serenity. Always proud and unruffled. Nothing rattled him.

Until now.

Maybe he was merely tired, hungry, and eager to go home, couldn't work out why his owners were taking so long to transfer him to the bus, out of the cold wind.

Or maybe he was trying to tell me something…

I let out a long-drawn-out breath.

Not my business. I had chores to finish off here at the show and a house and family to get home to myself. Instead, I bent down, told the poodle in a soothing sing-song voice that Chi and Stephen wouldn't be long, that he needed to be patient.

However, the moment I stood up and went to move away, the dog's barking became more frantic. Eyes wild, he bit at the wire, shaking it with his teeth, butting his head against the crate and then he let out a mournful howl that sent ice chips skittering along my bloodstream.

Oh. My. God. Was the dog trying to tell me something was wrong? But…what?

Teeth clenched, I forced myself to turn around and take a long hard look at the bus.

No, I'm being stupid, I told myself, letting my eyes wander from front to back and top to bottom. *This wasn't a premonition, a sign of trouble – the spoiled poodle was merely acting up because he was cold and tired of lying in his crate. The dog was a diva not a psychic.*

I half closed my eyes and squinted at the vehicle. From where I was standing nothing appeared amiss, but maybe I should take a closer look, a quick one – just to satisfy my curiosity.

Not wanting to be caught snooping by either Chi or Stephen, I quickened my pace, scooted around the perimeter of the converted vehicle, checked underneath, peeked through the one and only miniscule front window, but found nothing to cause uneasiness.

The dog was definitely a diva.

With a sigh of relief, I turned away, ready to hurry back to my friends and finish cleaning up so I could go home and step into a warm refreshing shower, when I heard a whimper, a sort of strangled moan coming from inside the bus.

Someone or something in trouble…

"Who's in there?"

Silence.

"Is that you Stephen? Chi? Anyone?"

More silence.

"Whoever you are…I'm coming in."

Snatching a fortifying breath, I darted around to the rear of the bus, grabbed hold of both handles and threw open the doors.

And immediately wished I hadn't.

Cold sweat beaded across my forehead causing the stale hot dog with tomato sauce and mustard I'd eaten five hours ago to churn in my stomach like a cement mixer on high. My head spun. My legs, no sturdier than over-cooked spaghetti, didn't want to hold me up.

Maybe if I closed my eyes and counted to five, when I opened them again, I'd find the scene inside the bus merely an illusion.

One. Two. Three. Four. Five...

Nope. Chi was still staring at me, brown eyes wide and frozen, a keening animal-like sound radiating from this throat. The knife in his hand still dripped blood. And his partner, Stephen Channing, the love of his life, was still sprawled on the floor of the bus, arms lolling, mouth open, his pale pink satin show shirt now crimson with blood.

And he was still horribly, awfully, dead.

3

An hour and a half later, I slumped in one of Abi's kitchen chairs, the sharp rim digging into the back of my legs.

My greyhound's head lay heavy in my lap, her worried eyes never leaving my face, while Abi's long-nosed dachshund and Molly's bouncy fox terrier wriggled and whined at my feet. Obviously perplexed by my lack of response.

Their high-pitched barks on the periphery of my mind, I continued to sit and stare at the kitchen floor. But I didn't see the gray and blue square of carpet that I'd bought Abi last Christmas with the small scuff marks made by sharp doggy claws. I didn't see the tiny lemon flowers scattered across the blue and gray texture of the carpet. All I could see was Chi's devastated face as he'd lifted his head and stared bleakly back at me when I threw open the rear doors of the bus.

Although he held the murder weapon in his hand, Chi could not have been the perpetrator of the crime. I'd never seen a man so shattered, so utterly destroyed, his heart in a million pieces, as I watched him return his gaze to the lifeless body of his lover, then lean forward and gently close both Stephen's wide unseeing eyes.

When the police came to arrest him, Chi refused to leave Stephen's side. Three flat-faced, burly cops surrounded him; their chins tipped forward to accentuate their authority. And then a fourth dived in, quick-legged, handcuffs at the ready.

Finally, they dragged him, wailing, from the bus, away from Stephen's body, away from the scene of the crime and into the back seat of a waiting police car. Bowed, beaten and desolate.

I doubted if even the astute Detective Lightfoot would be able to break through Chi's protective shield and find out what really happened.

"You okay, Dana?" It was Molly, one arm around my shoulders.

"Want me to add a dollop of brandy to your coffee?" Abi knelt on the floor between the anxious dogs and took my hands in hers. "Or do you want me to ring Peter, ask him to come get you?"

I shook my head, dispelling the last of the fug-like mist. "No, no, I'm fine. Peter has his hands full with Kayla and Jake and-and I don't want them to see me like this."

"Fair enough."

Looking into Abi's concerned eyes, I squeezed her hand. "You know how it feels, Abs. When you found Petra's body in the lane at the back of the *Pussycat Parlour*, you went to pieces." I shifted my gaze to Molly whose arm was still draped across my shoulders. "And I remember you drinking yourself into oblivion after finding Harry's body in the dog trailer. But I thought I was the strong *Gumshoe Chick*. You know, the one who can cope with whatever life throws at her. After all, I've given birth twice, while you two start sweating if I mention the word *womb* in your presence." I let out a sigh. "So, for some crazy and utterly inexplicable reason, I thought seeing a guy I knew with his life essence drained, gone forever, I wouldn't fall apart." I sniffed, shook my head. "But, of course, I was wrong."

Abi squeezed my hand again. "So, I guess that means you're only a Supergirl knockoff after all."

Molly squeezed my shoulder. "Or a Buffy wannabe."

"In that case," I said, love for these two wonderful friends making me sniff. "Another coffee wouldn't go astray. In fact, why not make it half coffee, half brandy? Might be enough to restart my brain cells."

"Or blast your head right off your shoulders." Abi stood up and crossed the room to her new espresso machine sitting in pride of place on the kitchen counter.

I let out a laugh and immediately felt better for it. "Look, I'll admit, I was in shock, but I'm okay now and I'm ready to start investigating."

"Investigating?" bleated Molly, snagging first a glass and then a bottle of wine. "Again?"

Abi selected a clean coffee mug from her cupboard. "Which means you don't think Chi stabbed Stephen to death, even though he was kneeling beside the body and the murder weapon was in his hand."

"Chi isn't a killer. He loved Stephen."

"Jails are full of people who kill their lovers in anger, or jealousy, or because they're going to leave them. And you heard Chi threaten to kill Stephen when the two of them were arguing."

"Just words. You weren't there when I opened the back door of the bus. You didn't see Chi's face. He was a broken man. The only words he said to me were, 'Dana, please, find out who did this.'" I took a sip of the doctored espresso and felt a ping in the synapses leading to my brain. "Anyway, we need to find the real killer so Chi can come home and look after his dogs. While he's in prison, all the *Windswept* poodles are in limbo. Confused and distressed."

Our eyes automatically zeroed in on the stunning apricot standard poodle stretched out on Abi's sofa. Head resting on a pillow, long legs dangling over the edge, he was snoring softly. Neither *distressed* nor *confused* were words I'd use to describe him. Of course, when the police were arranging for the *Windswept Kennels* show dogs to be taken away and cared for by the local RSPCA, Abi had snaffled *Fly-By-Me* from his crate and settled him in the back of her van to bring home. No way was she letting Stephen and Chi's beloved top show and stud dog spend even one night in the Rescue kennels. Not while she had a warm house, a freezer full of dog food and a comfortable lounge for him to doss down on.

Typical Abi.

Molly pointed her full glass of wine at me. "You can't blame the police for charging Chi with Stephen's murder. One – he was the only person in the bus with Stephen, two – the bloody knife was in his hand, and three – lots of people witnessed their full-on argument earlier in the day."

"All good points, Moll." I nodded. My shy romance author friend had blossomed as a sleuth during our last case.

Abi took a sip of her coffee and frowned. "So, if it's not Chi, who else could it be?"

I laughed. "Come on, Abs, how many feathers has Stephen ruffled in the show world? One hundred? Two hundred? Heck, there's a list of competitors as long as the Strzelecki track who he's upset over the last year with his bullying and cruel words."

"But why now? Why specifically on *this* day? There has to be a reason."

Molly skulled half her glass of wine before placing the glass on the table and leaning forward. "And who kills a man because he calls them 'a tub of lard' or says their dog has 'cauliflower ears'?" She shrugged one shoulder and pulled a face. "Heck, we all know what Stephen's like – *was* like – and we merely shrugged our shoulders and accepted that was just Stephen's way."

"Maybe he went too far with his bullying this time and the murderer snapped."

"But if it was a spur of the moment act, wouldn't the perpetrator just punch him out? Kick him in the gonads? If it wasn't premeditated – why would they be carrying a knife?"

Abi and I stared thoughtfully at our coffee. Molly's question was something to chew on. She was right – who carries a lethal weapon in their backpack at a dog show unless they planned on using it? Or was the knife already in the bus?

Molly glugged down the remainder of her wine, let out a loud burp and, pleased with her logic, slumped back in her chair and closed her eyes. This was her first glass of wine for the evening – one more and she'd be asleep.

"What about Rick?" I placed my coffee cup back on the table. "Our cute Beagle guy *was* hanging around after the show finished."

"But where's the motive?" Abi smoothed a hand over her sleeping dachshund's ears. After getting little response from me, Chloe had given up and jumped onto her owner's lap where she'd turned in a tight circle, let out a contented sigh, and promptly closed her eyes. "You don't kill a person because they forget to show up for an appointment."

Molly opened one eye and trained it on Abi. "Maybe there was more to it than that. Maybe Rick was lying about asking Stephen to design a website for him. Stephen could have been blackmailing Rick?"

"*Blackmailing Rick?*" Abi laughed. "Molly, this isn't a book you're plotting, it's real life."

"I don't *plot* – I *pants*. And I write *romance* – not *mystery*."

Abi grinned at Molly's fierce frown and dropped bottom lip. "Just teasing."

"But Molly's right," I put in hoping I wasn't fuelling the fire. "It wouldn't hurt to ask Nathan to check on Rick. You know, court history, business interests, associates, financial problems. Who knows what secrets are hiding in his past?"

Nathan Forrester was not only Abi's smart, hot, and caring lover, but a successful private investigator who came in handy when we needed background checks on our suspects.

The headlights of a car lit up the kitchen window and came to a stop outside on Abi's driveway. Surely not the police. I'd already answered a grocery-list of questions at the dog show. If my two best friends hadn't rescued me, insisting that I was in shock and needed to rest, I'd probably still be there becoming more and more distressed.

A light knock sounded on the front door. Immediately Chloe, Busta, Penelope and even the snoozing poodle woke up and beat Abi to the door.

It was my husband, Peter. I could see him just inside the doorway, hear him talking softly to Abi, while unconsciously ruffling Penelope's ears and tickling Chloe under the chin.

Inexplicably, tears threatened, just at the sight of my other half. My soulmate. The guy I'd loved and declared I'd marry way back when we were both in eighth grade at Woodville High School. All thoughts of his latest slackness in helping-around-the-house dissipated.

Peter, concern written across his face, hurried toward me, both arms outstretched. I moved into their comfort, snuggling into his chest, a sigh pulling at my lips.

"You okay, Shooter?" he whispered, using the nickname he'd come up with years ago when I'd used my excess energy to shoot winning goals in the school basketball team. Now, I used that same excess energy to run a mobile doggy-wash and chase after our two exuberant offspring.

"Mmm."

His arms tightened, hefting me up against his chest where he could easily drop a kiss on the top of my head. "I came as soon as I could."

"What about–?"

"The kids are with my mum. They're having a sleepover tonight, complete with four bedtime stories that Kayla made sure she slipped into her backpack together with her fairy wand."

I kissed him on the lips and snuggled closer, the familiar smell of his Jimmy Choo aftershave, patchouli, suede, pink pepper, and honeydew, calming me down. "Thanks, Pete. I'm glad you're here."

Abi stretched up and snaffled an extra-large King Presley mug from her top cupboard. "Hey, what do you think of my new coffee maker? On sale last week at Harvey Normans for 50% off. Absolute steal."

"Umm…" Peter blinked in the direction of the coffee maker.

Abi placed the King Presley mug beside the bubbling machine and continued her spiel. "So, are you game to try my *Abigail Truelove* special?"

"Umm…" Peter blinked again.

"You'll love it," Abi assured him. "It's an eye-watering double espresso."

Molly growled and shook her head. "Say no, Pete. Abi's double espressos are so potent the hairs on your chest will run screaming to the nearest Safe House and hide in the basement." She held up the wine bottle. "Have a glass of this and chill out – like me."

"As tempting as that sounds, Molly, I'd better stick to coffee. I'm driving." He dragged a chair up to the table, made himself comfortable before turning back to me. "So, what do the *Gumshoe Chicks* think about this latest murder?"

I couldn't suppress a chuckle. Peter might annoy me by forgetting to put the bins out on bin night, but he was always supportive of my life choices. "Actually, we were discussing possible suspects when you pulled up."

"What? You don't think it was '*Chi, with a knife, in the bus*'?"

"We're still debating that one." Abi carefully placed a full mug of coffee on the table in front of Peter. "Dana says a definite no, but Molly and I aren't totally convinced. We're at the stage of trying to work out if it wasn't Chi, who, out of a conga-line of Stephen-hating suspects, finally decided they'd had enough of his poisonous tongue."

"At the moment, it's looking like a lucky dip," added Molly carefully pouring her second glass of wine. If she didn't call 'time' after this one, she'd be spending the night on Abi's sofa, again.

Peter took a sip of coffee, blinked twice and then frowned. "Come to think of it, I did see something a bit odd today. It was while I was strapping Kayla and Jake into their car safety seats in the showgrounds car park."

We all spun to look at him.

"It was just a woman slinking out of the showgrounds. But it seemed like she didn't want to be seen."

"What did she look like?"

"I was a bit busy trying to settle Kayla down at the time. She'd left one of her fairy wings inside the showgrounds and it was taking some serious diplomacy on my part to convince her Mummy would see it and bring the fairy wing home with her." He took another sip of coffee, swallowed, then surreptitiously wiped his eyes. "All I remember is the woman was tall. Sort of looking over her shoulder and hunching down as she walked. In a bit of a hurry."

"Young or old?"

"Umm…not much good at telling ages. Mid-thirties, I guess."

"What was she wearing?"

"Umm…something greenish. Dress, I think. And she had long blonde hair done in a sort of plait that reached all the way down her back. Quite unusual."

"And then what did she do?"

"Well, after she almost tripped over her own feet due to looking over her shoulder instead of where she was going, she got into this old white Holden sedan and drove out of the car park."

"Did you get the number plate?"

"Number plate?" Peter laughed. "Abi, it's easy to tell you've never had to deal with a little girl who's lost her fairy wing, plus a toddler who's vomiting orange fruit juice all over the back seat of your car."

Abi's face screwed up into a look of horror. The typical single, no-children-in-the-mix-yet expression. "Orange juice? Ugh!"

"Hmm…" I said, thoughtfully swirling a spoon in my by-now, cold coffee, while hoping Peter had cleaned up the mess on the back seat and not left it for me. "A highly furtive woman in her mid-thirties, seen running from the showgrounds about ten minutes before I discovered Chi cradling Stephen's dead body in the back of their bus."

I let my speculative gaze fall on each of the *Chicks* in turn. "Clue or red herring?"

4

The trauma of finding a blood-splattered murder victim didn't get me out of going to work the following day. It was Monday morning, and I had a fully booked list of clients, all booked in for a warm relaxing shampoo, to have their nails clipped, ears and eyes cleaned and to smell like the Chelsea Flower Show.

During the night, in between short restless naps, I'd played the scenario over and over in my head. Forced myself to picture the crime scene, the area outside the bus, inside the bus, anyone I'd seen hanging around or darting away when I was walking toward the bus...

And I'd come up with nada.

All I could think of was poor Chi languishing in a cell at the police station, shattered over the death of his beloved Stephen. Didn't matter that most people thought Stephen was an obnoxious pain in the butt, to Chi he could do nothing wrong. Until yesterday. I'd never seen him so upset as he was when arguing outside the show ring. Chi, a placid Asian-Australian was always smiling, always ready to help his fellow competitor, always attempting to deflect his lover's barbs away from their intended victim.

So, what happened to get the little guy so mad he threw not only a brush, but his fist at Stephen, even if it did only glance off his arm? Was I wrong about Chi? Could the fight have escalated later in the day, until Chi snapped, drew out a knife and stabbed him?

No, not possible. Not Chi. Not after seeing how broken he was when I yanked open the back doors of the bus and found him kneeling beside Stephen's body. Poor Chi must have found Stephen covered in blood, eased the knife out of his chest thinking it would help, then realized there was nothing he could do because his lover was already dead.

Which is where I came in.

I sighed, forced myself to concentrate on the road and the traffic around me. I still had to drop the two Munchkins off at day care, it was already 8.00am, and my first *Hydro Hound* client, Ellie Beeswax's adorable black Labrador, was due for his make-over at 8.30am – on the other side of town. Barney, the Labrador, enjoyed his shampoo and blow dry so much by the time I finished, my face would be devoid of make-up, all licked off by the lovable long-tongued dog.

I glanced at the clock on the dashboard. Damn. 8.05. I was *so* going to be late.

Okay, don't panic...

When you reach Baby Bunting's, slap on your, 'don't-talk-to-me or I'll bite your head off' face, dodge the Yummy Mummy posse, drop the kids off, and get straight back into the car.

Easy peasy...

Slowing down, I manoeuvred the *Hydro Hound* outfit into a parking space between a whopping big SUV, so new, I wouldn't be surprised if it still had the price tag attached, and a tiny red bubble car not much larger than the toy car Jake drove around the backyard, and turned off the engine. Diving out of the van, I checked the surroundings – *not a Yummy Mummy in sight* – so I quickly proceeded to extricate the two littlest Foxes from their car seats.

"Where Doggo?" Jake's bottom lip began to quiver.

"Mummy got." I closed my eyes. Wow, great vocabulary, Dana. The joys of conversing, day in, day out, with two little munchkins under the age of four.

To cut Jake's tears off at the pass, I rummaged deep into my tote and dragged his battered stuffed dog out by its half-a-tail, before scooping my baby boy up over my shoulder and snagging Kayla's hand so she couldn't dart off on those hundred-dollar sparkly sneakers she'd insisted she couldn't live without.

I checked my surroundings again.

All clear. Except for the two large brightly-colored wooden baby motifs mounted on the front fence and the even larger sign: 'BABY BUNTING DAY CARE CENTER – where *your* jewel is the center of *our* crown.'

"Here, sweetie." I handed Kayla her newly glued-together magic wand before she could start asking for it.

The biggest trick to conquering motherhood – anticipate!

"Thanks, Mummy." I was rewarded with one of my daughter's beatific smiles which highlighted her adorably kissable dimples. "My fairy wand's all better now."

We'd almost made it to *Baby Bunting's* front gate, when out of nowhere, Twitchy Tania Turner, the germophobic member of the Yummy Mummy gang, accosted me. She was known for not only carrying a giant bottle of sanitizer in her bag, but for using it to spray everything in her path, including animals and humans.

"Don't touch that gate!" she screeched, so loudly, I jumped back, expecting sparks to fly from the metal latch.

Panting, she slid to a stop beside me, dust rising in her wake. "Did you douse yourself in disinfectant?"

I shot her one of my super-charged scowls. The one I kept mainly for muggers and other irritants. "Forget to take your morning medication, Tania?"

This woman, always dressed from head to toe in eye-dazzling white, was becoming whackier every day. I'd heard on the grape vine she visited a therapist three times a week and couldn't help wondering if her therapist needed to visit her own counsellor afterwards.

"Did you cleanse your body before coming here today?" Sanitizer spray in hand, Tania forced herself between me and the gate and stood, legs wide, spray at the ready. Cerberus guarding the Gates of the

Underworld. "I heard you grabbed the knife from the killer and stabbed that poor dead man ten times before the police pulled you away, and I refuse to let you contaminate my darling Myron, with your dead-man cooties. My son has an IQ that's only equalled by top professors at the University."

"More like top ball-boys at the local tennis center." Patricia Stamford of the *Canberra* Stamford's, self-made Queen of the *Yummy Mummy Mafia*, her expensive *Chanel No. 5* perfume preceding her, had decided to join our little huddle. And judging by that caustic comment, Twitching Tania might soon be dispatched to scrubland instead of the perfectly manicured environs of the Yummy Mummy establishment.

Not waiting for the Queen Bee to dip her feelers into my business any further, I shook my head at Tania. "Where did you hear that rubbish? From a daily comic strip?"

Head high, nose tilted as though smelling something the cat might have dragged in from a nearby dumpster, Patricia nodded in Tania's direction. "Leave us, please, Tania. I wish to speak with Dana. In private." The voice was smooth, ultra-polite, with a slice of diamond-hard ice deep in the center. When Tania didn't instantly comply by somersaulting into the distance, Patricia continued, her voice now sharp with warning. "Or I'll spread it around that I saw you drinking a McDonald's chocolate thick shake *and* there was also a packet of their ghastly 'fries' in the mix."

Tania's face blanched, her hands fluttered like a helpless bird as she backed away from the gate, stuttering something incoherent about the devil on her shoulder.

"Now," said Patricia, always one to round her vowels and show off her expensive private school education. "I have a proposition for you, Dana."

"You do?" I almost told her where to stick her proposition and how many times to stir it, but I was intrigued. What was the woman was up to? In the past, the only times Patricia Stamford deigned to speak to me was to ridicule, set me up, or create problems between me and the manager of *Baby Bunting*.

"This murdered man, Stephen Channing. A very unpleasant creature I'm led to believe. However, I may have some information to help with your murder investigation."

"And why would you do that?"

"As I said, I have a proposition for you."

My two munchkins were getting restless so I opened the gate and made my way along the path toward the main building, Jake singing some unintelligible ditty to Doggo while Kayla skipped along beside me.

Patricia tagged along, her regal stance making it difficult for her to keep up with the running-late Fox family.

Once inside the doorway, I watched Jake toddle off in the direction of the sand pit, his cute little derriere wobbling from side to side as he ran. Kayla headed for her favourite nook, the doll's dress-up area, where she was greeted with a big hug from her best friend, Prada. Then, after assuring the Manager, Mrs. Tyler, who spoke to mothers in the same voice as she addressed her under-five-year-old clients, that I'd return on the dot of 4.00pm to pick up my children, I re-joined Patricia outside.

"Where's your boy, Noble, today?" I asked. "I didn't see him in the play room with the others."

"His Nanny has taken him for piano lessons."

"But he's only two-and-a-half years old."

"And your point is?" She frowned but due to an over-supply of Botox, nothing much happened.

I shook my head, gave up. "Okay, well, why are *you* here?"

"I came to see you."

I rolled my eyes. "Me?"

"There's something I want you to do for me."

My mouth gaped like a thirsty goldfish. Was this woman for real? She'd treated me like the backside of a cow for the past two years and now had the cheek to ask for my help?

"Let's go for a coffee," Patricia continued, completely impervious to my bottled anger. "I'm not comfortable talking here. Too many spies."

I glanced around at our normal everyday surroundings. *Spies?* Had the FBI recently installed hidden cameras behind the wooden baby motifs mounted on the front fence? Were those two homeless guys currently squabbling over a cigarette butt one found in the gutter, actually undercover agents checking that *Baby Buntings* wasn't a front for illegal gambling?

"Sorry, Patricia," I said and blew out a sigh, "but unlike you, I have to work, and I'm running late. If you have something to say, walk back to the car with me and just spit it out."

She took a deep breath, had another quick look over her shoulder as she followed me to the gate. "I think my Edward is cheating on me."

"And?"

"I don't wish to employ a private detective. Too tempting to pass the information on to the press, make themselves a lucrative deal. Which is why I want to employ you and the other two members of your investigative team to follow my husband, place him under surveillance, catch him in the act."

I stopped, spun inwards to face her. This woman, with the condescending arrogance of the ultra-rich, was freaking unbelievable. "And why would we do that, Patricia?"

"Because I have information which will facilitate your present case." She paused, flashed her expensively cared for pearly whites before continuing. "I know who killed Stephen Channing."

5

Twenty minutes later I parked in the driveway of a conventional cream brick suburban home, complete with front lawn and neatly pruned red, white and yellow rose bushes. Still trying to come to terms with Patricia's latest revelation, I scrambled out of the car and, going to the rear of *Hydro Hound*, my doggy beauty parlour on wheels, I carefully let down the ramp and ambled inside.

Why, what, and *how-the-hell* did the Queen Bee of the *Yummy Mummies* know anything about Stephen Channing's murder – a poodle-breeder – a man so far outside her circle of friends he may as well live in Siberia?

This conundrum had been churning around in my head, driving me crazy, ever since I'd left *Baby Buntings*. At the time, I was unable to follow through with questions due to running late for work, plus, agreeing to track her cheating husband in return for information wasn't a decision for me alone to decide. All I could do was set up a meeting at 2.30 this afternoon, between Patricia, myself, and the other two *Chicks*, at our usual headquarters, *Pampered Pooch,* Abi's one-of-a-kind exclusive doggy boutique inherited from her Aunt Tilly, who'd died of a heart attack while kayaking in the North of Queensland.

"Morning, Dana. Barney's all ready for you." It was petite Ellie Beeswax, on one end of a tartan dog lead while on the other end was a grinning black Labrador whose tail was wagging like a windscreen wiper on a rainy day.

"Sorry I'm a few minutes late, Ellie. Got held up." I quickly removed brushes, trimming scissors and nail clippers from the wall cupboard inside the mobile and arranged them on the grooming table.

"When Barney woke up this morning, I told him you were coming and he's been like a flea on a hot grill ever since. He *loves* his Dana."

"More like he loves his warm bubble bath and pampering." I took the lead from Ellie and bent to kiss the top of Barney's head. "It's like checking in to a day spa, isn't it, Barney?"

"I didn't think you'd be here today." While watching me use the slicker brush to remove dead hair from Barney's black coat before securing him in the hydro bath, Ellie leaned against the side of my mobile salon ready for a gossip. "My friend, Bunty, who breeds *Lakeview* Labradors, was on the phone to me last night. She said you found a dead guy at the dog show yesterday. *And* he'd been murdered." Her golden curls bounced energetically as she shook her head. "How are you holding up?"

"Fine," I said and quickly changed the subject. "Did you hear about my Penelope winning runner-up to Best in Show?" I gave a low chuckle. "Thinks she's too good for us now. Wanted me to serve her breakfast in bed this morning." I pocketed the slicker brush and led Barney up the ramp and into the hydro bath.

Was it going to be like this all day? Clients wanting to know more about what it was like to come across a dead body covered in blood?

Should have expected it, I suppose. Most people never get to see a murder victim during their lifetime, so I guess curiosity is a natural reaction when confronted with someone who has had that grisly experience.

But I didn't want to talk about it.

After using the retractable hose attached to the hydro bath to douse Barney in warm water, I followed up by squeezing his favorite shampoo – Liquorish Lavender – all through his wet coat and massaged it in with both hands. He smiled up at me, eyes at half-mast. This was the part he loved the best. I had to be careful not to massage for too long as some days the sweet-natured Labrador would relax so much his legs would buckle and I had the devil of a job lifting him out of the hydro bath.

Every time Ellie attempted to bring the conversation back to the murder at the show, I changed the subject. Finally, the penny dropped and she chatted on about the roses in her garden and Barney's new trick of barking at the postman.

And it was like that all day, right up until I blow-dried my last dog, clipped my last nail and fed my last natural doggy treat as a reward for good behaviour.

The only useful information I uncovered was via the mother of another poodle breeder/show competitor, who'd booked her retired standard poodle, Anthony, in for his bi-weekly bath. Mrs. Stewart, in a hush-hush tone, said she'd seen Chi talking to a travel agent two days before Stephen's death. While she'd been booking a week away with her husband to celebrate their fortieth wedding anniversary, she'd overheard Chi booking a single flight to Taiwan.

A single flight? Was Chi leaving Stephen? Going home to his mother country? Was this the reason the two men were arguing so heatedly at the dog show?

I hauled in a deep breath, held it for ten. Was my gut instinct completely out of whack? Was Chi just going home to visit his family – or did this new information somehow make him guilty of killing his lover?

I exhaled, letting the breath out slowly until my shoulder muscles relaxed. Lots of 'maybes' up on the crime-scene board. Lots to mull over with the other two members of the *Gumshoe Chicks*.

When I pulled up outside *Pampered Pooch*, Patricia's silver Lexus was already showing off its ultra-smooth lines by the curb, so I carefully slotted my rig into the two parking bays beside her. I closed my eyes, breathed slowly in and out a few times to center myself before climbing out of the car. This meeting could go one of two ways – it could be illuminating, or it could belly flop. I had so many questions to ask

Patricia, starting with, 'if she knew who killed Stephen, why hadn't she gone to the police?'

Because Patricia Stamford was full of excrement. That's why.

As I shouldered my way inside and breathed in the subtle scent of vanilla, dog treats and cossetted pooch, the bell over the front door tinkled the first line of, *Doggie in the Window*. Hmm…bell was new. Something else Abi thought up to add to the congenial ambience of her beloved place of business.

Chloe, Abi's dark-eyed black-and-tan dachshund, trotted over to meet me, her thin tail whipping from side to side and her long soft ears flapping. She grinned up at me and rubbed against my legs, refusing to let me go any further without admiring her new soft pink *Gucci* doggy coat.

"You look amazing," I told her, squatting to ruffle her ears and kiss her on the nose. "That coat definitely brings out the twinkle in your eyes."

I spotted Patricia checking out a pair of designer-brand doggy pjs over in the clothing display, which made me wonder if she owned a dog. Didn't really seem the type to risk hair on her clothes or coming home to a surprise parcel in the middle of her five-thousand-dollar iceberg-white quilt. Holding the pjs in the air, Patricia was in deep conversation with Veronique, Abi's assistant, who'd virtually come with the stock. When Abi's Aunt Tilly died and left *Pampered Pooch* to her, Veronique had been invaluable as both assistant and friend. Abi was the first to admit, without Veronique's expertise and knowledge, *Pampered Pooch* would have hit the rocks within a month.

On seeing me, Abi, the ever-cheerful, bubbly member of our team, left her task of attaching price tags to fluffy puppy slippers and sashayed across the room toward me, her long blonde ponytail bouncing with every step. She indicated Patricia with a lift of one eyebrow, her favorite party trick, before turning the sign on the door from OPEN to BACK IN FIFTEEN. "So, how come we get to meet your nemesis?"

"Not my idea. She has a proposition for the *Chicks* and I figured you and Molly might want to hear it."

"A proposition?" Abi tweaked a cord to lower the venetian blind over the door. "I'm all ears."

"Has she mentioned Stephen's murder yet?"

"Hasn't spoken a word to me but seems to be getting along with Veronique."

"*Everyone* gets along with Veronique."

Molly, propped up on the customers' lounge, pillow at her back, typing furiously on the laptop perched precariously on her knees, looked up when I nudged her foot. She blinked, as though reluctantly returning from her fictional world of hot sexy men, star-crossed lovers and the strong but flawed heroines she created for her avid readers. "Umm, hi Dana. How long you been here? What have I missed?"

I grinned as she blinked again. An owl woken from sleep. "Two minutes tops, so you haven't missed a thing."

Although shy and more comfortable inside one of her own romance books, Molly had come out of her shell recently and shown a much tougher side to her personality. In fact, as well as finding herself a hot biker boyfriend with a day job as a policeman, she had solved our last investigation, confronted the killer in his kitchen – and survived unscathed.

"Patricia says she knows who killed Stephen," I told them, eyeing the woman still holding up a pair of flowery pjs on the other side of the store. "But she refuses to divulge her information unless we act as Private Eyes and tag who she claims is the mistress of her adulterous husband. Take a photo, or better still, a video, of the two of them *hard at it*."

Abi sent a scowl across to the pyjama-waving woman on the other side of the store. "She wants us to do *what*?"

"You heard me."

Molly closed her laptop with a snap and shook her head. "But that's not what we do."

"Hey, don't shoot the messenger, I'm only relaying the facts."

As though realizing we were ready for the meeting to start, Patricia sailed across the room toward us. "Good afternoon, ladies. Have you discussed my proposition?"

"No point in discussing it, Patricia. Following adulterous husbands or their bit-on-the-side, is not what we do," said Abi, scooping Chloe up in her arms and cuddling her close to her chest as though protecting her from Patricia's cooties. "Plus, if you know something important about the investigation, you need to go to the police."

"I agree," put in Molly. "This is a murder investigation – not a game of Cluedo."

I shrugged one shoulder at the woman still grasping the doggy pjs as though choking the life out of them. "Looks like it's a three-way *no*."

"Why *haven't* you gone to the police?" Abi persisted.

Patricia's lips tightened into a thin line. "I made a promise that I wouldn't."

"Who to?"

"I can't say."

"Yet you were going to give *us* this information."

"You're not the police and-and I hoped you'd assist me in return." She wiped under her eyes with the back of one finger being very careful not to smudge her eye-makeup. "What if Edward leaves me? I know he only married me for my money, but we-we've been together since he escorted me to the Debutante's ball, the year I graduated from college. And-and I love him."

This was not the woman I'd locked horns with on a regular basis at day-care. Not the woman who continually criticized and mocked the way I fed, clothed and disciplined my children. If you'd asked me last week whether the Queen Bee of the Yummy Mummies actually had a heart, I'd have answered in the negative. That she must have been playing under a rock with her rattle when God allocated hearts to the batch of babies coming through that day. Looking at her now, I actually felt a smidgen of compassion for the woman.

Or was Patricia merely a brilliant actress, dragging us into her web of lies? Was there more to this story than she was letting on?

I nudged a tapestry-covered stool featuring a motif of laughing collie-dogs in her general direction before she embarrassed herself further by slipping to the floor. At the moment Patricia looked more like a wingless blow-fly than a Queen Bee.

"You say you know who killed Stephen. How? No way you could know that – unless you were there, at the show, yourself."

"No, I've never met the man, but I've heard enough about him from my cousin to relegate him to the compost heap at the bottom of our garden. My cousin said her best friend paid Stephen Channing $100,000 for a top stud dog so she could set up her own poodle stud."

"Lot of money for a dog."

"My cousin's friend wanted the best available and was willing to pay the going price. However, after several matings with no puppies, she took the dog to the vet, only to discover she'd paid $100,000 for a sterile stud dog. Stephen must have known this before he sold her the dog, yet he refused to return her money. She'd over-invested in setting up her dream poodle-breeding establishment and has since lost her property and been declared bankrupt."

"But how do you know it was your cousin's friend who killed him? And what's the woman's name?"

"I can't give you her name, but I can tell you this woman was so angry she went to the show yesterday to have it out with Stephen."

"And?"

"She told my cousin that if she couldn't get Stephen to return her money – she'd kill him."

Wheels turned in my brain. Clanked to a sudden stop. Was this the woman Peter had seen slinking from the showgrounds as though the devil himself was looking for her – not ten minutes before I discovered Stephen's dead body in the back of his bus?

SIX

The moment Patricia's silver Lexus roared off up the street, I flopped, boneless, on the shop sofa next to Molly. "Well, *that* was a wonderfully warm experience. Not."

"How did she end up getting us to spy on her husband?" Molly shook her head and stared at the ceiling. "We told her it's not something we *Chicks* do."

"Several times," I added with a sigh.

"Yet we're still doing it."

"Only because we need the name of her cousin's best friend," put in Abi collapsing on the other side of Molly, Chloe still clasped against her chest. "And for that to happen, we get down and dirty and take a video of her Edward in cahoots with his floosy."

"Preferably *in flagrante* with said floosy."

I joined Molly in staring up at the ceiling. Plain unadorned white. The color of innocence, of purity. As opposed to the color of murder, which was...black? Red? I shook my head. "You know, the more I hear about Stephen's devious activities, the more I wonder how someone hasn't done away with him sooner."

"*Alleged* devious activities," corrected Molly, always the one to see both sides of a person's character, no matter how on-the-nose their philosophy of life might be. "Especially as he's not around to refute their allegations."

"You're right," Abi agreed letting go of Chloe so the almost-purring dog could settle comfortably on her lap. "And even if the claims are valid, *someone* snuffed out a man's life – and that's never okay."

Molly's gaze left the ceiling and settled on me. "So, Dana, what's our plan?"

I blew out a deep sigh. "Our plan?" Reluctantly abandoning the serenity of ceiling-gazing I frowned down at the tiled floor, all the better to think. "Well...according to Patricia, she's planning to check the texts on Edward's phone while he's under the shower, find out where he and his lady-friend are hooking up next. She'll let me know and then we arrange to be at the rendezvous beforehand. Stake them out, and if necessary, follow them."

Abi held out her hand, palm up. "Let me have another look at Edward's photo."

I unzipped a pocket on the side of my extra-large Mummy bag and produced the photo Patricia had left with us for identification purposes. A photo of a well-dressed businessman with a smooth chin and tinted hair that touched his collar – a love-rat who wanted to hang onto his own rich piece of cake and eat someone else's too.

"Looks a smooth operator," commented Abi, checking out the man in the photo before passing it on to Molly. "Did you get the feeling Patricia has no intention of kicking Edward to the kerb even if we do secure a tell-all video for her? That she'll merely confront him with the evidence, threaten to cut his funds if his extracurricular activity doesn't cease, and then continue on as though the crashing breakers on the ocean of their marriage were merely soft, breezy ripples?"

I nodded. "And that she's more likely to take revenge on the woman involved rather than her two-timing adulterous husband."

"It's all to do with reputation," continued Molly in her wise author voice as though she were creating backstory and flaws for her current romance protagonist. "Patricia wouldn't want to rock her standing in society, therefore she'd rather turn the other cheek than let anyone know her husband is cheating on her."

"Can't get my head around that dumb way of thinking." I knew if ever Peter cheated on me, he'd be toast. Badly burnt binned toast. Only one time I'd doubted him was the middle of last year when he appeared to be visiting a lady's house a little more regularly than normal – turned out he was taking piano lessons so he could surprise me by playing my favourite song, *As Long as You Love Me* at our fifth wedding anniversary dinner. Sweet guy. Even if he was forever leaving his smelly socks on the bathroom floor and entertaining clients when I needed him for fatherly duties.

Abi held out the photo to her smartly dressed assistant who was in the act of tugging the cord inside the front door and watching the blind shoot up. "What do you think of this guy, Veronique?"

Veronique flicked the sign on the door back to OPEN and walked across to study the photo. She rolled her eyes, which is very effective on a forty-something female with life experiences. "Smooth and arrogant and as empty as a beer bottle on a hot day." She handed the photo back to Abi with a shrug. "The sort to love 'em and leave 'em on a regular basis."

"So, why's Patricia so obsessed with *this* particular woman?" I put in, shaking my head as I considered the absurdity of Patricia Stanford coming to me for help when she'd done nothing but belittle me since the first day I enrolled Kayla and Jake at Baby Buntings. "She's had to deal with other women in the past. What is it about *this* one that's got her knickers tied in so many knots it's making her itch?"

"Maybe she senses it's more than a fling this time," said Veronique. "The other women didn't threaten her marriage – perhaps this one does."

The door swung open and two identical ladies of indeterminate age marched into the boutique. Needle thin, gray hair hauled back in tight buns, their black ill-fitting stockings ending in pointy witch-like shoes, they were trailed by four ancient dogs, one so slow it seemed to pause and go to sleep between each step.

"You're wrong, Aggie. Today is Beef Wellington day," declared lady number one adjusting her tortoiseshell spectacles more comfortably on her hawk-like nose.

"No, that's not until Friday, " countered lady number two dragging her tatty fawn cardigan around her bony body. "You're getting forgetful, Bitzy. On Mondays we eat Irish stew for dinner."

"Do not."

"Do so."

"Do not."

"Do so."

"The Bobbsey Twins," whispered Molly, with a grin.

"And their gang of four – Huey, Dewy, Louis, and Pumpernickel. All of mixed breeds, all over thirteen and all incontinent," finished Veronique, her gaze centered on the mop and bucket in the far corner of the store.

After settling her sleepy dachshund on a cushion in the middle of the lounge, Abi hurried across the room to greet the twins. "Good afternoon, Miss and Miss Robertson. What can I do for you today?"

Molly and I exchanged a smirk. This could be entertaining. The twin sisters could never agree on anything.

Twin One tugged at the neck of her loose-fitting top and peered myopically at the closest shelf. "Vitamins."

Abi nodded. "And what specific vitamins are you after today, ladies?"

"Something with a bit of a kick," said Twin Two.

"Something to calm Pumpernickel down," said Twin One.

"No, to give him a boost."

"To help him sleep at night."

"No, to get him moving," insisted Twin Two with a shake of her head. "Yesterday he fell asleep in the middle of a walk."

"But only because you stopped to pick a flower."

"It wasn't a flower, you silly moo, it was a weed. A yellow soursob that invades every garden in our street. And the only reason I stopped to pull it out of Mrs. Barton's front lawn was because–"

The front door crashed open with a thud and before Twin Two could close her mouth, Detective Lightfoot, followed by two of his burliest constables, stormed into *Pampered Pooch*, all high rank and flashing badges.

Startled, Abi and both Bobbsey Twins spun around at the intrusion, while Huey, Louis, and Dewy each gave a shrill bark of welcome and tottered across the room, stumpy tails wagging, to greet the newcomers.

The largest of the two burly constables, clearly not a doggy fan, stuck his lower lip out and scowled down at his doddery welcoming party. "Someone put these flea-bitten, mangy dogs on leads!"

"Mangy?" gasped Twin One, her voice deceptively low and thin.

"Flea-bitten?" snarled Twin Two, her eyes lasering a hole in the constable's bullet-shaped head as she and her twin both slid their solid-looking lethal leather handbags off their bony shoulders into their gnarly hands and took a step forward.

"Oh-uh!" With a throaty cry, I threw myself off the lounge and into the fray, hoping to intercept the next feature on the program, *The Battle of the Handbags*.

No-one derided the Bobbsey twins' dogs without losing the use of at least one part of their anatomy.

A couple of feet behind where the constable hovered, I could see Pumpernickel, the oldest and slowest-moving member of the gang of four. He'd just finished depositing his calling card on the boutique's smooth tiled floor. A calling card of quite large proportions. The dog must have sensed the unrest in the air, or sussed out the belligerence of the man glaring down at his beloved owners, because he shook his head, let go a gargantuan fart, then shuffled forward until he was standing directly behind the oppressor. Opening his mouth wide, he wrapped his toothless gums around the bottom of the policeman's trousers, then, seemingly proud of himself, shook the trouser-leg and farted again.

"Hey, get your filthy mutt away from me!" With a flick of his hand, which the dog completely ignored, the red-faced policeman took a large step backwards and his foot landed in a rather mushy and potent-smelling mess. His feet went from under him as he slid, floundered, windmilled his arms wildly and finally ended up bottom-first on the floor, slap-bang in the middle of Pumpernickel's calling card.

Hand over my mouth, I smothered a giggle, made harder by the sight of Abi's face, plum-colored and bug-eyed, as she wrestled to withhold a belly laugh, while Molly, ever the diplomat, handed the fallen constable a packet of paper tissues.

Detective Lightfoot was quick to react. Before the Bobbsey twins could dive in, their fully-loaded handbags swinging, he stepped between them and his prone officer. "Outside, Constable Everest!

Now!" His steel glare and the anger behind the four words sent the constable skittering to his feet and bolting through the open doorway back to the police car, leaving the twins to re-holster their weapons.

As the door closed behind the chagrined constable, Abi fronted up to Detective Lightfoot, annoyed, and like me, full of questions. "What's going on? Why are you here, detective?"

He dismissed Abi without a word and turned to her assistant who'd made a dive behind the counter when the police arrived. "Veronique Claire Garnier?"

"Yes."

"We need you to accompany us to the police station to answer questions in relation to Stephen Channing's murder."

Face the color of dirty chalk, Veronique let out a gasp and made a grab for the shop counter, hands shaking. Her eyes, like two popsicles on sticks went from the detective to Abi and back to the detective. "Stephen Channing's m-murder?"

"Stop!" Abi pushed herself between Veronique and the detective, scowling up at six-foot-two wrapped in a tailored pearl-gray Hugo Boss suit. Hands on hips, chest puffed out, a Mumma Bear defending her cub. "What rubbish are you talking, Detective? Veronique isn't into handling or owning show dogs, she doesn't even *know* Stephen Channing."

Detective Lightfoot's eyebrows hiked upwards as he glanced from the white-faced Veronique back to Abi. "If Ms Garnier doesn't know Stephen Channing, why is there a text from her on his mobile phone? A text saying, she refuses to pay any more blackmail money and if he goes ahead and reveals her secret, he'll wish he were dead?"

6

The moment Patricia's silver Lexus roared off up the street, I flopped, boneless, on the shop sofa next to Molly. "Well, *that* was a wonderfully warm experience. Not."

"How did she end up getting us to spy on her husband?" Molly shook her head and stared at the ceiling. "We told her it's not something we *Chicks* do."

"Several times," I added with a sigh.

"Yet we're still doing it."

"Only because we need the name of her cousin's best friend," put in Abi collapsing on the other side of Molly, Chloe still clasped against her chest. "And for that to happen, we get down and dirty and take a video of her Edward in cahoots with his floosy."

"Preferably *in flagrante* with said floosy."

I joined Molly in staring up at the ceiling. Plain unadorned white. The color of innocence, of purity. As opposed to the color of murder, which was…black? Red? I shook my head. "You know, the more I hear about Stephen's devious activities, the more I wonder how someone hasn't done away with him sooner."

"*Alleged* devious activities," corrected Molly, always the one to see both sides of a person's character, no matter how on-the-nose their philosophy of life might be. "Especially as he's not around to refute their allegations."

"You're right," Abi agreed letting go of Chloe so the almost-purring dog could settle comfortably on her lap. "And even if the claims are valid, *someone* snuffed out a man's life – and that's never okay."

Molly's gaze left the ceiling and settled on me. "So, Dana, what's our plan?"

I blew out a deep sigh. "Our plan?" Reluctantly abandoning the serenity of ceiling-gazing I frowned down at the tiled floor, all the better to think. "Well…according to Patricia, she's planning to check the texts on Edward's phone while he's under the shower, find out where he and his lady-friend are hooking up next. She'll let me know and then we arrange to be at the rendezvous beforehand. Stake them out, and if necessary, follow them."

Abi held out her hand, palm up. "Let me have another look at Edward's photo."

I unzipped a pocket on the side of my extra-large Mummy bag and produced the photo Patricia had left with us for identification purposes. A photo of a well-dressed businessman with a smooth chin and tinted hair that touched his collar – a love-rat who wanted to hang onto his own rich piece of cake and eat someone else's too.

"Looks a smooth operator," commented Abi, checking out the man in the photo before passing it on to Molly. "Did you get the feeling Patricia has no intention of kicking Edward to the kerb even if we do secure a tell-all video for her? That she'll merely confront him with the evidence, threaten to cut his funds if his extracurricular activity doesn't cease, and then continue on as though the crashing breakers on the ocean of their marriage were merely soft, breezy ripples?"

I nodded. "And that she's more likely to take revenge on the woman involved rather than her two-timing adulterous husband."

"It's all to do with reputation," continued Molly in her wise author voice as though she were creating backstory and flaws for her current romance protagonist. "Patricia wouldn't want to rock her standing in society, therefore she'd rather turn the other cheek than let anyone know her husband is cheating on her."

"Can't get my head around that dumb way of thinking." I knew if ever Peter cheated on me, he'd be toast. Badly burnt binned toast. Only one time I'd doubted him was the middle of last year when he appeared to be visiting a lady's house a little more regularly than normal – turned out he was taking piano lessons so he could surprise me by playing my favourite song, *As Long as You Love Me* at our fifth wedding anniversary dinner. Sweet guy. Even if he was forever leaving his smelly socks on the bathroom floor and entertaining clients when I needed him for fatherly duties.

Abi held out the photo to her smartly dressed assistant who was in the act of tugging the cord inside the front door and watching the blind shoot up. "What do you think of this guy, Veronique?"

Veronique flicked the sign on the door back to OPEN and walked across to study the photo. She rolled her eyes, which is very effective on a forty-something female with life experiences. "Smooth and arrogant and as empty as a beer bottle on a hot day." She handed the photo back to Abi with a shrug. "The sort to love 'em and leave 'em on a regular basis."

"So, why's Patricia so obsessed with *this* particular woman?" I put in, shaking my head as I considered the absurdity of Patricia Stanford coming to me for help when she'd done nothing but belittle me since the first day I enrolled Kayla and Jake at Baby Buntings. "She's had to deal with other women in the past. What is it about *this* one that's got her knickers tied in so many knots it's making her itch?"

"Maybe she senses it's more than a fling this time," said Veronique. "The other women didn't threaten her marriage – perhaps this one does."

The door swung open and two identical ladies of indeterminate age marched into the boutique. Needle thin, gray hair hauled back in tight buns, their black ill-fitting stockings ending in pointy witch-like shoes, they were trailed by four ancient dogs, one so slow it seemed to pause and go to sleep between each step.

"You're wrong, Aggie. Today is Beef Wellington day," declared lady number one adjusting her tortoiseshell spectacles more comfortably on her hawk-like nose.

"No, that's not until Friday, " countered lady number two dragging her tatty fawn cardigan around her bony body. "You're getting forgetful, Bitzy. On Mondays we eat Irish stew for dinner."

"Do not."

"Do so."

"Do not."

"Do so."

"The Bobbsey Twins," whispered Molly, with a grin.

"And their gang of four – Huey, Dewy, Louis, and Pumpernickel. All of mixed breeds, all over thirteen and all incontinent," finished Veronique, her gaze centered on the mop and bucket in the far corner of the store.

After settling her sleepy dachshund on a cushion in the middle of the lounge, Abi hurried across the room to greet the twins. "Good afternoon, Miss and Miss Robertson. What can I do for you today?"

Molly and I exchanged a smirk. This could be entertaining. The twin sisters could never agree on anything.

Twin One tugged at the neck of her loose-fitting top and peered myopically at the closest shelf. "Vitamins."

Abi nodded. "And what specific vitamins are you after today, ladies?"

"Something with a bit of a kick," said Twin Two.

"Something to calm Pumpernickel down," said Twin One.

"No, to give him a boost."

"To help him sleep at night."

"No, to get him moving," insisted Twin Two with a shake of her head. "Yesterday he fell asleep in the middle of a walk."

"But only because you stopped to pick a flower."

"It wasn't a flower, you silly moo, it was a weed. A yellow soursob that invades every garden in our street. And the only reason I stopped to pull it out of Mrs. Barton's front lawn was because–"

The front door crashed open with a thud and before Twin Two could close her mouth, Detective Lightfoot, followed by two of his burliest constables, stormed into *Pampered Pooch*, all high rank and flashing badges.

Startled, Abi and both Bobbsey Twins spun around at the intrusion, while Huey, Louis, and Dewy each gave a shrill bark of welcome and tottered across the room, stumpy tails wagging, to greet the newcomers.

The largest of the two burly constables, clearly not a doggy fan, stuck his lower lip out and scowled down at his doddery welcoming party. "Someone put these flea-bitten, mangy dogs on leads!"

"Mangy?" gasped Twin One, her voice deceptively low and thin.

"Flea-bitten?" snarled Twin Two, her eyes lasering a hole in the constable's bullet-shaped head as she and her twin both slid their solid-looking lethal leather handbags off their bony shoulders into their gnarly hands and took a step forward.

"Oh-uh!" With a throaty cry, I threw myself off the lounge and into the fray, hoping to intercept the next feature on the program, *The Battle of the Handbags.*

No-one derided the Bobbsey twins' dogs without losing the use of at least one part of their anatomy.

A couple of feet behind where the constable hovered, I could see Pumpernickel, the oldest and slowest-moving member of the gang of four. He'd just finished depositing his calling card on the boutique's smooth tiled floor. A calling card of quite large proportions. The dog must have sensed the unrest in the air, or sussed out the belligerence of the man glaring down at his beloved owners, because he shook his head, let go a gargantuan fart, then shuffled forward until he was standing directly behind the oppressor. Opening his mouth wide, he wrapped his toothless gums around the bottom of the policeman's trousers, then, seemingly proud of himself, shook the trouser-leg and farted again.

"Hey, get your filthy mutt away from me!" With a flick of his hand, which the dog completely ignored, the red-faced policeman took a large step backwards and his foot landed in a rather mushy and potent-smelling mess. His feet went from under him as he slid, floundered, windmilled his arms wildly and finally ended up bottom-first on the floor, slap-bang in the middle of Pumpernickel's calling card.

Hand over my mouth, I smothered a giggle, made harder by the sight of Abi's face, plum-colored and bug-eyed, as she wrestled to withhold a belly laugh, while Molly, ever the diplomat, handed the fallen constable a packet of paper tissues.

Detective Lightfoot was quick to react. Before the Bobbsey twins could dive in, their fully-loaded handbags swinging, he stepped between them and his prone officer. "Outside, Constable Everest! Now!" His steel glare and the anger behind the four words sent the constable skittering to his feet and bolting through the open doorway back to the police car, leaving the twins to re-holster their weapons.

As the door closed behind the chagrined constable, Abi fronted up to Detective Lightfoot, annoyed, and like me, full of questions. "What's going on? Why are you here, detective?"

He dismissed Abi without a word and turned to her assistant who'd made a dive behind the counter when the police arrived. "Veronique Claire Garnier?"

"Yes."

"We need you to accompany us to the police station to answer questions in relation to Stephen Channing's murder."

Face the color of dirty chalk, Veronique let out a gasp and made a grab for the shop counter, hands shaking. Her eyes, like two popsicles on sticks went from the detective to Abi and back to the detective. "Stephen Channing's m-murder?"

"Stop!" Abi pushed herself between Veronique and the detective, scowling up at six-foot-two wrapped in a tailored pearl-gray Hugo Boss suit. Hands on hips, chest puffed out, a Mumma Bear defending her cub. "What rubbish are you talking, Detective? Veronique isn't into handling or owning show dogs, she doesn't even *know* Stephen Channing."

Detective Lightfoot's eyebrows hiked upwards as he glanced from the white-faced Veronique back to Abi. "If Ms Garnier doesn't know Stephen Channing, why is there a text from her on his mobile phone? A text saying, she refuses to pay any more blackmail money and if he goes ahead and reveals her secret, he'll wish he were dead?"

7

We watched in stunned silence as a visibly rattled Veronique – so shaken her legs looked ready to buckle – was escorted outside and bundled into a waiting police car.

She sat staring ahead, not looking our way, not meeting our eyes through the window. Pale. Withdrawn. Humiliated. Veronique had not only been accused of murder but of doing something blackmailable in her past.

For a long moment, we stood staring after the police car as it pulled away from the curb, almost afraid to move, to go on with our lives, as if this trouble, this awfulness with Veronique had never happened. Even the Bobbsey twins, standing side by side on the footpath, had stopped bickering.

"If Veronique's a killer, then so's Santa Claus," declared Abi at last, wiping at her eyes as she led the way back inside *Pampered Pooch*. "Veronique's the most honest, dependable person I know."

"Let's think of it as an added incentive to find the real murderer," I said, squeezing Abi's hand in support as I closed the door behind us. "It appears that our grubby poodle breeder was into much more than selling high-priced sterile stud dogs to gullible clients."

"But what did he have on Veronique? What was it Stephen knew about her past that had her paying to keep him quiet?" As usual, Molly blasted right through the elephant in the room, flipping him over and trampling on his long gray trunk.

"I can't imagine." And I couldn't. Veronique was a dependable level-headed, in-the-background sort of person. She wore simple but elegant clothes, rarely spoke ill of anyone and was always polite and helpful. Not the type of person to have a wild secret in her past. I let out a sigh. But did we know the *real* Veronique?

All very mystifying.

By the time I'd helped Abi go through all the bottles of vitamins until we found one that satisfied both the twins, joined with Molly to clean up after the gang of four left and made plans to meet at Abi's house later that night to discuss the latest turn of events, I was running late for pick-up at *Baby Buntings*.

Again…

In fact, it was 4.10p.m when I screeched to a halt in front of the child-care center, switched off the engine and slammed on the hand brake. Today was the third time I'd been late this month. An offence punishable by having my name printed in colored chalk on the Naughty Mummy's section of the blackboard. A violation that entitled every member of the *Yummy Mummy* brigade to gibe, mock, or taunt my lack of parenting skills.

In other words, it was a complete disaster that would probably scar me and my kids for life.

With a last look at the time on the dashboard, I scrambled out the car, coat and bag dragging behind and dashed toward the gate, where who should be waiting, their offspring already wrapped warmly in coats, chewing carrot sticks, and settled into their state-of-the-art strollers, but the most vicious threesome in the Yummy Mummy posse. Faith, Beatrice and Lark the Shark. All ready to tear me to shreds, all devoted followers of that wacky parenting bible, '*Raise Your Child like a Hot-House Flower*'. The book that advocated planning every waking moment of your child's life from birth to college. Its premise encouraging piano lessons for two-year-olds, plus swimming, yoga, mindfulness and mathematics from the age of 6 weeks. Utter bollocks in my opinion. Children raised via this deranged book were being robbed of their childhood.

"Hey, forget you gave birth to two children?" enquired ferret-faced Faith reluctantly moving from in front of the gate when my elbow connected with her breast bone.

"Statistics state that children who are neglected turn to crime as a way of getting attention," added Beatrice, quoting the 'book' from memory.

I raised one eyebrow. "The philosophy I follow states that those who are coddled and smothered all through childhood end up on the dole queue, unable to care for themselves."

"Which book does that come from?" growled Lark, circling me, her eyes narrowed.

"The book of Dana. Now, out of my way. I'm here to pick up my children and take them out for a pizza and chips, not debate with you three goons. So, go home, make your toddlers a green smoothie and let me pass."

We were actually having roast chicken and vegetables for dinner but throwing the words 'pizza and chips' at them like spears to the heart would give them something to rant about, keep them busy, allow me to get through the war zone.

Ignoring Beatrice's nose hike and dodging Lark's shark-circling tactics, I pushed through the gate and strode up to the front door of *Baby Buntings*, ready to get down on my knees and beg to keep my name off the blackboard, if necessary.

"Mummy! Mummy! I felled off the big bike and got my mouth blooded!"

Nooo! Not what an already stressed-out parent wants to hear when she barrels through the doorway of her children's day-care center.

Kayla, fairy wings at half-mast, skipped toward me holding a tooth in the air for my inspection and, so I could inspect the gap from whence the object of her pride came, grinning like a toothpaste commercial.

"Look, Mummy! Look!"

I studied the tooth as though it were from a rare collection of dinosaur bones before letting out a relieved breath and hugging her to me. Thank God, it was that loose tooth in front that would, if left to its own devices, have fallen out sometime in the next couple of weeks.

Jake, trailing his sister, padded across the room, his yellow and green Robot backpack dragging along behind him. Full of puffed-up importance, he clutched a drawing of what appeared to be a cross between a one-legged dinosaur, a squashed tomato and a bundle of sticks.

"Wow!" I grinned down at the eager baby face as he held the paper up to me, hoping he'd fill me in on the nature of his latest creative artwork so I wouldn't have to play the twenty guesses game.

"Dadda on pot."

"Shh…" I shushed him, expecting Mrs. Tyler to intervene, demanding to know if we were drug lords.

"Dadda on pot!" His voice grew louder as though noise decibels would get the message through to his dim-witted parent. And then it hit me. I was looking at my husband, Peter, giving a hands-on demonstration of potty training.

"Oh, Jake, that's-that's um…wonderful." I forced the words out through the bubble of laughter percolating in my chest.

"Mummy…will the tooth fairy come tonight?" asked Kayla, hefting her Disney Princess backpack onto her back, her face glowing with excitement. "'Cos if she does, I want to stay up and meet her. Tell her I *love* fairies. Can I Mummy? Can I?"

"Me up too?" put in Jake, eyes widening at the thought.

"No, that wouldn't work," I told them, putting on my sad face. "The tooth fairy won't come if either of you are awake."

"Wanna see fairy!" My little man's voice was getting teary. First sign that he was overtired.

"Come on, let's go home, Batman." I picked Jake up and breathed in his sweet baby smell as I cuddled him against me, tickling him until he giggled.

One child sorted.

Now for the second. "Kayla, sweetie," I said, looking down into my daughter's disappointed eyes. "What you're holding is a *magic* tooth."

"*Magic?*" Her eyes immediately lit up, her quivering bottom lip stilled.

"So, when you go to sleep tonight, a beautiful fairy will collect your magic tooth and take it back to fairyland."

"Oooh!"

"And in its place, she'll leave a present under your pillow."

"Will she *really*, Mummy? Will she?"

I nodded. "And a present from a fairy is *very* special."

Geez, I was good…

"Mrs. Fox." The manager bustled over, breaking up our magical moment. She was all Mary Poppins bright-eyed and cheery – not the greeting I was expecting. A furtive glance at the blackboard proved my name wasn't up there either. Hmm… had Clarence Clock, the cartoon time-piece used to teach the children the time, malfunctioned, and I wasn't late after all? Mrs. Tyler's smile cranked up an extra notch. "We had a little accident, I'm afraid. Kayla fell off the bike a short while ago so we had the nurse check her out. Sorry about the tooth, but the nurse said it's a baby tooth and was ready to come out anyway. Kayla, brave girl, merely jumped up, popped her tooth in her pocket and went on playing, so I didn't worry you by ringing."

Ah. So, it wasn't Clarence Clock's malfunction, it was guilt that kept my name off the *Naughty Mummy* board and triggered the manager's extra wide smile.

I looked her in the eye and frowned. "In future, Mrs. Tyler, regardless of what the nurse says, I would like to be informed if one of my children gets hurt," I told her, drawing Jake closer and taking Kayla's hand in mine. "Is that clear?"

"Yes, but–"

Before the Mary Poppins wannabe could elicit her standard Baby Bunting puffery, the Fox family swooped out the door and headed for the nursery's gate…where Faith, Beatrice and Lark had been joined by Patricia Stamford.

What was the Queen Bee doing back at the nursery? Her son, Noble, hadn't attended today, so she wasn't here to pick him up.

"Hey, Dana, which disgusting pizza have you decided to inflict on your children tonight?" demanded Faith in a voice dripping with so much horror you'd think I was planning on force-feeding Kayla and Jake poison from the hemlock tree.

"Do you know how many calories are in a store-bought pizza?" added Beatrice, her tone equally as derogatory.

I blinked, disorientated for a moment, and then, remembering I'd goaded them earlier about buying pizza for dinner, quickly decided to choose one of the most-calorie laden pizzas on the market. Just to pee them off. "Mmm…thought we'd try a Mega Meatlovers with extra pepperoni and Italian sausage." I sent them a beatific smile to counter their combined gasp of horror at the combined calorie count in my chosen pizza. "And maybe we'll follow up with chocolate ice cream and sprinkles for dessert."

"Typical," scoffed Patricia in her usual patronising tone. No way was she letting on that she'd been at Abi's boutique earlier, enlisting our help to catch her husband in an uncompromising position with his cheap floosy. Instead, she turned away as though to ignore me, but as I pushed past, she unobtrusively slipped a crumbled piece of paper into my pocket.

Without acknowledging the exchange, I quickened my pace. The sooner I got away from this clique of judgemental women the better. Claws out, teeth sharpened, they were never happier than when ripping apart any mother whose views differed from their own. It was even worse on social media where they'd formed a group called, 'Raising your Child to be Whole'. I'd snuck a quick look this morning only to feel sorry for one new mother in the district who'd come to them for help. Poor deluded woman. Her question was: 'Is it okay to give my 4-year-old Froot Loops for breakfast occasionally, as a treat?' The answers came thick and fast, all informing her how store-bought breakfast food is loaded with poison, or how they themselves spent an hour every morning making a special and wholesome breakfast for their offspring, and how only lazy mothers allowed their child to eat Froot Loops. All bollocks. If I was that new mother, I would immediately unsubscribe and block any more posts from their page.

Jake, overtired, wriggly, and still a bit teary, was making it difficult for me to strap him into his car seat. "Sit still, Jake," I told him, dodging another foot to the face. Even after giving birth to two children, it always amazed me how quickly a toddler can go from smiles and giggles to screams, kicks and fist throwing.

"Stop it Jakey!" Kayla admonished giving her brother's arm a pinch. "Mummy won't take us for pizza and ice cream if you don't be good."

Oh, my wobbly Aunt! I cursed under my breath and counted to ten. While I'd been giving the *Mummies* the proverbial finger, Kayla had been listening, and naturally thought the menu for tonight's dinner was pizza and ice cream. Serves me right for letting the women get to me. Now, if I wanted any peace, any cooperation from the munchkins, we'd be heading to The Pizza Hut on Port Road, instead of home so I could cook up a meal of roast chicken and three veg.

It wasn't until I'd settled in behind the wheel and dragged my car keys from my pocket that I remembered the note Patricia had surreptitiously tucked into my pocket. The crumpled piece of paper tumbled out onto the car seat with my keys.

What now?

I flattened out the paper so I could read Patricia's printing more easily:

'Text came in this afternoon – Mr. Can't-Keep-It-In-His-Trousers is meeting up with his floosy beside the Port Adelaide Lighthouse at 9pm tonight. Be there!'

I frowned down at her snarky words.

Events were moving faster than I'd like.

Now, as well as getting Chi out of jail and Veronique's name cleared

– both achieved only by catching the real assassin – the *Chicks* had an unwanted surveillance job on their hands.

I fossicked through my bag – the largest bag I could find when shopping at Target for a tote bag suitable for a mother with two always-hungry, always thirsty kids – juice boxes, fruit bars, Doggo, spare diapers, plastic bags, two picture books, comb, brush, lipstick, until I unearthed my phone and texted the other two chicks in regard to our extra activity tonight at the Port Adelaide lighthouse.

Then, thoughts still on Patricia Stamford's message, I turned the key and started the car's engine. As I cranked my head around to check for traffic before pulling out of my parking bay, a chill prickled its way up my spine and formed a cold lump under my breastbone.

There was something about this whole surveillance set-up that was on the nose. Why hadn't Patricia, or her cousin, gone to the police with their evidence?

8

A little over three hours later, I screeched to an untidy halt at the bottom of Abi's driveway and scowled at the blinking clock on my dashboard.

Late again…

Thirty minutes to be precise, as our meeting at Abi's was scheduled for 7pm. I sighed as I dropped the car keys into my bag. Was this going to be my way of life for the next ten, fifteen years or until Kayla and Jake took off for Uni? Always running late, striving to juggle multiple balls in the air without dropping and breaking one?

And then I thought of how Kayla had tucked her tooth under her pillow and gazed up at me with excitement in her eyes as she climbed into bed, her tattered fairy wings fixed to her pyjama top. And the soft baby kisses from Jake when he threw his arms around my neck to say goodnight. No, now was the time to treasure my children's magic, their love, their trust, the fact that I, Dana Fox, dispenser of Band-Aids and kisses to scraped knees, was my children's whole Universe. All too quickly the teenage years would arrive with an adolescent snarl and my once loving children would snub me, too ashamed to walk on the same pavement as their know-nothing, cringeworthy mother.

I peered in the back of the SUV at Penelope, the other love of my life. The one who'd always think I was special, no matter what age she lived to. "Come on, lazybones," I crooned. "Time to move."

Clearly comfortable curled up on her padded blanket behind the driver's seat, the black greyhound cranked one eye open and peered blearily back at me.

"Hey, don't you wanna play with Chloe and Busta?"

Ah. The magic words. Both eyes flew open, both ears cocked to high alert and she scrambled to her feet, urging me to hurry up and open the car door so we could start the visit.

Two exuberant bouncing dogs greeted us the moment we stepped inside the door. Chloe, little dachshund legs firing and Busta, displaying his characteristic wide toothy fox-terrier grin. Penelope bent her nose down to say a polite *hello*, then, unable to contain her excitement, set off around the lounge room at breakneck speed, the other two dogs after her.

"We're in the kitchen," said Abi, paying no attention to the chaos in her lounge room.

"Ohmygod, I love you, Abigail Truelove," I said collapsing at the kitchen table in front of a giant cornflake cookie and a mug of piping hot coffee. "I'm *so* in need of caffeine!"

"Heard you pull up," explained Abi with a grin.

"Sorry I'm late, but you wouldn't read about the night I've had," I said rolling my eyes after first sampling the coffee which Abi had made exactly how I liked it. "Either of you ever had to play the part of the Tooth Fairy?"

Abi's nose squished. "No, but I once dressed up as a donkey in a school Nativity play. Does that count?"

"And I wore a pirate costume to a fancy-dress book party a couple of years ago," said Molly. "The alpha hero in my book was a pirate, so I thought I'd use the costume as a marketing ploy."

"And, while you were dressing up, did either of you have two over-stimulated children to contend with, one swinging on your legs, while the other danced around the room declaring she was never going to sleep again until she'd seen a *real* fairy?"

Abi grimaced while Molly gave me a sympathetic half-grin.

"And it wasn't *only* due to the pizza and chocolate ice cream they'd eaten for dinner," I assured them. "I substituted Vegetarian for Meat-lovers and the chocolate ice cream only consisted of one small scoop."

"Where was Peter during this tooth-fairy shemozzle?"

"Out in the shed playing at using a hammer, glue, and nails to supposedly fix a leg on a chair." I took another sip of coffee relishing the taste as it hit my tongue and continued on into my caffeine-deprived bloodstream. "When I checked later, the *fixed* leg was so wonky it fell off at my touch. But I can't complain, he's home on sentry duty now. Even if he *is* sprawled out in front of the television, feet up on a pouffe, two giant-sized packets of Sour Cream and Chives potato chips and a glass of wine on the coffee-table beside him, praying the munchkins stay asleep until I get back."

"Does Peter know about our latest surveillance job?" asked Abi bustling over from her new coffee-maker, a frothy cappuccino for herself in one hand and a notebook in the other.

I shrugged, hoping to convey indifference. "Didn't think he'd be interested," I said, crumbling off a minute corner of my biscuit to slip to Penelope who'd snuck in beside me while the other dogs weren't looking. I could write a book about what Peter would say in regard to me getting involved in an adultery case, so I quickly changed the subject. "Abi, any news from Veronique? Do you know if she's okay?"

"Police car dropped her back at the shop half an hour before closing time."

"Poor Veronique," said Molly. "How was she?"

"Still shaken up and she didn't want to talk about it. All I could find out was the police let her go after confirming her alibi checked out. When Stephen was murdered, Veronique was at a friend's 40th birthday party with several other guests, almost fifty miles from the showgrounds."

"Well, that puts her in the clear."

I frowned. Maybe, but she still had some explaining to do. "Did she mention *why* Stephen was blackmailing her?"

"Not a peep. And it didn't feel appropriate to come right out and ask her. She was so tight-lipped and shaken I told her to go home, that I'd finish up for the day."

"Hmm...it'll be the elephant in the room until she spills the beans though."

Abi picked up a biro lying beside the notepad and twirled it in her fingers. "I just can't see Veronique having a secret in her past."

"A secret so dire she paid Stephen blackmail money to keep it that way," I added.

Abi placed both elbows on the table and leaned forward. "I've known Veronique since I was twelve years old when I used to help Aunt Tilly in the shop during school holidays in return for pocket money. And Veronique was always my friend. In fact, like a big sister. She was only in her twenties then, but she'd listen to my school problems and even my boyfriend woes as I grew older. And now, since I took over *Pampered Pooch*, we've become even closer." Abi's chin firmed and her eyes narrowed. "Veronique Garnier is a good person."

"I know, Abs," I leaned over to squeeze her hand. I knew there had to be a good reason behind Veronique's dark secret. But now it was time to move on. "Okay, fellow *Chicks,* like we always do, let's write down our list of suspects." I lifted my chin at Abi. "You got a clean page in that notebook you're hogging over there?"

Abi nodded, sent me a weak grin, and, opening the notebook at a fresh page, printed: *Who killed Stephen Channing?* across the top.

"Chi has been charged with the crime, so we have to put his name down first," said Molly, giving me a side-eye. Probably in case I jumped down her throat.

But I refrained. "Fair enough," I said watching Abi write Chi's name next to the number one. "Even though he's innocent," I added. Neither Abi nor Molly had seen Chi's face when I found him leaning over Stephen's body, nor heard him mouth a plea for me to find Stephen's killer.

"And what about the woman who paid Stephen $100,000 for a sterile stud dog? She'd be angry enough to rip him apart." Molly was on a roll. My shy romance-writer friend had blossomed over the last few months, mainly due to single-handedly apprehending our last villain, a cuckolded Schnauzer breeder, plus – and this was a big one – she'd found the love of her life in the form of a biker-slash-cop called, Hudson Driscoll. A guy who looked at Molly like she was the softest, tastiest chocolate in the box.

"Whoever she is – she's definitely a suspect," said Abi writing: *Woman who Stephen fleeced of $100,000 for a sterile stud dog* beside number two on her list.

"Wonder if she has fair hair done up in a long plait and drives an old white Holden car?" I said thinking of the stressed-out woman Peter had seen sneaking out of the showgrounds.

"Would Peter recognize her if he saw her again?" said Molly.

"Doubt it. When the woman made her dramatic exit, he was half-way inside the car attending to his stroppy son. I'm amazed he remembered the color of her hair, dress and car."

Abi glanced up from the notebook to shoot a wry frown in my direction. "Unfortunately, I can't give this woman a name until we've fulfilled our sleazy bargain with your uppity day-care friend."

"Not *my* friend," I growled. "Queen Bee of the *Yummy Mummies* is more like a prickly thorn in my side. Never happier than when she's firing accusatory barbs at me or mocking my parenting skills."

Molly shifted her chair closer to Abi and leaned over to inspect the suspect list. "What about Corey Black?"

"What about him?" I asked her. Corey Black was a harmless, invisible sort of a guy. Always at the dog shows competing with his scraggy, but loveable, miniature poodle, Pablo. He rarely got a ribbon, mainly due to Corey's lack of dog-grooming skills and Pablo's propensity to lie down and refuse to move when the judge asked to see him gait around the arena. But that didn't worry Corey. Apart from Stephen's continual jabs and ridicule, Corey Black seemed to enjoy the social side of showing his dog. "Why Corey?"

"Because Stephen's always treating – um – *treated* Corey like gloop on the end of a kid's nose," said Molly. "Did you see the way he bumped the poor guy head-first into a steel pole while arguing with Chi? Gashed his head and didn't even apologize."

Abi nodded. "And he continually made fun of him and his dog. Called him Cack-Faced Corey and his dog a flea-bitten hairball with legs – amongst other nasties. If Stephen said those things about my Chloe, I'd have splattered him against the wall like an irritating mosquito."

I shook my head. "You might have punched him in his smug, smirking mouth if he dissed Chloe, but would you snatch up a knife and stab him?"

Abi's gaze settled on the floppy-eared, big-eyed, long-bodied sausage dog who was blatantly begging to be picked up and installed on her lap. She screwed up her face in thought. "Mmm…"

"No, you wouldn't." I got in before she could finish processing the thought of anyone badmouthing her adorable, much-loved, dachshund. "So, being called Cack-Faced Corey with a hairball on legs for a dog, doesn't really give Corey a strong motive for murder, does it?"

"However," put in Molly from over by the counter where she was busy selecting another cookie. "Earlier in the day, I saw Stephen and Corey having a full-on argument." She picked out the largest choc-chip and settled back in her chair. "And," she continued, nibbling on a corner of the cookie, "Corey was waving his arms around and Stephen had that smug look on his face that makes you want to smack it off. And when Stephen finally swaggered off, Corey was in tears."

Abi nodded. "And later, when Stephen went too far and shoved Corey's head into that steel pole, maybe Corey decided he couldn't take it anymore and cracked."

"Maybe." I hadn't witnessed the big argument. Probably too busy at the time keeping Jake from being eaten by large dogs and Kayla from wandering off looking for fairies. "Better put Corey on the list then. But we need to interview him and find out more about the argument before we cement his name as suspect number three." I watched Abi write Corey's name down and when she looked up, I shot her a wide grin. "And then, of course, there's Rick."

"Rick?"

"Yes, your hot Thor look-alike and good friend is a suspect too."

Abi's mouth opened and shut like a beached fish.

"Well, Rick said he had a meeting with Stephen after the show but couldn't find him. What if he was lying? What if he found Stephen, they argued about something completely unrelated to designing a new website and then he killed him?"

"No way," said Abi. "What motive could Rick possibly have to kill Stephen?"

While I was carefully choosing my words, Molly answered for me. "Maybe Stephen was blackmailing Rick too."

The biro dropped out of Abi's hand, rolled and clattered on the floor. "Ohmygod," she gasped. "What if Stephen found out about the drugs?"

"*Drugs?*"

Frowning, Abi shook her head. "I'm sure he doesn't do drugs now, but when he was a crazy off-his-face teenager, Rick got done for drugs." She dragged in a deep breath, let it out slowly. "And if his employer found out, he could lose his job."

Molly, who'd bent to retrieve the biro, broke off to stare up at Abi. "How do you know that?"

"When I met Rick at that party a couple of years ago, there was a lot of booze on tap and when I say a lot, I mean the birthday boy's father was a publican. So, by the end of the night, tongues were loosened and secrets divulged. In fact, at one stage there was a betting competition going on to see who had the most shocking secret." Abi grabbed another breath. "And that's when I found out about Rick being done for drugs."

Molly sat back in her chair with a thud while I continued to stare at Abi, open mouthed. This case was becoming more and more complicated at every turn. As for the dog show world, it was rife with secrets, so Stephen could have been blackmailing every one of our suspects.

Question was – which suspect decided to put an end to the poodle-breeder's greedy, money-making racket?

And make the ending permanent.

9

"Molly, for goodness' sake take that balaclava off. We're supposed to be incognito, not the main attraction." It was an hour and a half later and while I'd been securing an empty table in good view of the historic Port Adelaide lighthouse and our target's rendezvous, Molly, possibly thinking it made her look more like a PI on surveillance, had slipped a black balaclava over her head. "You'll have people wondering which bank we're planning to rob."

I placed my coffee, bought from a nearby food van, on the solid wooden table, eased onto the hard wooden planks that made up a seat, and let out a sigh. I'd already confiscated Abi's ostentatiously large sunglasses because they made her ninety-nine percent blind in the shadows of the night. Even though there was muted lighting in the area surrounding the lighthouse, she'd bumped into several people, knocking one poor lady's pie with sauce right out of her hand.

At times, dealing with my fellow *Chicks* was akin to herding cats.

Switching back to the job at hand, I clicked on my phone. Ten minutes to the planned meeting between Edward and his bit-on-the-side, leaving us plenty of time to settle unobtrusively nearby. Everything in readiness. Phones on laps primed to take photos of the adulterous couple, cardboard cups full of the most god-awful coffee I'd ever tasted, and Edward Stamford's photo on the table in front of us.

"Act natural, but be alert," I told my fellow sleuths. "And when you do see Edward, keep him in sight until his lady-love shows up and then take photos of the pair of them together."

"Especially if he leans in for a hello kiss," added Abi.

"Right," I said. "But don't be obvious. Make it look like we're taking lots of photos of the area for our Facebook page, especially of the historic lighthouse."

"Didn't think there'd be so many people out and about at this time of night," said Abi gazing at the couples wandering along the wharf, hand in hand, and the small cluster gathered at the bottom of the lighthouse.

"Guess the history of the place attracts tourists at all times of day." Molly took a large swig of her coffee and immediately pulled a face that resembled a guinea-pig's bottom. "Oooh, that's disgusting."

"Just pretend to drink," advised Abi with a wink. "I've added six heaped sugars to mine and it still tastes like cat's urine."

Molly grinned. "And you know what cat's urine tastes like, because…?"

"Ooh, sharp." Abi rolled her eyes and stuck her tongue out the side of her mouth. "You'd be surprised what initiation ceremonies I've been through, Moll."

"Oh, you *haven't*?" Molly's face twisted in disgust. "Who? What? How?" She shook her head. "Nope. I don't wanna know."

"I was eight at the time. We were on a school camp and this annoying boy we called Pickles dared me to–"

"*Ladies!*" I broke in sounding like the headmistress of an all-girls school. "Can we please lose the topic of cat's urine and get back to watching out for Edward Stamford. We can't afford to miss him."

Checking to see if our quarry had arrived while we'd been assessing our dishwater coffee, I cast my eyes across to the eighty-two-foot-high red and white lighthouse which had become the Port's first fixed navigational beacon way back in 1869. Made of cast iron with a hexagon tower and balcony, the lighthouse was later reassembled on Neptune Island and after eighty-four years of service there, finally returned to the Port Adelaide wharf under the care of the South Australian Maritime Museum. The structure now offered visitors an opportunity to visit the original keepers' quarters and climb to the lantern room for a bird's eye view of the river. However, having done the tour once myself and knowing how constricting the inner space and how exhausting the staircase, I was happy to remain on my hard timber seat and take in the view from the wharf. Listen to the merry chug of a tugboat passing by on its way to hook up with an outgoing cargo carrier, to smell and almost taste the diesel in the air and watch the eighty-year-old Birkenhead Bridge open to allow a high-masted sailboat to pass underneath.

"Anyone else feel like a hot dog from the van?" Abi stood and reached across the table for her sunglasses, shaking me from my reverie. "A hot dog smothered with sauce and mustard might take away the foul taste of whatever the guy's substituted for coffee beans."

"Not for me," I said watching Abi reinstate her PI sunglasses on her nose. "After sampling their coffee, there's no way I'm taking a chance on what's in their hot dogs."

"Might even *be* a hot dog," growled Molly who also shook her head to decline Abi's offer.

"Won't be long. I have my phone with me and can still keep an eye out for our perp from over by the van." Abi adjusted her dark sunglasses and tossed her head. "Don't care what you say, these babies are definitely part of a PI uniform."

"Ya reckon?" I squinted up at her. "All you need now is a Sherlock Holmes cap, a pipe and your trusty magnifying glass."

Abi smirked, lifting her chin in dismissal of my taunt as she took off for the food van.

"Look out!" yelled Molly, jumping to her feet.

"Abiii!" I warned.

Too late. She'd steamrolled straight into a long-legged red head coming the other way. Not content with knocking the air right out of the poor woman, Abi made to grab for the red-head's glittery gold purse as it flew high in the air, missed, bent to retrieve the missile and bumped heads with her victim.

I closed my eyes.

Once again, we were the main attraction on the wharf. People were pointing, laughing, stopping to watch the entertainment. Geez, I thought, discreetly nudging Edward's photo from the table into my bag, I should have sold tickets to the show and made a few dollars for charity.

"I'm so, so, sorry." While rubbing the lump on her head with one hand Abi handed the woman her purse. "I wasn't looking where I was going."

"Admit it, Abs." I bent to retrieve her sunglasses which had tumbled to the ground in the collision and slipped them into my bag too. "Wearing sunglasses at night makes you blind as a fence post."

The long-legged redhead laughed. Unlike my long thick auburn hair that took hours to dry and style after each shampoo, hers was short, curly and bright Ginger-Meggs red. She also sported freckles to match. Sparkling green eyes twinkled up at Abi who'd dropped her leather bag, picked it up, then dropped it again.

"It's okay," said the redhead, standing up and leaning against the table to steady herself. "It's just as much my fault as yours. I was looking out for my friend. I'm meeting him by the lighthouse." Her grin widened. "By the way, I'm Gemma Haines and I hope you don't mind me asking, but do you ladies own show dogs?" She looked more closely at Abi and then Molly and me. "I'm sure I saw you handling dogs at the dog-show last weekend."

"Yes, we do," said Abi, sitting down and inviting the red head to join us. "It's our hobby. I show an award-winning dachshund, called Chloe, adorable, but can be a bit of a drama queen, Molly here tries to show a cheeky fox terrier called Busta, who is never happier than when he's up to mischief, and Dana owns the gentlest and most stunning greyhound in the state. She actually won runner-up to best-in-show last Saturday."

Gemma turned her smile on me. "Congratulations. I actually saw you and your dog parading in the ring and thought she should have beaten the Maltese Terrier."

I returned her smile. "Thanks."

"I own a gorgeous black standard poodle bitch." Gemma laughed. "Or should I say, she owns me. Samantha's beautifully bred and I thought I might show her. In fact, for a while there, I had the brilliant idea of buying a top stud dog and setting up my own poodle stud."

Instantly my ears pricked. In fact, they pricked so quickly and so hard, I thought for a moment they were going to fly off the sides of my head. "*You* bought a stud dog?"

She nodded. "Didn't pan out though. But that's another story."

Molly leaned forward, fingers twitching as though she wanted to grab Gemma's sleeve and hang on tight so she couldn't get away. "Did you buy the stud dog from Stephen Channing?"

Gemma blinked, a frown appearing. "As a matter of fact, I did. But how did you know?"

"And did you kill him because the dog he sold you was sterile and Stephen scammed you out of $100,000?"

Gemma's fists closed. "I beg your pardon?" Her frown deepened and for a moment I thought she was going to exhibit the proverbial hot temper that went with red hair and upend a half-full cup of cats-urine coffee right over Molly's head.

I flicked my fellow *Chick* a warning frown to indicate her questioning methods were way down there with magic mushrooms and poison ivy. In fact, since hitching up with a certain bikie-slash-policeman called, Hudson, my friend, Molly, had not only lost her shyness and her virginity, she'd become a female Philip Marlow on steroids. "Sorry, Gemma," I said hoping to keep the redhead's temper in check. "Molly didn't mean to accuse you of murder. It's just that we heard that Stephen sold someone a sterile stud dog for $100,000 and refused to return her money, and-and-well, we were wondering if that was you."

Gemma's shoulders sagged and she let out a sigh. "Yes, that was me.

Gullible Gemma Haines."

"And did you go to the show last weekend to have it out with him?"

Gemma settled back down on her seat and nodded. "Yes, I went to the show, but I didn't *see* Stephen, nor did I *kill* him. Instead, I spoke to his partner, Chi. Lovely guy. He said he'd told Stephen to return the money, apologised when he realized that hadn't happened, and immediately wrote me out a cheque." She opened her glittery gold purse, poked around inside and finally placed a cheque for $100,000, signed by Chi, on the table in front of us. "There's the proof."

After we'd all had a quick look, she folded the cheque in two and slipped it back into her purse. "Anyway, I thanked him and then I left." She shook her head. "Chi is so sweet, so different to his rat of a partner."

Abi put her hand over Gemma's. "I'm glad Chi did the right thing for you. Now you can set up your poodle stud after all."

Suddenly a smile lit up Gemma's face and her eyes twinkled like fairy lights. "Changed my mind about the poodle stud," she told us. "You see, I've fallen in love. And me and Eddy are leaving the country." At the word *Eddy*, my ears stood to attention. "We're going away, starting a new life together." She peered across at the lighthouse, the light from its lamp reflecting on the ripples of the dark river, and jumped to her feet, waving both arms in the air. "Eddy," she called out. "Over here! Come and meet my new friends."

I followed her line of vision and immediately knew I was right. The man waving back, a wide grin crinkling his aristocratic face, was Edward Stamford, Patricia's husband. And this was the couple we'd agreed to film committing adultery in return for the name of a suspect to help our case.

Gemma Haines.

I quickly shook my head at Molly, who'd evidently clicked on the scenario as well and appeared ready to spill the beans.

It wasn't the time yet.

Looking at these two lovers, I had a feeling Patricia was in for a bit of a face-plant. Edward wasn't dressed at all like he was in the photo she'd given us. Not a tailored suit, a pressed tie or a pair of expensive hand-made Italian shoes in sight. Instead, he wore faded jeans and a sloppy tee, and funky green and orange sneakers that glowed in the dark.

And by the goofy look on both their faces, and the tender kiss exchanged when they came together, Gemma Haines wasn't just another of Edward Stamford's long line of indiscretions.

These two were very much in love.

In fact, it was so obvious, I wouldn't have been surprised to see a flock of Disney bluebirds tweeting and fluttering around their heads, one with a love-heart wedged in its beak.

Did Patricia know Edward's 'other woman' was the same person she'd accused of murdering Stephen?

Had she set Gemma up to take the fall? And set us up too?

Or what if Patricia killed Stephen herself?

Too many what ifs.

Gemma could even be in danger herself, so I squared my shoulders, took one last sip of godawful coffee, screwed up my face and began to confess.

Both Gemma and Edward listened in quiet acceptance, as if this wasn't the first time Patricia had tried to separate them, until I came to the part where Patricia had told us of her and Edward being lovers from college days.

"That's rubbish!" exclaimed Edward shaking his head. "We've been married for four years and I only met Patricia two months before the wedding. It was actually an arranged marriage. I know, in this day and age that sounds ludicrous, and I admit, I married Patricia for her family money, but hey, she married me for my title."

"Title?"

"My parents are low-level aristocrats, Lord and Lady Beaumont of Beaumont Hall. Completely impoverished and relying on U.K. government handouts to keep the old pile of stones from falling down around their ears. The Stamford money paid for a new roof, new wiring and plumbing. It was the least I could do to help out Mother and Father. Patricia's plan was once my father conveniently kicked the bucket, we'd move to England and live in the big house, spend millions to bring it back to its original grandeur and Patricia would become Lady of the Manor." He turned to Gemma and squeezed her hand, smiled into her eyes. "That won't be happening now as Gemma and I are going to live in the old gardener's cottage on the Beaumont Hall grounds." He turned back to us and lifted his nose as though smelling dirty socks, so on the nose, they'd grown a covering of mold. "But do you know the most degrading part of this deal? I had to relinquish my surname and change it to Stamford when we were married. How's that for belittling a man?"

Abi gave him the death stare. "Which is something we women have suffered ever since cavemen first started dragging us around by the hair."

For a moment Edward scowled, and then burst out laughing, a laugh that rocked his whole body, made him look ten years younger. I could actually see how Gemma had fallen for this man, even after the mental damage caused by the four years of derision inflicted by Patricia and her family. "I'm sorry, Abi. Let's put it another way, I now know how you women feel. Okay?"

Abi nodded and sent him a wink.

"But how are you and Gemma going to live?" Molly asked. "How are you going to help your parents pay taxes and continue to renovate Beaumont Hall without the Stamford millions?"

"From the divorce settlement." Edward grinned. "In exchange for changing my name so Patricia could retain hers, I didn't have to sign a prenup."

"Hmm…" murmured Abi. "A name-change with benefits? Must remember that one."

Edward's grin widened. He seemed happier, more laid back – sitting so close to Gemma she was half on his lap – than he did in the pompous photo now residing in a dark and grubby corner of my Mummy bag.

With one hand each side of her face, Eddy drew Gemma closer and kissed her. A kiss so intimate, so passionate, I quite expected to see steam rising from their lips, hot and billowing, curling the ends of their hair.

"Gemma," I broke in, after putting up with their get-a-room kissing session for all of two minutes. It was time to continue with the case. "When you were at the show can you remember anything about your surroundings? Anything suspicious? Out of the ordinary?"

Gemma came back to earth slowly and let out a contented sigh before turning to me, a goofy look on her face. "Sorry?"

I repeated my question.

She leaned back in Edward's arms, thought for a moment, and then shrugged. "Not really. After the show finished, I wandered around looking for Stephen. Couldn't find him anywhere. Then I caught up with Chi and as they say in the movies, all ended well. When he wrote out the check, I was so happy I just floated off home."

"Did you see another woman hanging around near the Windswept bus?" I asked, thinking of the woman Peter had spotted skulking from the showgrounds. "A woman with long fair hair done in a thick plait that hung all the way down her back."

"No, sorry, as I said, I…hang on, yes, I *did* see a woman like you described. I remember wondering at the time, how many years it would take to grow hair that long." Gemma frowned in thought. "She was standing by the Secretary's office reading from the notice-board. Had her back to me so I didn't see her face." She grinned, scrunching up her freckled nose. "Hey, with a $100,000 check neatly folded in my purse, all I could think about was what Edward and I could do with that money. I was floating on air, singing Chi's praises. He's such a sweet guy. Nothing like his partner."

I nodded in agreement. "Which is why we need to find the *real* murderer. Chi is in jail for Stephen's murder, but he's innocent. He loved Stephen, regardless of the man's self-opinionated, snarly personality. And whoever did murder Stephen is still out there, maybe getting ready to kill again."

Edward drew Gemma closer, kissed her on the right ear lobe. "This man, Chi, he was good to Gemma. If it hadn't been for him, she'd still be one hundred thousand dollars out of pocket." He nuzzled Gemma's neck with his nose making her purr. *Geez, these two couldn't keep their hands off each other.* "What do you say, Dumpling? Shall we help our new friends get Chi out of jail?"

Gemma's purr turned into a contented sigh. "Whatever you say, Pussycat."

Abi, struggling to contain an eye-roll, nodded. "Umm…the more the merrier."

"Welcome to the team," added Molly.

"Thing is, Gemma," I said, looking from her to Edward, "You need to be careful. Not only is there a murderer out there, but I think Patricia is out for revenge. She knows you're different than Edward's other er – indiscretions – and doesn't want to lose him–"

"Lose my title you mean. And those *indiscretions* as you call them, were merely my way of provoking the Stamford family. Gemma and me – we're soulmates."

"What's Stephen's murder got to do with Patricia?" asked Gemma.

"I don't really know, but Patricia knew we were investigating Stephen's murder and by saying you were a friend of her cousin and refusing to tell us your name, she used us to help implicate you. In her words, you had means, motive, and opportunity but she'd only give us your name if we went along with her plan."

Edward nodded. "My wife is accustomed to getting her own way."

"Which means her next move, now that we've seen through her deception, will be to go to the police with her story."

"And if that doesn't work?" Molly's voice caught in her throat. "What else is your wife capable of Edward?"

"She'll do whatever it takes to get her own way." Edward's fingers closed around Gemma's hand. "Which means, I'm going to move in with Gemma today and file for divorce tomorrow."

10

At 6.30 am, the following morning, I flopped back on our bed, still unmade, and half-listened to Kayla and Jake arguing over the iPad in their bedroom next door. If I was lucky, I had about half a minute to myself before our bedroom door crashed open and a dummy-sucking toddler, followed by a disgruntled fairy invaded my space, both demanding I sort out their unsolvable iPad problem.

Where the heck was Peter?

I hadn't seen him since he climbed out of bed and disappeared to supposedly collect the newspaper from the front lawn. That was over twenty minutes ago.

Inhaling deeply, then letting it out ever-so-slowly, breath by breath, I blocked the hostile vibes gathering momentum in the next room and let my mind drift to the facts relating to our latest *Chick's* case.

Gemma's name had been scrubbed from our suspect list – since Chi had reimbursed the money for the sterile stud dog, Gemma had no motive for killing Stephen. Which meant we were now down to three potential suspects. The mystery woman with the long fair plait seen both inside the show grounds and sneaking out the exit. Rick, the hot Thor look-alike who showed beagles and had arranged to meet Stephen after the dog show but said he hadn't turned up. And Corey, the little guy who'd been bullied relentlessly by Stephen over the last few months and who'd finally been pushed headfirst into a steel pole.

Oh yes, and we'd pencilled a *maybe* beside Patricia Stamford's name. Only a *maybe* because I couldn't see her associating with the likes of Stephen Channing without a peg on her nose and a ready supply of antibacterial wipes.

Luckily, we now had two extra gumshoes on our team, both ready and willing to assist in the case. Gemma and Edward – aka *Dumpling* and *Pussycat*. However, judging by their non-stop snogging at the Port Adelaide lighthouse the previous night, I had a feeling my biggest problem would be keeping these two apart long enough to actually 'detect'.

Before disbanding the night before, Molly, Abi and I arranged to meet outside Corey's apartment block at 7.30 this morning, hoping to catch our suspect before he left for work. Plan A was to use our collective wiles to shake some answers from Corey. With three seductive women on his doorstep, we figured there'd be no way he'd refuse to let us in.

And if Plan A didn't work, hey, there were always 25 more letters in the alphabet.

Our new friends, Edward and Gemma, had a busy day ahead of them shifting house and talking to lawyers, so they weren't joining us until tonight, when we planned to follow up our enquiries by visiting Rick and hopefully squeezing a few answers out of him. Of course, we three *Chicks* would rather be squeezing his pecs to see if they were as hard and deliciously powerful as they appeared to the naked eye, but I guess we'd just have to shove our hands in our pockets and keep it all professional.

We had it all arranged. Peter was dropping our two munchkins off at Day-care on his way to work this morning and my first *Hydro Hound* client wasn't due for his shaggy coat to be shampooed, brushed and polished until 10am. Abi, having told Veronique to stay home today, had decided not to open *Pampered Pooch* until 9.30 and Molly was the lucky one. Writing romance books for a living, she could easily schedule her work around our investigations.

I cast a quick glance at my bedside clock/radio which told me it was time to haul myself off the bed, sort out the munchkins, prepare breakfast and finish dressing. Corey's apartment block, on Junction Rd., Rosewater was at least a 20-minute drive away, it was now 6.35 am, and the noise decibels in the next bedroom had reached window-shattering intensity.

Where the heck was Peter?

Was he deaf? Fallen over one of Jake's toys and lying unconscious on the front step? Or, so absorbed in reading his daily Horoscope he'd zonked out from reality? Being a Taurus, and supposedly a bull, I sort of agreed Peter was strong, semi-dependable and yes, quite sensual, especially in bed – all the attributes his star sign depicted – except for the last one on the list. Creative.

The most creative thing Peter has ever done in his life happened the night he proposed to me. He took me for a candle-lit dinner and when I slipped my shoes off under the table to ease my aching feet – yes, I'd made the mistake of wearing my normally pushed-to-the-back-of-the-cupboard too-tight high-heeled shoes just because the color matched my new dress – he unobtrusively dropped the ring into my right shoe. Of course, when I forced my feet back into my shoes, stood up and began tottering in the direction of the restroom to freshen up, the ring dug into the tender part of my foot. I stumbled and went sideways on my ankle. Cursing and in pain, I hobbled back to the table, sank down in my chair, dug out the engagement ring and held it up in the air. *What the–?* And that's when my future husband grinned that irresistible grin of his and said, 'Yes, I know it's going to be painful, but I love you, Dana Moore, so, will you take a chance and marry me?' The rest of this special night was spent at the local hospital getting my ankle x-rayed and finally treated for a bad sprain.

And that's how I became a Fox.

Right on the dot of 7.30am, I parked my SUV behind Abi's white van and Molly's fully restored classic red Morris Minor and eyed the run-down 20-unit apartment block in front of me with misgivings. This is where Corey Black and his ragamuffin black poodle, Pablo, lived. The thought of so many people residing in such close proximity to each other always made me claustrophobic but more and more of these poverty-stricken buildings were springing up across suburbia Australia. Where building blocks used to have one house and a large backyard, now there were three units built on that same block, or, like this, a three-story building with 20 or more basic units, all identical.

"Okay, so what's our plan?" asked Molly, as she and Abi walked across to talk to me through my open car window.

"Simple. We interview the guy while being very polite and sweet," I said climbing out of the car and letting Penelope jump out before locking all the doors. "Get Corey to talk about Stephen's abuse. Where he was after the show ended. Whether he went straight home and has someone to collaborate his alibi – or whether he hung around the showgrounds long enough to stop Stephen's bullying stone-dead."

"Hmm…" Abi rolled her eyes. "As you say … simple."

"Let's go." Penelope and I led the way toward the eastern side of the building, checking door numbers as we went. Well, I checked the door numbers while Penelope investigated the clumps of dead lilies on each side of the gravel path.

Unit 3 was on the ground floor and after knocking on the warped front door, I had to check my knuckles for splinters.

When there was no answer, Abi took over and whumped against the wood so loudly I worried about the door's health. But still there was no answer.

Molly peeked through one of the windows. "Can't see anyone in there."

"No wonder," said Abby, rubbing her bruised hand. "Probably more dirt than glass."

"Should I get out my tools?" asked Molly, referring to her two lock picks, Harry and Meghan. "Maybe Corey's lying on the floor in there, unconscious, unable to yell for help."

"Umm…" I frowned, tossed up between how much against the law breaking-in would be against maybe finding Corey in need of help. Or even a clue to help solve our case.

"Hey! Whaddaya think ya doin'?"

I spun around as the presence of a tattooed granite-jawed giant appeared out of some bushes behind us. Shoulders wider than two beer barrels and legs related to tree trunks, the man's bald head was so shiny, the sun's reflection made me squint.

Late twenties, he had that bad boy bullishness about him that made me glad our first meeting hadn't occurred in a dark alley, at midnight, with only a few partying rats for company.

"Waddayadoin'?" the giant repeated, his voice louder and his eyes so dark and penetrating, I instinctively reached out to place my hand on Penelope's head for security.

"Um…w-we're looking for Corey Black," bleated Abi taking a step back, while Molly froze, open-mouthed. "H-he lives here in number three."

"Waddya want 'im for?"

With my dog still glued to my left leg, I forced my shoulders back, dragged in a lung full of air and decided to front up to Mr. Scary-on-Steroids and, like they advise in self-confidence books, show no fear. "Not that it's any of your business, but we need to talk to Corey."

Gigantor's scowl deepened. "Waddabout?"

"Hey, hey, down boy." A petite woman, no taller than your average ten-year-old, came bustling through the doorway of unit 4. Dressed in holey jeans, a tee-shirt that told us exactly how much she didn't like mornings, and long black leather boots, she was all eye-rolls and hand waving as she strode up to the glowering giant and punched him on the thigh. "Benny," she growled. "How many times have I told you not to go all Sylvester Stallone and scare people off? One day you'll give a little old lady a heart attack and then how will you feel?" She turned to us and tipped her head to one side. "Hi, I'm Tuesday. Don't mind my friend, Benjamin Eli Stark, better known as Big Ben, he's actually all custard and cream once you get to know him. Bit rough round the edges, but I'm working on ironing them out." She stood on tiptoe and punched the giant a little higher than the thigh this time. "Thinks he's the caretaker around here. But he's not."

"Aww, Tuesday, I was just lookin' out for Corey." The big guy's bottom lip quivered like a five-year old. "These gals could be hustlin' him for money."

"No, no, we're not," Abi assured him, shaking her head so vigorously her ponytail started doing the tango. "We just want to talk to him. Honest."

"Corey's gone," said Tuesday and sighed. "Lost his job a few weeks ago and then some mongrel fleeced him of all his money. He's broke. Had to move out."

Corey had lost everything? I frowned. Did that make him more likely to be our killer? Or not? I watched Big Ben carefully hunker down beside Penelope and gently scratch her behind the ears. The greyhound looked up and gave him a goofy smile of thanks. I smiled too. The big guy might be granite on the outside but there couldn't be too much wrong with his heart if Penelope accepted him so readily. "Do you know where Corey's gone?" I asked him.

"Under the bridge with the others, last I saw 'im."

"Under the bridge? What bridge?"

"And what others?" asked Abi.

"The other homeless guys," explained Tuesday, also reaching out to add to Penelope's pleasure by scratching her tummy. "There's a sort of colony who've got together and camp out under the Nautical Bridge at the back of the old tyre factory."

"On Shipwreck Road?"

Tuesday nodded. "Corey's not the first from here. We've had a couple guys get kicked out cos they couldn't pay their rent and they live under the bridge too." She shrugged. "There's shelter, water nearby and no one bothers them."

"Gotta be careful though," cautioned Ben, pulling thoughtfully at his ear lobe. "They're leery of strangers."

"Need to watch your back," agreed Tuesday. "There's a couple of dodgy guys hang out there sometimes. Been known to pinch money or grab your phone right out of your hand. And it doesn't pay to stand up to them."

Big Ben flexed his muscles in a show of strength. "Want me to come with ya?"

Both Abi and Molly sent me horrified, "no, no, no!' glances leaving me with the task of politely turning the giant down. "Thanks, Ben, really appreciate your offer," I said, before indicating Penelope with one hand. "But as you can see, we have our own protection."

The big guy's eyebrows lowered as he peered down at my killer greyhound who'd decided it might be easier for Tuesday to tickle her tummy if she lay on the ground with her four legs in the air. "Um…cheers then, mate," he said, "but if anyone does get outta line, just tell 'em Big Ben's gonna bang heads. That'll back 'em off."

For all his badass hulking exterior, Benjamin Eli Stark was basically a good guy.

I must have looked as though I might change my mind about bringing him with us, because Abi immediately bustled us back to our cars, reminding us time was ticking on and if we wanted to check on Corey before work, we didn't have a minute to lose.

Nautical Bridge, at the back of the old tyre factory on Shipwreck Road, was quiet when we pulled up. Three homeless guys with supermarket trollies laden with all their worldly goods and a middle-aged woman dressed in several layers of clothing squatted around a makeshift fire. They were toasting what looked like dead rats, but on closer inspection proved to be soggy, well-past-their-use-by-date crumpets, probably rescued from a curb-side bin before the garbage-collector made his rounds.

"Good morning," I called out as we locked our cars and approached the breakfasters, Penelope on the end of her lead, tail wagging, eager to discover what was on the menu. "Anyone know where we can find Corey Black?"

The woman with multiple-layers of clothing reluctantly lifted her head and pointed to a large cardboard box parked under the bridge about fifty meters further on.

The other three didn't even look up and meet our eyes, although I could feel those same guarded eyes boring into my back once we'd gone past their camp fire.

Maybe they were wary about us stealing something from their supermarket trolleys which they kept within grabbing distance. Two were full of clothes and other personal belongings while the grizzled man in the furry cap on the far side of the fire had loaded his trolley up with firewood and old bicycle wheels.

Once we'd picked our way through the scrub, rocks, and rubbish to the thick cardboard box which had once housed a family sized refrigerator – according to the faded printing on the side – we stopped, unsure what to do next. None of us knew Corey that well. What to say? 'Hey Corey, did you finally blow your stack and kill Stephen Channing?' didn't sound quite right as a greeting.

There was a greenish-colored blanket hanging across the entrance to the box and a supermarket trolly loaded with bits and pieces from Corey's former life parked outside.

Abi knocked on the side of the box. "Corey, are you home?"

"Go way…"

"We're friends from the dog show," put in Molly, making her voice soft and hard-to-refuse.

"Corey, we only want to talk to you," said Abi.

"Won't take up much of your time," I added, closing my eyes so I could pretend I didn't see Penelope, who I'd let off the lead, stick her head around the side of the blanket and stroll inside the box.

After a welcoming yap from inside, I watched Penelope carefully back her way out again. She was followed by Corey's scraggly black miniature poodle, Pablo. Always a happy dog with a grin on his face, Pablo danced around our feet, begging to be picked up and cuddled, and when we declined, due to the dead fish smell and river-mud caked through his coat, he danced up and down on the spot, yapping at Penelope who was zooming round and round the cardboard box, legs a blur. Finally, after at least twenty laps, she ran out of steam and flopped on the ground beside me, mouth wide, tongue lolling to the side.

With a roll of my eyes, I looked down at her and sighed. So much for my sensible, well-mannered, protective bodyguard…

A round face, almost as dirty as Pablo's blinked up at us as the blanket was lifted and Corey Black poked his head around the side of the box. He frowned. "Go 'way! Don't want you coming here and seeing me like this. It's embarrassing."

"Being poor is nothing to be embarrassed about," I said, diving into my voluminous bag and passing him a juice packet and an energy bar from my kiddy-stock.

"But committing murder is," said Molly, one eye on the woman who'd got up from the camp fire and pushed her trolly full of old newspapers and magazines closer. All the better to hear.

"Murder?" yelped Corey. "What are you talking about?"

"We're investigating Stephen Channing's murder and you have to admit he wasn't a friend of yours," continued Molly, the worst interviewer in history.

"It's okay, Corey," I said, giving Molly the back-off glare, which naturally flew over her head. "Chi's in jail for Stephen's murder and we think he's innocent, so we're just asking a few questions, checking out anyone who had reason to hate him."

Corey crawled the rest of the way out of his box and stood up. His shoulders were slumped, his eyes tired and he looked beaten. "Well," he said bending down to pick up his furball, mud and all. He cuddled the little dog to his chest as though Pablo was the only creature left in the world that loved him. "I definitely qualify. I hated the bully's guts. He swindled me out of all my money, he treated me like snot and after slamming my head into a steel pole didn't even bother to apologize." He let out a long-drawn-out sigh and his shoulders sagged even further. "But I didn't kill him."

I met Corey's eyes. Scowled my scepticism at his denial. "Are you sure about that?"

For inside the cardboard box he used as a home I could see a thin mattress, a pillow, a blanket and an open suitcase. And spread out on top of his clothes, like a creepy souvenir, was a familiar chunky gold chain.

Identical to that worn by Stephen Channing the day he was murdered.

11

"That's Stephen Channing's gold chain." Stressing each word separately for emphasis, I pointed at the indisputable evidence lying in plain sight in Corey's suitcase. "Where did you get it? From around his neck after you stabbed him to death inside his bus?"

This changed everything...

"No, no, I didn't kill him," Corey bleated, tears trickling down his cheeks. "The chain broke when Stephen pushed me into the pole. He didn't notice when it fell to the ground. Please, I know I shouldn't have taken it but when he didn't even say sorry, I thought, damn you Stephen Channing, you've taken all my money, so I'm going to keep your favourite gold chain for myself."

"You've got to be kidding me," I told him in my scariest voice, the one I'd perfected while dealing with the Yummy Mummies at *Baby Bunting*.

"Honestly, it wasn't me. Stephen was awful to me and Pablo, called us all sorts of nasty names and he was blackmailing me, but I didn't kill him." Corey's cheeks were wet with tears. "I-I can't even kill spiders and they scare the heck out of me. I use a jar and relocate them outside."

By now, both Pablo and my Penelope were all over the little man. Pablo licking the tears off his owner's face while my soppy greyhound rubbed up against his legs and tried to push her head into his open hand in commiseration.

"You'd better sit down, before you fall over," said Abi wrapping one arm around both Corey and his dog and leading them across to a faded blue plastic crate that had seen better days before being dumped under the bridge. "Then you can tell us about how Stephen was blackmailing you." Once Corey was perched on the crate Abi produced a handful of clean tissues for him from her pocket. "And please, stop crying, or you'll have me in tears too."

"Sorry." Corey sniffed as he wiped his eyes with the tissues. "I'll try not to."

"So, if you didn't kill Stephen," I said, not completely won over by his tears. 'Where were you at the time of his murder?"

"You don't believe me," he wailed. And started crying again.

"No, no, it's not that we don't believe you," soft-hearted Molly assured him, patting his head as if he were a distraught dog. "We just want to establish whether you went straight home after the show finished or stayed to help clean up, and…and maybe saw something or some*one* acting suspiciously."

While focussing on Corey, we'd forgotten the breakfasters sitting around the campfire, but when I glanced up, away from Corey's tear-smeared face, I noticed the three homeless men, plus the woman wearing several layers of clothing, had moved closer. In fact, one, a man whose scruffy beard bore the remains of his crumpet breakfast, was so close, his hot breath scorched the side of my neck and the rancid smell of his unwashed clothes forced me to take more shallow breaths.

"Corey doesn't want to talk to you," Bearded Guy said, muscling his way into my space, his eyes hard as he returned my stare with one of malice.

"I think that's up to Corey," I told him, tamping down my fear and refusing to take a step back. Which left us nose to nose. Not a wonderful place to be as his nose, struggling its way through his equally wild unkempt moustache, showed traces of a recent violent sneeze.

"It's okay, Bluey. I'm fine," said Corey, looking up at his glowering rescuer with leaking eyes. "I *want* to talk to the *Gumshoe Chicks*.

They're good at solving mysteries. They'll find Stephen's murderer and then I won't be a suspect and no one will bother me anymore."

"You sure, ducky?" The woman moved closer to Corey and gently lifted his chin with one finger, forcing him to look into her eyes. "'Cos if you want us to run these gals outta here so they'll never come back, just give us the word. We're all brothers and sisters here under the bridge."

"Thanks, Matilda. You're the best." With another sniff, Corey grabbed the homeless woman's hand and lifted it to his lips. He looked up at the others. "In fact, I love you all, but I want to help these ladies find out who murdered Stephen. Not because I liked him – the man was nothing but a bully and a crook – but because his lover, Chi, is a good guy and he's in jail for a murder he didn't commit."

Abi tipped her head to the side. "You told these people about Stephen's murder?"

"Of course." Corey nodded. "No secrets here under the bridge. It's our motto. What we live by."

"You know," said the guy with the furry cap, leaning on the handle of his trolly full of firewood and bicycle wheels. "Like in that movie with the three macho guys in fancy dress. 'All for one and one for all…'"

Molly grinned. "The Three Musketeers?"

Furry cap guy nodded.

"But there's five of you."

"So," he said, his wide grin revealing three remaining teeth. "All the better for us."

Corey stood up, his little dog sliding to the ground where Penelope was waiting, anxious to check him out, make sure he was okay. After licking Pablo's face, she lay down beside him, his head resting on her shoulder. Both dogs seem to sense the tension in the air.

Corey wiped his face clean of grime and tears and visibly straightened his shoulders. "I'm sorry I lost it, ladies. Been a few bad weeks and when you showed up accusing me of Stephen's murder, it was all too much. I'm okay now and ready to answer any of your questions."

"My fault." Molly looked ready to cry herself. "Dana keeps telling me I need to work on my interrogation techniques. Go ahead, Corey, call me some bad names. I deserve it."

Corey smiled at her, his smile lighting up his face and revealing an inherent sweetness that few people possess. "The only names I can think to call you, Molly, are cute, pretty, and lovable."

"She already has a boyfriend, Corey." Abi grinned. "And as well as being a Harley-owning biker, her boyfriend's a cop."

"Damn." Corey's eyes twinkled. "My loss, I guess."

"Now we've established that Molly isn't girlfriend material for you," I put in, "can you think back to what happened after the show last Saturday? Did you hang around for a while or go straight home?"

"I stayed to help clean up."

"And did you go near the Windswept Kennels bus?"

Corey blew out a breath before answering. "Yes, I went looking for Stephen. I think the final bang on the head made me realize I was acting like a dumb jerk. I wanted to tell him I couldn't pay any more money and that I had proof he was blackmailing me. See, I'd recorded our last phone conversation and intended taking it to the police if he didn't stop hassling me." Corey's eyes never left mine. "But I couldn't find him. Neither Stephen nor Chi were anywhere near the bus, which I found a little strange as they're usually very particular about leaving their dogs unattended."

"Was anyone else hanging around near the bus when you were there?"

"No one." He shook his head and then frowned. "Although, I thought I heard a noise *inside* the bus, but when I called out, there was no answer, so I thought it must have been one of their dogs already loaded up ready to go home."

"You heard a noise?" Abi leaned forward, ears virtually twitching. "What sort of noise?"

Corey's brows furrowed. "Not sure. Maybe a bump. But I really wasn't paying much attention at the time because I was desperate to find Stephen, and as I said, I thought it was a loose dog in the bus, so I left and went hunting for him in the cafeteria."

"Hmm…" Molly chewed on her thumb-nail in thought. "So, the killer might have been inside the bus when you were there. Either with Stephen dead at his feet or waiting for him, knife in hand."

Corey's face paled. "And if I'd opened the back doors to investigate…" He gave a little choking sound, his legs wobbled and he sank back down on the crate, his breath coming in gasps.

"Sorry, sorry." Molly pulled a face as she danced on the spot. "I'm doing it again. I'm scaring you."

"What if the killer saw me? What if he decides to murder me, too?"

Humming to herself, Matilda removed one of her layers, a khaki-colored coat and wrapped it around Corey's shoulders. "It's okay, dearie," she crooned, like Mumma Bear to Baby Bear. "Just keep yourself warm and think of a juicy piece of steak surrounded by fat brown chips."

"But what if the killer saw my face?" Corey tugged at the collar of Matilda's coat. "My face is one of a kind. When I was little my mum always told me, I've got a face like no one else."

I had to agree with his mother. Corey's round child-like face was a one-off.

"No one is going to hurt you, dearie," said Matilda as she and the three homeless men drew closer, virtually wrapping themselves around Corey in solidarity. "You're safe with us."

I studied their 'safe' environment and a chill prickled down my spine. We were surrounded by dry scrub, salt bushes and piles of rubbish, likely dumped by those who couldn't afford the rising prices charged by legitimate rubbish tips – or Waste & Recycling Centres as they now called themselves. Their home was under the shelter of an old cement foot-bridge, rarely used since the large tyre factory nearby closed down, the arches decorated in colorful tags and epistles left by local graffiti artists. One such message assuring us in foot-high purple letters, 'HUMPTY DUMPTY WAS PUSHED'.

But I guess 'safe' has different connotations in different circumstances. This homeless group considered themselves safe because they were united. Because they lived by the motto, 'All for one and one for all', words as strong today as they were almost two hundred years ago when penned by Alexandre Dumas.

"Whoever was in that bus when you went calling wouldn't have seen you, Corey," I told him. "When Chi and Stephen had the bus converted to a dog carrier, all the windows were closed in along the sides and a barrier built between the driver's seat and the dog area."

"But they would have heard my voice."

"Maybe, but unless you know a person intimately, it's almost impossible to recognize anyone by their voice alone."

"There ya go, mate," said Fur Hat clapping Corey on the back with a teeth-rattling thump. "Nothin' to worry about."

Whether it was Fur Hat's confidence, Matilda's mindfulness, the Alexandre Dumas motto, or that Corey had finally decided it was time to man up, when he looked back at me, he'd grown visibly taller. "Dana," he said, eyes holding mine like he was drawing extra strength from me. "I may not be your classic James Bond devil-may-care movie character, but if there's anything you need me to do to help with your investigation, I'm up for it."

"Appreciated." Refraining from telling him exactly how far removed he was from being a classic James Bond devil-may-care movie character, I decided to push my luck a little further and see if I could prod more information from him. "Corey, you don't have to say anything if you don't want to, but I just can't see you as some badass crim. What I mean is…I'm struggling to believe that Stephen could dig anything up in your past bad enough to blackmail you."

"But I am. A badass crim, that is."

"No way," scoffed Abi.

"Way." Corey gave a loud sniff. "Years ago, I was the lookout at a robbery. See, the two Campbell brothers, tough guys in our neighbourhood, guys you couldn't say no to, stole my dog, a bitzer called Sausage, and threatened to chop his tail off with a blunt axe if I didn't stand lookout at the supermarket while they broke in and stole cigarettes." He shook his head and let out a sigh. "And I couldn't even do that right. I was such a useless pathetic lookout. I stood there shaking, eyes closed, hands over my ears. And when this cop who'd been passing by spotted me and tapped me on the shoulder to see if I was okay, I actually wet myself with fright." He tipped his head back and stared at the sky. "Sooo humiliating."

"How old were you?" asked Molly clearly affected by his story.

"Ten."

"Oh, Corey," she said, her voice close to breaking. "You were a victim. Not a badass crim."

"I still took part in a robbery."

I could imagine Corey as a frightened ten-year-old being forced into crime to save his little dog, but what I couldn't work out was how Stephen found out about his consequent arrest. "Your juvie records would have been sealed so who told Stephen?"

"One of the Campbell brothers, Des, happened to be repairing a broken window at Windswept Kennels when I rocked up with a delivery of fifty-five bags of kibble from the warehouse." Corey shrugged as though being in the wrong place at the wrong time was the story of his life. "First time I'd seen either of the Campbell brothers since leaving the Northfield area over twenty-years ago. And naturally, Des couldn't wait to tell Stephen the amusing story of 'the lookout who peed himself while on duty'…and it went from there. Wouldn't be surprised if old Des got a cut out of the blackmail money himself."

"So, how long have you been paying Stephen to keep quiet?" I asked.

"Just on six months. He cleaned out my bank account, I ended up taking too many days off from work due to depression, lost my job, lost my unit because I couldn't pay my rent…" He indicated the bleak landscape underneath the old foot bridge with one hand. "…and ended up here."

Corey was more than a victim, if left too long in this environment, he could end up a suicide statistic. I exchanged a quick glance with Abi and Molly and could see my own thoughts reflected in their faces. Diving into my voluminous bag, I pulled out five more energy bars, a business card displaying my phone number and a two-dollar piece. After handing out the bars, I tucked the card and the coin into one of Corey's coat pockets. "Now, listen up, Corey. If there's anything we can do to help you or your friends, or you feel down and want to talk to someone, promise me you'll get to a phone box and give me a call. Right?"

Eyes on the ground, Corey nodded.

"Enough chit-chat, ladies and gentlemen. It's ten o'clock," said Matilda, slipping her energy bar somewhere in amongst her many layers of clothing while frowning up at the sky, evidently checking the time by the position of the sun. "We'd better skedaddle. If we don't get to the Food Bank drop-off early enough, that greedy mob of lefties from the park will bag all the best tomatoes, potatoes, and apples."

"Thieves," grunted the guy with the grotty whiskers, "last time we were late, all they left us was a couple of squashed loaves of bread."

Feeling overfed and inadequate, I watched the five Musketeers collect their trollies and move off, chattering, laughing and heading down the track toward the road and to wherever the Food Bank met weekly to make sure those in need at least had tomatoes, potatoes, apples and bread to live on.

"Don't know how lucky we are, do we?" said Abi her eyes still on the departing trolly-pushers.

Her phone buzzed from deep inside one of her pockets. When she checked the caller ID, her face broke into a huge grin. "Nathan, baby. Can't manage without hearing my voice for more than a couple of hours, heh? Though, I must admit we didn't do much talking last night."

Molly and I rolled our eyes and let out a groan. Once Abi got on the phone with her P.I. boyfriend, Nathan Forrester, it was time to block our ears and tune out.

We began walking back to our parked cars, with Abi trailing behind, still chatting away on her phone.

Suddenly her voice grew sharp. "You found out *what*?"

I spun around to find Abi looking tense; her lovey-dovey air replaced by an alert *Gumshoe Chick* persona. "What is it Abs? Everything okay with Nathan?"

"It's Patricia," she said. "Nathan's done a background check on Patricia and she hasn't got a cousin."

I digested this piece of news and frowned. "Interesting, seeing all her information about Gemma supposedly came from her cousin."

"But that's not all." Abi had come to a standstill and the gleam in her eyes and the small twist to her lips told us the best was yet to come. "Patricia Stamford's bank account shows that for the last five months she's been transferring a thousand dollars a month into a special account set up by Stephen Channing." Abi's grin broke through. "And those payments stopped two weeks before he was murdered."

12

Another early morning meeting…
And let me add, getting two sleepy munchkins out of bed, fed, dressed, and into the car by 5.45am, while my other-half is still stretched out on the marital bed, snoring – probably for another blissful two hours – can be a test for any marriage. As I scowled down at my sleeping husband, the urge to accidently upend a glass of icy water over that bare muscular chest, had me fighting my inner demons with nail-biting determination, teeth-clamping grimaces, and good old iron will.

After Abi's PI boyfriend, Nathan, hit the jackpot when doing a background check on Patricia the day before, the other two *Chicks* and I decided to mull over our latest discovery, come up with ideas, and reconvene at the local dog park at 6.00am this morning. At that time, the park is always less crowded and therefore there's less chance of any doggy disasters – always a danger when multiple canine personalities are let off the lead in a dog park.

We figured, this way, we'd end up with three bonuses in one. The dogs would get exercised, my munchkins could play in the fresh air and we'd hopefully finish off with a solid brainstorming session.

Not that I'd come up with any useful ideas since yesterday. Instead, since Nathan's game-changing hit, I'd been up to my armpits in shampoo, wet dogs and distracting owners. Don't get me wrong. I love my clients, both human and canine, and my heart warms every time I see humans smiling and canine tails wagging, when they spot my car and trailer turning into their driveway.

But other than contacting Edward so I could bring him up to date with our latest 'find' and inviting him and Gemma to our early morning meeting, I hadn't come up with even one clue as to how the wife of a multi-million-dollar company and the flashy breeder of prize-winning show poodles had crossed paths, let alone become blackmail-*er* and blackmail-*ee* – if there is such a word.

"Mummy! Mummy! Look at Chloe-dog!" Kayla let out a squeal from her car carrier in the back seat. "She got Charlie Caterpillar. Oh, no! Look, Mummy! Busta took Chloe's caterpillar." She shook her head and tutted, so much like the animated Mrs. Tyler, from day-care, I had to stifle a giggle. "Naughty Busta!"

Jake bounced up and down in his carrier seat. "Me want *Cackypilla*!"

"Charlie is Chloe's toy and he's covered in dirt and spit," I told Jake, killing the engine and passing his beloved stuffed toy dog over the seat. Doggo wasn't in much better shape than Chloe's caterpillar but at least he wasn't covered in dog spit.

Kayla, undoing the seat belt on her carrier and eager to get out of the car, leaned forward, her fairy wings brushing against the back of my head. "Can I please go play with the dogs, Mummy?"

As we were parked less than five metres from the gate to the dog park, I nodded. "Uh-huh. But don't try to take their toys away. Remember what I told you. Not all dogs are like our Penelope."

By the time I'd unfastened my wriggly eager-to-get-going son and lifted him from the car, I could see Kayla was through the gate, down on her knees, arms spread out in front of her as both Chloe and Busta gave her a welcoming face-wash.

"Hang on, Jakey," I said, but Jake, eyes on Chloe's *cakypilla*, his own Doggo clutched to his chest, was already waddling across to the dog park gate, where Abi was waiting to let him in.

I sighed as I opened the car's rear door and watched an eager Penelope throw herself out. She was gone and through the open gate before I could say, 'take it easy, girl', and I was left alone to retrieve my ever-present Mummy bag of necessities, grab a large tartan blanket from the back seat, lock the car doors, and wonder if the new hand creme I'd used liberally this morning smelled of dead fish instead of the coconut the label had promised.

Gemma and Edward hadn't arrived yet and there were only two other early birds using the dog park. A stooped gentleman in his late seventies with an equally elderly Labrador, well-trained, as it barely left his owner's side, and a teenage girl with a scatty ginger-colored cocker spaniel. A real diva, the dog squealed every time Busta, in one of his mad flights, brushed past her. The teenager owner, sitting cross-legged on the ground, back up against a large rock, was so into her phone, she didn't even look up.

"Where's Fly?" I asked surfing the dog park and not seeing *Windswept Fly By Me*, the stunning standard poodle that Abi was babysitting for Chi.

Abi grimaced. "Wasn't game to bring him along. Fly's so valuable, every time he sneezes, I'm on the phone to the vet." She paused and shook her head. "It's not that Fly's any trouble – I'm just paranoid something might happen to him before we find Stephen's murderer and Chi's released from prison."

"Totally understandable," I told her, immensely glad I wasn't the one in charge of the valuable show dog as I visualized Kayla dressing Fly up as a fairy while Jake painted his beautiful long coat with a glue stick.

Molly came jogging up, Busta tucked under one arm. "Might have to put my boy on a lead. That dizzy cocker spaniel screams blue murder every time Busta gets within ten meters of her." Molly's face was red and sweaty and I could see a frown pasted between her eyes. She indicated the phone-obsessed teenager with a flick of her head. "If Madam over there would deign to glance up from her phone occasionally and check on her dog, it would make life easier for everyone else."

"Let's wander across to the other side of the park while we're waiting for Edward and Gemma," I suggested, refraining from giving Madam the rough edge of my tongue. I figured wresting a teenager from the gripping relationships on social media would require one hundred percent dedication and what with a zooming greyhound and two squealing munchkins already on my radar, I let it go. "There's a nice quiet spot on the other side of the dog park. We'll settle in and wait for the two lovebirds over there."

"You're right about Edward and Gemma. Can't keep their hands off each other," said Molly, still toting her wriggly fox terrier under one arm while frantically dodging his over-active wet tongue, as we made our way toward bushes, sprawling trees, a jungle gym and a covered sand pit, perfect for the dogs and the kids to play in. "They're quite sweet really."

"Aah...the first throes of love." Abi let out a sigh. "I remember it well."

"Remember it?" I let out a hoot. "Every time you and Nathan see each other you look like you 'need a room'."

"Yeah," Molly added. "Almost time you moved in together."

"Or is there a special announcement on the near-horizon?"

Abi's grin widened. The twinkle in her eye indicated that either one of those scenarios might be on the cards very soon. From the moment Abi climbed the stairs to Nathan's comfortable but high-tech PI office six months ago to seek help investigating a cheating boyfriend, it had been one of those Hallmark moments – you know, *love at first sight*.

By now we'd reached the other side of the park and while I spread the tartan blanket out on the grass, Molly placed a squirming Busta on the ground and watched him take off with Chloe, the little dachshund's colorful toy caterpillar bouncing along between them.

I glanced down at Penelope. Ears straining, eyes fastened on the other two dogs, she obviously wanted to join her friends, but instead, she stood motionless. Jake, one pudgy hand on her back, was leaning against her, and there was no way she would move while my youngest needed her support.

"Come on, Jakey!" Fairy wings flapping, Kayla skipped across the grass and took a dive into the sand pit, landing on her knees. "Help me build a fairy house in the sand."

Fairy house? Hmm…evidently sand *castles* were too last year…

With a squeal, Jake let go of Penelope and ran toward the sand pit, his fat little legs struggling to keep up with his enthusiasm. Penelope waited until Jake reached his sister's side, before letting out a joyful woof and zooming off to join in the current game of chase-and-toss-the-caterpillar-in-the-air. My heart warmed. The corners of my lips turned up in a smile that tugged at my chest. Just how special can one greyhound be?

Abi, who'd brought along a canvas folding chair, set her seat up next to the blanket, sat down, and began rummaging inside her bag, finally unearthing a hard plastic water bowl and a packet of dog treats.

"You make a good dog-Mummy," I told her, supressing a grin. "Which means you'll make a good baby-Mummy when the time comes."

Abi's right eyebrow shot upwards. She'd always declared her womb a baby-free zone, complete with an expression of horror whenever the concept of actually 'giving birth' was mentioned. Maybe now there was a possible baby-daddy on the horizon, her ideas might have changed.

Although, if that wide-eyed stare and violent head-shake were to be believed, maybe not.

It didn't take long for the dogs to run out of steam and flop down in the sand beside the children. While Penelope lay on her back, four legs in the air, Busta and Chloe stretched out, tongues lolling to the side, gazing with interest at the sand-structures that kept losing their shape, especially the house Kayla built for Doggo, which unfortunately caved in the moment Jake attempted to install his stuffed dog inside. Busta, ever helpful, dug a deep hole beside Doggo's collapsed house and called it a swimming pool.

6.51 am and still no sign of Edward and Gemma.

Just as I cleared my throat ready to start the meeting without them by bringing up the first item on our agenda, a shiny black Toyota Camry spewed gravel as it screeched to a halt in the car park next to my SUV. Immediately Eddy, Gemma and Gemma's poodle, Samantha, spilled out onto the tarmac. They waved excitedly, called out and after hurrying through the gateway into the dog park, Gemma let Samantha off the lead.

Twenty-one minutes late.

Although you wouldn't think it the way they came tripping across the park, hand in hand, all smiles, like a couple of high-school kids experiencing their very first love affair.

"Sorry we're late," said Gemma with a grin as they reached us. She giggled, definitely like a high-school girl and rested her head on Edward's shoulder. "We didn't get much sleep last night."

"T. M. I.," said Molly, flicking an eye roll in their direction. "Or you'll find yourselves starring in my next romance novel."

"As long as my badass picture is on the front cover," teased Edward, running a hand through his already tousled hair and posing as though for a camera shoot.

"So," I said, drawing the word out as I let my beady eye fall on each member of our team, determined to bring the meeting under control. "What do we do about Patricia?"

"Good question." Molly sunk down beside me on the blanket, pulling her legs up to her chin. "For which I have no answer. It's just too bizarre. How could Stephen have dug up secrets in Patricia's past? How does he even *know* the woman?"

Abi, who was filling the dog bowl with water from a public drinking fountain adjacent to the sand pit, looked up. "And did she kill Stephen to shut him up? Or because he got greedy and was asking for more money?"

"Or maybe she couldn't allow anything or anyone to tarnish her privileged lifestyle?" Edward's voice told us he was speaking from first-hand experience. He'd made himself comfortable on the tartan picnic blanket with Gemma tucked between his legs, leaning back against his body. His arms were wrapped around her waist, all the better to pull her closer whenever he wanted to nuzzle his lips against the soft skin on the back of her neck. An act that caused her to purr like a well-fed cat.

"What if *you* asked Patricia a few questions?" Abi said, looking at Edward. "You're in the best position, being her husband. Maybe she'd open up to you."

"Don't think so." Gemma shook her head. "When I said we didn't get much sleep last night, it wasn't *all* spent under the sheets." She turned her head to grin at Edward who leant forward so he could plant a light kiss on her forehead. "We actually *visited* Patricia last night. Together. Hand in hand. And told her that Edward and I were in love, that he wanted a divorce, and we were taking off for England at the end of the month."

I let out a gasp. Knowing Patricia's characteristically vitriolic response whenever thwarted, I leaned forward, eager to hear more. "And how did she react to that little bombshell?"

Edward shrugged one shoulder. "Well, if you don't count screaming obscenities, throwing whatever wasn't screwed down, and outlining how many ways she was going to prevent Gemma and me from leaving the country, including never allowing me to see my son again, then, yes, she was all for it."

"And what about Noble?" I asked aghast at the thought of never seeing your child again.

"I rarely see Noble now. His life is directed like a symphony orchestra by his mother and grandfather. His every waking minute is filled with planned activities – none of which include me, his father. Once our divorce is through, I'm hoping to get custody of our son. Or at least, have him with me for school holidays so I can show him that life isn't all work. That it can also include fun."

"But that's not all," said Gemma, looking ready to burst from withholding new information. "Even though Patricia would sooner eat cane toad than answer any of Eddy's questions after last night's visit, my clever *Pussycat* worked out the reason Stephen was blackmailing her." She dimpled at Edward who squeezed her hand and returned her grin. "Take it away, my darling."

Edward settled Gemma more comfortably between his legs before answering. "Well, about five years ago, Patricia was caught embezzling funds from some charity their Company runs. She let the secret out one night early on in our marriage. Evidently her father was furious at the time, but their slick, well-heeled lawyer managed to bury the information and pay off the charity, so it was never made public."

"But how did Stephen find out?"

"That's the best part. This well-paid lawyer, who tends to open his big mouth when plied liberally with vodka, has the same surname as Stephen." He nodded. "Yep. The lawyer's name is Tyson G. Channing."

"Tyson G. Channing?" Molly repeated, eyes wide.

He grinned at her. "Coincidence?"

"Easily enough confirmed." I turned to Abi who was leaning so far forward in her chair I expected her to overbalance and join us on the blanket. "Your mission for today is to call Nathan – no hard task – and ask him to run a more intensive background check on Patricia. Yes, and also to do a background check on the Stamford's lawyer, Tyson G. Channing."

"Aye! Aye! Captain." Abi lifted her right hand in a salute. "In fact, I'll grab sandwiches and coffees and take a run across to Nathan's office during my lunch break."

I rolled my eyes. "Umm… Maybe not a good idea."

"I second that." Molly let out a deep-throated giggle. "Once you walk through that office door, sandwiches, coffee, and background checks will be the last thing on Nathan's mind."

"And Molly," I said, thinking quickly. Time was running out and we all had to get organized for our busy working day. "Either before or after you start on your daily word count for your latest book, can you ring and organize an appointment for us at the Adelaide Remand Center? It's time we paid Chi a visit in jail. Listen to his side of the story. See if he has any clues we missed."

"On it."

"And as for you two." I poked a stiff finger into *Pussycat's* back and rolled my eyes while waiting for him and *Dumpling* to come up for air.

"Do you think you could concentrate long enough to take part in this investigation?"

Edward's grin was playful. "At your service, Ma'am."

"Mmm…" Gemma, eyes still closed, drifted back to earth more slowly, her smile dreamy.

I eyed Edward with barely contained exasperation as he leant forward to run his lips over Gemma's closed eye lids. "Edward!" I lifted both my voice and my eyes to the heavens, sitting on my hands to stop from shaking the pair of them. "Do you still have keys to your house or has Patricia changed the locks?"

"Yes, to the first, and no to the second. What's your plan?"

"We need evidence that Patricia is the killer," I told him.

"Like a personal diary," said Abi.

"Or an article of clothing belonging to Patricia, all screwed up at the bottom of a garbage bin, splattered in Stephen's blood," added Molly, always the more melodramatic member of our trio. Probably due to her being a best-selling romance writer.

"Look, Edward, I don't want you acting like a hapless fly waltzing into a spider's parlour." I frowned at him. He grinned back. I shook my head. Geez, if Patricia *was* the murderer, she would have no qualms in shooting her soon-to-be-ex in the back – just to stop him leaving and taking their son with him. Probably bury his body in her prize-winning petunia patch. "Wait until Patricia goes out and then sneak into the house and dig around. See what you can find." I waited for him to nod to show he understand. "And be extra careful."

"Will do."

"This should be fun," said Gemma, clapping her hands together. "I'll be the galah."

"Cockatoo," corrected Abi referring to the Australian slang for a 'lookout' - someone who keeps watch during an illegal activity.

"I want you reporting back the moment you find anything of interest. Okay?" I waited for Edward's nod. "As for me, I'm taking part in a 'get fit' session at the local gym later this afternoon, in between my last hydro bath client and when I pick the munchkins up from day-care."

"You are?" Abi grimaced. "Now you're making me feel guilty. The three of us were supposed to enrol in a gym so we could improve our fitness."

I pursed my lips to let her know there was more coming. "It's a one-on-one gym session. And guess who's the instructor?"

"No idea," put in Molly who didn't look one bit guilty about *her* lack of fitness.

"It's Mister Cute. Rick Starling. Our beagle-guy. I rang the gym and booked the session earlier this week as we hadn't got around to interviewing him yet. Thought I might slip in a few questions while I'm pumping iron."

Abi laughed. "I'd like to see that. You do realize how little breath you have left for talking, while lifting weights?"

"I'll find some." I stood up, grabbed my extra-large Mummy bag and shook out two boxes of juice and a couple of energy bars. Jake and Kayla were currently squabbling over who loved Gemma's black poodle the most, Kayla proclaiming she loved the little dog, *sixty-six times twice*, while Jake, bottom lip trembling, held both hands in the air, all ten fingers erect, while insisting, 'Me love doggy *that* many!'

Before the disagreement had time to escalate, I handed out the goodies, collected both pairs of shoes from the edge of the sand pit and slipped them back onto their feet, ready to go.

"Okay, let's race the dogs to that tree over there," I suggested pointing. "The one with lots of arms sticking out. Last one to the tree is a big fat wimp."

"Meeting officially over," I called out over my shoulder as I took off, Kayla one side and a giggling Jake on the other. All four dogs, plus the ditzy cocker spaniel who'd finally found us again, attempting to trip us over as we ran.

If Patricia was the killer and Edward found the evidence to put her away, Chi would soon be released from jail and the leader of the Yummy Mummies would be hassling the inmates at the Adelaide Women's Prison, instead of hassling me at *Baby Buntings*.

13

Our local gym, *Shape Up Fitness Center* was located between a doctor's surgery and a Krispy Kreme donut shop. Convenient, I thought, as I parked in front of *Shape up* and killed the engine. Sprain an ankle on the treadmill and there was a doctor on call. Suffer a low sugar episode while striving to lift those extra five pounds in weight and the best sugar-hit establishment in the Western World was right next door waiting to drop a Kookies N Kreme donut straight into your gasping mouth.

Due to a squeezed-in, last-minute booking at work today – an Afghan hound that had escaped the house and rolled in a neighbor's manure pit – I'd missed out on lunch. So, the drool-worthy menu of all those enticing donuts displayed on the sandwich-board out the front of Krispy Kreme', had my stomach growling in anticipation. But no. I was here at *Shape Up* to not only question Rick, but to get fit, not fat. Closing my eyes to the tempting menu, I forced my hunger pains back in their box and reached into the car for my gym bag.

Maybe after I'd sweated off a few pounds I could re-read the menu…

I barrelled through the front doors of *Shape Up*, noticing an interior shop displaying expensive-looking gym attire just inside the door, plus a small eatery that appeared to sell nothing more than smoothies, vitamins, and organic food. A bunch of beautiful people were sitting around a table conversing while showing off their muscles, flawless skin and the fact that they'd rather chow down on animal-fodder than be tempted by the sugary addictions of the shop next door.

After our meeting in the park, it had been a full-on day for me. Eleven dogs of various breeds were now much cleaner, odour-free, and prettier than they were when they woke up this morning. I pulled out my phone and checked the time. Ten minutes to change out of damp overalls into something more gym-appropriate. Ten minutes to get ready for my session with Rick.

The change room was at the rear of the building, of course, which meant I had to produce my membership card and pay in advance at the front desk and then traipse through the busy gym looking like something the cat dragged home after a rain-storm.

"Good *afternoon*! *Welcome* to Shape Up! Hope you're having a *wonderful* day!" The cosmetically enhanced twenty-something, flouncing her bonhomie behind the front desk like a cheer-leader on steroids, had to be a robot. No flesh-and-blood creature could still be that preppy, that positive and look as though she was going to break out singing the first bars of Mary Poppins', 'Let's Go Fly a Kite', after a full shift of working with the public.

I mumbled a greeting, waved my member's card under the Disney Princess's pert little nose and completed the transaction by swiping my bank card. Then, before *Mary Poppins* could begin her upbeat spiel concerning all the extras I'd acquire if I became a Gold Star Member of the gym, as opposed to my current lowly Bronze star, I left her to her peppiness and headed for the change room.

Before leaving for work that morning I'd stuffed a pink tee with the words *I Hate Mornings* plastered across the front, a pair of black shorts – the only pair that didn't exhibit a permanent stain, be it marmalade, vegemite or juice – all child-related – and my favourite pink and white $99.99 Nike cross-trainers into a gym bag. The only thing I'd forgotten in my hurry this morning was my sports' bras. Never mind, this was my first one-on-one session, so I wouldn't be asked to do anything too strenuous and the rather ill-fitting bra I was wearing would have to suffice. If I survived the more intensive work-out and decided to make Rick my regular trainer, I'd invest in a specially fitted sports' bra. Maybe even one of those sweat bands and a pair of yoga pants as well.

It didn't take long to wriggle out of my work overalls and dog-haired tee and even though I was running late, I couldn't resist a two-minute shower before dressing for action. As for my damp hair, a quick brush and a rubber band to pull it into a pony tail and I was ready to show Rick Starling not only how fit the mother of two energetic munchkins could be, but how to question a maybe-suspect without him cottoning on.

My personal training session was scheduled to take place in Room 6 – the sixth door along the passageway. I knocked, opened the door and peeped inside. Soft music gave ambience to the room while a treadmill, a glute machine, a stationary bike and a few other machines I had no name for indicated the sweaty part of what was to come. There was a bench running along one side with several barbells from small to large, a heavy-looking medicine ball and a couple of skipping ropes.

But no Rick.

I poked my head out the door, checked to see if he'd wandered off down the passage looking for me, couldn't see him, so I strolled across to the bench and before sliding my gym bag underneath, removed my water bottle and towel. Two absolute necessities when working out.

Okay. Now I was prepared for whatever barbaric torture he threw at me.

As Rick would be arriving at any moment, I decided I'd better warm my muscles while waiting. We could then get stuck straight into the interesting stuff. Dubiously, I regarded the equipment scattered around the room. Some I knew from my previous rare visits to the gym, while others were completely alien. I pulled experimentally at a handle on one machine and when it sprang back with a clang loud enough to be heard in room 4, or even 3, I took a hurried step back and surveyed the equipment again. Finally, not wanting to either break a bone or an expensive machine before my trainer arrived, I settled for the treadmill.

Any gym dummy knows what to do on a treadmill.

I had just turned the walker up from 'we-might-actually-arrive-somewhere-one-day', to 'look-out-I'm-coming-through', when the door crashed open and a frazzled-looking Rick arrived.

"Sorry, sorry, Dana," he said tossing his gym bag onto the bench where it slid along and took my water bottle out like a skittle. His hair was tousled as though he'd been dragging his fingers through in frustration, one shoelace was undone and there were several raw scratches on his right cheek. "You wouldn't believe the day I've had," he growled rescuing my water bottle from the floor and replacing it on the bench. "And to cap it all off, Birkenhead Bridge was up and traffic was held up for almost fifteen minutes because the damn bridge got stuck and couldn't close."

I nodded in sympathy. I'd been in the same situation a couple of time myself and could commiserate. The Birkenhead Bridge over the Port River was a bascule bridge that opened in two parts to allow tall ships to pass underneath. And yes, occasionally it got stuck on open.

He glanced at me walking on the treadmill and nodded. "Ah, good girl."

"*Girl*?" I let my raised eyebrows do the talking. It was at least twelve years since I'd considered myself one of those.

He turned back to me, a smile ghosting his lips. "Ma'am? Lady? Mrs. Fox? What would you like me to call you?"

"Dana will do nicely."

"Okay, Dana, you've already warmed up. That's great. So, let's proceed with your fitness programme." He glanced down at his notes and frowned. "It says here you're not actually a regular at the gym."

"I've been a few times. Taken a couple of classes."

"Your last class was two years ago. So, why book a one-on-one session with me now?"

"Thought it was time to get serious."

He lifted one eyebrow and visibly flexed his muscles. It was like this guy thought I, like all his other groupies, had a crush on him.

Time to throw that one in the trash. "Plus, you were the only instructor available at this time of day."

"Hmm…"

At the show, we'd found Beagle Guy Rick cute and full of banter. Trainer Rick…not so much. Still cute, dressed in a grey tee shirt with the *Shape Up* emblem on the front and grey jogging pants, but the expression on his face said he was anticipating applying a little extra torture. I switched off the walker and squinted up at him. Not only was his hair tousled, his shoelace undone, but it looked like he'd had a run-in with a an eaglehawk on his way to work. "What happened to your face?"

"Oh, that?" he lifted one hand to his cheek and grimaced. "Never take on a cat that everyone else has rejected. Only brought him home from the Rescue Center three weeks ago, and I've already discovered a dozen reasons why so many families have returned him, pronto."

Aww. Rick Starling was one of the good guys. How many men would put themselves out to rescue any cat, let alone a cat that had a well-established bad boy title? "What's his name?"

"Sugarlumps."

I let out a chuckle. "You're joking."

"Nope." His eyes twinkled. "Never owned a cat before but I figured anyone called Sugarlumps had a reason to be a jerk." He shrugged. "So, I renamed him Tiger."

"And did it work?"

"Nah. In fact, he's taken the name to heart. I'm sure that feline's great-great-great-grandfather was a large striped man-eater." He lifted two barbells from the bench as though they were lolly papers and passed them to me, one in each hand. "Okay, Dana, I want to see four sets of alternating bicep curls. No more. We don't want you deciding to quit after the first five minutes, do we?"

I flipped him my narrow-eyed Mummy-glare. If he thought I was going to give up after four sets of curls, he was delusional. Lifting a squirming toddler at least fifty times a day meant curls with those tiny little barbells would be a piece of cake.

After two sets of eight I was cruising. Three sets – my motor gave a few hiccups. And by the last set, my arm muscles had begun to burn and breathing became a priority. Forcing a smile between breaths, I placed the barbells back on the bench and straightened, forcing myself to continue smiling up at Trainer Rick.

"How's the investigation going?" he asked as he unrolled a deep red gym mat and placed it on the floor.

I blinked. "Investigation?" Hey, I was here to ask questions, not to answer them. And how did he know we were investigating Stephen's murder?

"Well, I know you and the other two *Chicks* are into solving murders, so I guessed you'd be feet-first in the middle of Stephen Channing's grisly murder."

"How do you know about the *Gumshoe Chicks*?"

He laughed. "Everyone at the dog shows knows you, Abi and Molly solved Petra Sullivan's murder and then followed up by catching old Harry's killer." He looked down at my frown and laughed again. "Dog show competitors are like the inhabitants of a small village where gossip spreads like peanut butter on jelly."

"Good analogy."

"Thank you. Now it's time to give your triceps a workout."

"It is?"

He nodded, eyes twinkling, his grin pure evil. "Or in layman's terms – push-ups."

Okay...push-ups weren't too hard. I could do that.

"Now, place both hands on the mat, shoulder-width apart, feet together on the mat behind you while resting on your knees."

I knelt down on the mat before answering his earlier question. Surely someone who rescues unlovable cats could be trusted. "We're actually closing in on the killer."

"That so? Nice one. Now, inhale, bend your elbows and lower your torso towards the mat, ensuring that your elbows remain in close contact with the sides of your body." He paused. "And does this killer you're presently closing in on have a name?"

I didn't answer, instead I bent my elbows and lowered my body to the floor. Until we had proof, it would be wrong of me to divulge Patricia as the killer. Anyway, I was falling down on my job. I was here, sweating and straining my muscles, so I could question Rick yet somehow, he'd turned the tables and was questioning me.

"Good. Now, exhale and extend your elbows to lift your body back into the starting position." I could feel his eyes on me as I pressed upwards. "And repeat for ten repetitions."

Talking while executing push-ups is nigh on impossible. Instead, I concentrated on working those tricep muscles until I'd completed the ten repetitions, then stood up on slightly wobbly legs and puffed my way across to the bench.

I grabbed my water bottle and took a sip. "When you left us at the show, did you go looking for Stephen?"

"Nah. Figured it was easier to ring the guy and make another appointment to discuss a new website."

"Don't suppose you saw anything suspicious when you were leaving? Anyone hanging around Stephen and Chi's dogs?"

"Nah, sorry. Wish I could be of more assistance. But look, if you ever need support, someone to talk to, or even another set of muscles to help in your investigation, you have my phone number."

"I do?"

"Well, you do now." His grin, as he snaffled my phone from the bench and entered his number, emphasized the two ever-so-cute dimples that probably had females of all ages gagging for him.

Um…except for the married ones, like me, of course, who refuse to allow mere cheek craters to send heat flooding to all areas below the belt.

Having added his number to my contacts, he dropped my phone into my gym bag and handed me my towel to wipe the sweat off my face. "When Stephen didn't show up for our meeting in the cafeteria, I let it go." He shrugged one muscly shoulder and I couldn't help noticing a chain reaction going on underneath that tight grey tee shirt. "Didn't bother checking to see if he was still around. And after talking to you and the other two *Chicks* at the showgrounds, I left by the front entrance. Wish I could be more help."

"That's okay."

"Although…" a wrinkled frown appeared between his eyes. "I did call into the Secretary's office before I left, you know, to return my number and now I think of it, there was someone over by the *Windswept* bus. Didn't think much of it at the time – just thought she was admiring the dogs. Tall woman. Fair hair done up in a long fair plait." He shook his head. "Forgot all about that. It was just a flitting vision that didn't really register at the time."

The mystery woman again…

But how could Patricia be the mystery woman? Patricia didn't have long fair hair. Her hair was shoulder-length, chocolate-brown and treated by a prominent celebrity stylist at least twice a week. And as for flaunting a plait – far too bohemian for her.

Unless…

My head spun. My breath caught in my throat. I let out a gasp. Nothing to do with Rick instructing me to perform twenty squats while holding a medicine ball heavier than a bag of cement in front of me…

No, it was the sudden lightbulb that went off in my head.

What if Patricia had been wearing a wig?

14

Three-quarters of an hour later, I sat outside *Baby Buntings* staring morosely through the windscreen at the colorful wooden motifs attached to the day-care center's front fence while attempting to work out how I could move myself from the car into the nearby building without shattering into a squillion pieces.

Every muscle in my body ached. Every. Single. One. I lifted my hands off the steering wheel, only a couple of inches, that's all, and I swear someone or something with long sharp metal teeth chomped into the ridge that runs across my shoulders. Hard.

Due to sitting while driving from *Shape Up* to *Baby Buntings* I'd stiffened up. I'd felt fine when the one-on-one gym session ended. Rick had quickly shown me a couple of cooling-down exercises to do on my own while he moved on to his next victim – er…client – who was waiting for him in Room 4. However, when I checked the time on my phone, I realized I only had twenty-five minutes to shower, change, and drive to *Baby Buntings* to pick up the munchkins. No time for stretches. And although there was a slight burning in my muscles at the time, I'd felt pleasantly pleased with myself. I hadn't wanted to quit once.

So how come twenty-five minutes later I'd metamorphized into one giant pain?

Before I could come up with a way to get my children *into* the car without me actually moving *out of* the car, there was a sharp knock on the window beside me.

I turned my head slowly, painfully, half-inch by half-inch, until I was looking up at two grinning faces. Edward Stamford and his soulmate, *Dumpling*.

With gritted teeth, I wound down the window. "What are you two doing here?"

"Picking up Noble," said Edward.

My raised eyebrows must have sent him the message that I needed more information. Gemma leaned closer, her curly red hair brushing her *Pussycat's* shoulder. "Eddy got a text from Patricia a couple of hours ago. Yeah, I know, strange. She ordered him to pick Noble up from day-care. Said it was the Nanny's day off and she had an unexpected but important meeting with a client this afternoon and she didn't know how long it would run."

"Does she often do this?" I asked Edward.

"First time. Normally, she won't allow the Nanny to take the day off, not if it in any way disturbs her own day's plans."

"Sounds like she wants the house to herself and doesn't want anyone to know who she's meeting."

"Maybe she has a secret lover," I said.

"No need to keep him secret. She's welcome to him." Edward opened the car door for me to get out. "Okay, let's go get these kids."

When I didn't move, he frowned. "You okay?"

"Define 'okay'. If it means, can I get out of this car without help? The answer's no."

Gemma leaned in further. "What happened?"

"A one-on-one session at the gym with Rick is what happened. Here give me your hand," I held out one hand to Edward. "Just give me a pull. And make it gentle. Once I'm on my feet I'll be good to go."

Edward's worried frown disappeared. He laughed as he took my hand and helped me ease myself onto the roadway and then onto the footpath where he propped me up against the fence. "Gave you a bit of a workout, did he?"

I nodded as I grabbed a breath, carefully rolled my shoulders and prepared to put one foot in front of the other. "Just need to soak in a bubble bath for an hour or three," I told him. *And maybe bribe my ever-loving husband into giving me a full body massage.*

Gemma linked her arm through mine. Must have looked like I needed someone to lean on as I couldn't bring the fence with me. "Did you wring any information out of your cute trainer while performing those squats and weight-lifting sets?"

With Edward on my other side, ready to link arms at the first sign of faltering, we walked toward the front gate. Thankfully, with each step, my body loosened up. "A couple of things," I told them. "Firstly, Rick rescued this feral cat that no one wanted from a rescue-center, which puts him in the good guy category. And secondly, he also saw the mystery woman hanging around the *Windswept* dogs."

"The woman with the long fair plait?" Gemma asked.

"Yes. And if Patricia is our killer, that doesn't make sense." I paused for effect. "Unless she was wearing a wig."

"Of course." Edward nodded. "She wouldn't want anyone knowing she was at the show planning to kill the leech who was blackmailing her."

"And I guess she arrived when the show was almost over and most people had gone home," Gemma added. "Less chance of a witness."

"Talking of Patricia, did you manage to get inside the house to check for evidence?"

Edward sighed. "No, not yet. Both Gemma and I were involved in a drawn-out meeting with my divorce-lawyer all morning and I received a phone call asking me to come into work this afternoon. A client changed his mind on a business transaction and we had to negotiate a new deal."

"So, while Eddy was working, I decided to spend the afternoon making myself beautiful." Gemma, tossed her head and grinned. "First a spa and a massage, then a freshen up at the hair-dressers and finally a manicure."

"You, my darling, *Dumpling*, would look beautiful dressed in an old sack and rolling in the mud," Edward told Gemma, adoration lighting his eyes. After blowing her a kiss over the top of my head, his attention turned back to me. "Don't worry, Dana, I'll see what I can arrange when I drop Noble off this afternoon. Once inside the house, I'll insist on packing a few of my belongings and while Patricia's organizing Noble, I'll check out her bedroom, see if I can find any clues. And before you ask, yes, we each have our own bedroom. Have done since the day we were married."

By now we'd arrived at the front gate, manned, as usual, by Twitchy Tania Turner, dressed from head to toe in dazzling, eye-blinding white. She was brandishing a mega-sized bottle of sanitizer spray like a shotgun.

"Hi Tania," I said, suppressing a grin. This should be fun. "Let me introduce you to Patricia Stamford's husband, Edward, and his girlfriend, Gemma Haines."

"P-P-Patricia's h-husband?" For a moment I thought Tania's eyes would pop out of their sockets and go running down the street. And then she turned to blink open-mouthed at Gemma. "G-girlfriend?"

"Nice to meet you too, Tania," said Edward stepping past her to open the gate and usher both Gemma and me through.

"Why is that strange woman in white waving a giant spray bottle?" whispered Gemma when we were out of earshot.

"Better not to ask," I told her.

"Is she Baby Bunting's official hand-sanitizing monitor?"

"Umm...no..." More like a Germophobe Detector or a Cootie-Catching Inspector. I shook my head. "As I said...better not to ask."

Acting the gentleman again, Edward opened the brightly painted front door of the day-care center and indicated for Gemma and me to pass through first. I sighed. Why is it the English seem to have a monopoly on good manners? Maybe Lord Edward could give my laid-back husband a quickie course on the topic before he and Gemma left Australia to return to his stately home in Devon.

Jake spotted me as I followed Gemma through the doorway. I watched his deep-blue eyes – inherited from his Dad – light up, as he came scooting across the room towards me. "Mummy! Mummy!" he yelled, his fat little legs working double-time to reach me before Kayla realized I'd arrived. "We paint wall!"

He grabbed my hand and tugged me outside to the play area where a newly painted mural stretched along one wall of the building. A mass of brightly colored squiggles, odd looking stick figures, planes, trucks and lop-sided dwellings with creatures that could have been dogs, cats, family members, or aliens from outer space, posing out front.

Kayla, who'd been washing a paint brush in a bucket of soapy water over by the taps, looked up and saw me studying the wall with Jake. Her face lit up. Dropping the brush on a bench to dry, she danced across to us, eager to point out her painting in the middle of the long mural. "See, Mummy? See my fairy house?"

A whimsical-looking square painted in blue, green, pink and yellow stared back at me. There was a tall chimney with wings, stick figures with long yellow hair and wings and even the table in the garden and what looked like a toadstool seat had wings.

Jake, a dob of red paint on his nose, dragged me by the hand to the other end of the wall mural, eager to show me his amazing green squiggle with bright red eyes. "Snake!" he declared, his little chest pumped out with pride.

"Wow!" I looked from one painting to the other, making sure I showed the same rapt attention to both the air-borne fairy house and the squiggly red-eyed snake. "These are amazing. Did everyone get to paint on the wall today?"

"All 'cept Myron." Kayla tutted like a little old woman. "Mrs. Tyler couldn't get Myron to take his thumb out his mouth so he could hold the paint brush."

As we walked back into the building, still discussing the paintings and Myron's thumb, I could see Edward over by the front desk talking to the manager, Mrs. Tyler. He looked agitated. He was waving his arms, while his son, Noble sat high on his shoulders, arms entwined around his neck.

"What's up?" I asked Edward who looked ready to explode.

"This stupid woman won't let me take my son home, that's what's up." He glared at the manager who must have been accustomed to parental glares and insults as she didn't flinch. "I've already shown her two forms of ID – my driver's license and passport – to prove I'm Noble's father, now she wants to know my social security number."

"I can vouch for him," I told Mrs. Tyler, giving her my best trust-me smile. "This man is Edward Stamford and he's Noble's father."

"Well why does it say here on his passport that his name is Edward James *Beaumont*?"

The silence that followed was deafening.

Edward finally shuffled his feet and looked down. "Um… Beaumont is my er maiden name. You know, um, before I was married."

Mrs. Tyler blinked, confusion splattered across her face, while I couldn't stop the grin from tugging at the corners of my mouth.

"Look, I'm sorry, Mr. Stamford, or Beaumont, or whatever you call yourself, but I have never laid eyes on you before today. Noble seems to know you, but I can't allow him to leave these premises with you without first contacting his mother. It's against the company's rules." She snaffled her mobile from the desk and started sorting through what looked like a long string of contacts. "I'll just give Patricia a quick ring to confirm you're picking Noble up today and then we can all get on with our lives." She lifted her eyebrows at Edward and smiled. "Agreed?"

Edward raised his eyes to the ceiling, gently pried a couple of his two-year-old son's more taxing fingers from his windpipe and finally nodded. What else could he do? If he took Noble without Mrs. Tyler's permission, she would contact the authorities. If he let her ring Patricia, this would all be over and he could take his son home.

After a few minutes on the phone, Mrs. Tyler looked up at Edward and frowned. "Keeps going to voice-mail."

"I know Patricia's home," said Edward, his frustration causing him to jiggle up and down on the spot, which made Noble giggle. "Look, she's probably busy with her visitor, and it's the Nanny's day off." He gritted his teeth and glared at the woman behind the desk. "Which is why I'm on pick-up duty today."

Mrs. Tylor shrugged. "If you say she's at home, I'll try again." She pressed redial then tapped one finger on the desk, and waited.

"You're wasting your time," Edward told her, rolling his eyes. "If Patricia doesn't want to answer her phone, she won't."

Mrs. Tyler frowned; her attention caught by whoever was speaking on the other end of the phone-line. "No, I want to talk to Mrs. Stamford, please."

Her frown deepened.

"Who's that?"

She sat forward in her chair, knuckles white as the grip on her phone tightened. "Is Mrs. Stamford alright? Why are the police–"

"Police?" Edward leaned over, snatched the phone from the manager's fingers and slammed it to his ear. "This is Edward Stamford, Patricia's husband. What's happened? Where's Patricia?"

His body stilled as he listened, the color draining from his face. "Are- are you positive?"

He swallowed, cleared his throat, as though a stone had lodged in his windpipe and he was having difficulty in getting his words out. "Of course. I-I'll be there in twenty minutes."

Slowly placing the phone back on Mrs. Tyler's desk, he turned to Gemma and me. "Can you give Gemma a ride home please, Dana?"

When I nodded, he blinked, as though disoriented.

"What is it, Eddy?" Gemma reached up to brush her fingers across his cheek. "Whatever's happened?"

Edward looked down at her and shook his head. "Patricia, my wife, has gone and got herself murdered."

15

Molly let out a loud gasp. "Murdered?"

I flicked a quick glance at the diners seated at tables nearby to see if they'd stopped eating and drinking to gape at Molly's shocked response. No one looked up. No one appeared interested in our conversation. All either too immersed in their own personal exchanges or busy tending to their dogs.

Molly, Gemma and I were sitting around a small wooden table inside *Paws A Moment*, our favorite dog-centric coffee-shop situated on a quiet street away from the main thoroughfare of Port Adelaide. The owners, a friendly Greek couple with four rescue dogs of their own, had converted a run-down, sprawling hardware store into an eating place for dog owners. While we sipped on our coffees and munched fresh still-warm bakery treats, Penelope, Busta and Samantha sprawled at our feet, chewing on freshly cooked doggie treats supplied by the staff.

Abi hadn't shown up yet. Which was strange. She was usually first to arrive on the scene. Maybe a consignment of Gucci doggy scarves had arrived at the last minute and she had to sort them before leaving the boutique.

Finally, convinced we didn't have an attentive audience, I nodded at Molly. "Well, that's what the police said."

"What happened then?"

"Edward was the one on the phone so we only heard his side of the conversation, but evidently the police instructed him to go straight home."

"And he did?"

I nodded. I could still see Edward's shocked face and his disorientated movements as he stumbled out the door, his two-year old son, Noble, bouncing on his shoulders. "Well, that's where he said he was going."

"And we haven't heard from him since," put in Gemma, her voice cracking. Since the news of Patricia's death, Gemma had morphed from a bright, starry-eyed *Dumpling* into a dull, blah regurgitated lump of kale. How would this chilling set-back affect the passionate romance between her and Edward? Would it draw them closer together or become the sharp prickly wedge that drove them apart?

I stretched out a hand and squeezed her arm. "Edward hasn't really disappeared, Gemma. We know where he is. You were there. We heard him tell the police he'd be home in twenty-five minutes."

"And it's now two hours later. Is he still at his home? In hiding? Or has he been arrested?" Gemma, looking close to tears, grabbed a rough breath and sniffed. "Eddy will be their top suspect, you know. It's always the husband they blame in cases like this, and after the big blow up he and Patricia had when we told her he was leaving, he's probably slumped on one of those uncomfortable looking bunks in a prison cell right now."

"How bad was the argument?" Molly gently pushed Busta's paws down off her lap. Her cheeky fox-terrier had evidently finished his own treats and was now keen to check out Molly's choc-chip cookies.

"How bad?" Gemma repeated. "It was ultra-bad. Especially when Patricia threatened to not let Edward see Noble any more. She said she was taking Edward to court, and even if she had to lie on oath and say he'd been abusive to his son, she was determined to win."

Molly's eyes widened. "Holey Moley, what did he say to that?"

"Not much, but I think the three smashed wedding photos he flung against the wall let Patricia know his feelings on that score. When we left, the Stamford's next-door-neighbors, both sides, were outside in their garden, all agog, looking as if they were ready to call the police."

I checked the time on my phone and looked up, a little upset that we still hadn't heard anything. "It's been two hours since Edward left *Baby Bunting's*. Why hasn't he contacted one of us? Especially Gemma. Even if the police charged him, he'd still be allowed one phone call."

"With only one phone call he wouldn't ring us, Dana." Gemma's her voice was soft, almost a whisper. "He'd ring his lawyer."

Penelope, who'd been standing beside me, nudged my leg with her nose. I looked down. My over-sensitive greyhound seemed to be listening to our conversation. She was watching us, eyes flicking from one to the other, sensing tension. "It's okay, sweetie," I said smoothing my hand across her head, ruffling her ears until she relaxed. "We're fine."

"What I don't understand," mused Molly, nibbling around the edges of a donut with pink icing. "Is how Patricia could have gotten herself murdered? I mean, she was our chief suspect. Without her, we're back to square one."

"Even worse," I said. "This means our killer is still out there and although we have no idea who he or she is, they know we've been investigating." A frisson of fear zipped up my spine sending icicles crashing into every nerve-end. I grabbed a quick breath to steady myself before gently removing Penelope's head from my lap, then I pushed my chair away from the table and stood up. With my mind still on our unknown killer, I lurched through the open doorway and into the shop. I was in need of more coffee. Coffee so strong the spoon stood up and danced a tango in the middle of the cup.

While waiting to be served, I spotted Abi scurrying along the footpath towards us. Her black and tan wiener dog Chloe was on the end of one leash, stumpy little legs firing like pistons, while Chi's exquisite apricot-colored poodle, Fly, floated regally along on the other.

Being a dog-centric eatery, *Paws A Moment* encouraged patrons to bring their dogs along with them. There were half a dozen chairs and tables arranged outside the shop under the verandah, more seating inside, and another half dozen out the back under a shady patio for diners who weren't particularly dog lovers.

"Sorry, sorry, I'm late." I could hear Abi apologizing as she and her two tail-wagging canines arrived at our table. After letting the dogs greet each other with woofs and slurpy kisses, she collapsed in a vacant chair, a dog each side, and appeared to deflate like a pricked balloon.

While ordering a strong coffee for me, doggy treats for Chloe and Fly, and Abi's usual – cappuccino and two extra-large hazelnut cookies – I could hear Molly and Gemma filling Abi in on the latest baffling turn of events.

So, by the time I arrived back at our table, Abi was overflowing with questions.

"Are you sure it's Patricia the police found? Do they know how she was killed? What will happen to Noble now?"

Being careful to avoid Penelope's paws, I settled back in my chair and shook my head. "Noble still has a father, Abs."

"But what if Edward's arrested for Patricia's murder?"

Out of the corner of my eye I could see Gemma's bottom lip begin to wobble. Why did everyone expect Edward to be arrested for Patricia's murder? Didn't he have an alibi? I turned to Gemma, ignoring her quivering lip. "After you left the lawyer's office, Edward went back to work. Right? Didn't he say he was at a meeting all afternoon?"

Gemma's eyes lit up. "Of course, which means no matter what time Patricia was murdered, Eddy has an airtight alibi for the entire day."

"Did you see him actually go inside his work building?"

Gemma hesitated. "Um…no, he dropped me off in the city so I could spend the afternoon treating myself…but I was with him when he was called back into work. I heard him speaking on his mobile."

"His alibi is easy enough to check," said Molly. "All it would take is a phone call to his workplace."

I nodded. "Which the police would have already done."

"So why isn't he home?" Gemma's voice faltered. "Wh-why hasn't he rung me?"

"He's probably still at the police station answering questions," Molly put an arm around Gemma's shoulders and hugged her. "Don't worry, Gemma. We've been there before. We know how the police keep you waiting, hoping you might confess out of boredom."

"Yeah," I said, trying to lift everyone's spirits. "It's Inspector Lightfoot's specialty. And if he can't get a confession out of his suspect that way, he'll try the long cold stare routine. You know, like Gibbs in the TV series, N.C.I.S."

Abi, who'd been quiet, just listening, lifted Chloe onto her lap and ran her fingers over the little dog's fur, almost like she was seeking comfort from the connection. "Patricia might have been a bitch, but she didn't deserve this," she said. "Does anyone know *how* she was murdered or by *whom*?"

I shook my head. "Haven't heard a thing from Edward yet and there's been nothing about the murder on the news."

"It's just..." Abi's frown deepened. "It's just that something a bit weird happened to me before I left home. It's the reason I'm running late."

A smiling waitress, balancing two cups of coffee plus a plate of hazelnut cookies on a tray decorated with pictures of comic canines in humorous poses, stopped at our table. "What gorgeous dogs," she said placing the food and drink on the table before bending to ruffle Penelope's ears and tickle Busta under the chin when he jumped up at her, clearly smelling treats. She dug into her pocket and unearthed a bag of doggy-treats. "Thought I'd better bring enough for the other three as well. That okay?" When we nodded our agreement, she tore the bag open with her teeth and handed a treat to each dog. "Don't want any grumbles, do we?"

The moment the waitress left, I instinctively leaned toward Abi. "What do you mean? Weird as in odd or weird as in scary?"

"A bit scary, actually." She gave a nervous titter. "I was getting ready to come here and called the dogs so I could put their leads on. But I couldn't find Fly. I knew he'd been in the lounge earlier as I'd put a video on for him to watch, you know, 'Cats and Dogs', that funny spy-movie where Buddy gets captured by the cats. Fly loves it. He'll curl up on his beanbag for hours watching that movie, over and over again. He also likes me to put a bowl of potato chips beside him, you know, the unsalted ones, and gets rather annoyed if Chloe takes more than her share, which is quite hilarious to watch, especially–"

"Abi!" I growled. "Will you get on with it?"

She blinked and I could see a flash of something that looked a little like fear, or confusion, hiding behind her usual bubbly persona. "Anyway," she drew the word out. "I couldn't find Fly. I checked underneath the beds 'cos sometimes he hides there when he steals Chloe's green ball, behind the sofa, inside cupboards and even behind the shower curtain in the bathroom. Of course, I immediately panicked. Big time. Chi would have my head on a platter if I let anything happen to his beloved stud dog."

"So, where was he? Where did you find him?" Gemma, leaned forward in her chair.

Abi didn't answer. Instead, she pulled Fly's head towards her, leaned down and kissed him on the nose.

"Abi? Where was he?"

Abi looked up, eyes huge as she stared back at me. "I-I found him in the backyard."

Molly shrugged, still puzzled. "So…he pushed the back door open and took himself out while you were busy in another room."

"What?" Abi's voice cracked. "And tied himself with a hunk of rope to my rotary clothes line?"

Silence greeted this announcement. Silence and growing unease. Was this a prank by neighborhood kids? Or was it something a lot more sinister?

Something like a cold-blooded killer warning us to butt out of the investigation.

16

The Port Road was busy as we headed toward Adelaide City Center the next morning on our way to visit Chi at the Adelaide Remand Center.

Two important topics topped our list of questions to ask Chi. One – did he know the mystery woman with the long fair plait? And two – we needed Chi's input in sourcing a 'safe house' to hide Fly, so the killer couldn't get his hands on him.

At the moment Fly was holed up in an apartment with Abi's boyfriend, Nathan, and his bratty canine furball, Mimi. The little Pomeranian might be mouse-sized compared to the large regal-looking poodle, but her teeth and personality, which were sharper than ice picks, would keep him in line. And as for anyone breaking into Nathan's apartment, they'd need to burrow underground with earth-moving equipment to get past his state-of-the-art security.

However, this arrangement was only temporary. Fly couldn't stay on his own in the apartment during the week, and although Mimi accompanied Nathan to work every day, another dog in the office wouldn't go down well with his clients.

So…we had until Sunday evening to find another safe home for Chi's prize-winning, apricot poodle.

Molly, who'd been elected driver – we drew straws – was behind the wheel of her classic red 1963 Morris Minor, a car that had been meticulously and lovingly restored by her neighbor. When he died, his wife had put the car up for sale and now it was Molly's pride and joy. Personally, I found it hard to get comfortable in a car, so tiny, passengers needed to ingest Alice's magical shrinking tablets before climbing aboard.

Molly rarely drove when the three of us were out on a job. And yes, we'd been known to cheat with the straws. Not only because her car was barely big enough to fit three ants and their siblings let alone three humans and their dogs, but we'd found in the past that Molly was inclined to drift off occasionally, not to sleep, but to mentally puzzling out the plot of whichever book she was currently working on. I guess when you have a heroine with commitment issues and a hero with an ex-wife and six children to bring together in a happily-ever-after scenario, your mind can sometimes take a left turn.

"Hey, Abs." Molly flicked Abi, who was sitting knees under her chin in the back seat, a troubled glance via the rear vision mirror, which immediately sent the car dangerously close to the monstrous four-wheel-drive in the next lane. I gripped the toy-sized door handle and held my breath until we were back in our own lane. Molly, barely registering our close call, shook her head. "Did you work out how the perp got Fly out through your back door when the door was locked?"

"Um…" Abi's voice sounded unusually high, her knuckles white as she gripped the seat in front of her, eyes glued to the hulking vehicle beside us, so close we could reach out and touch the shiny metal. "I, um…found scratch marks around the lock. And there was some damage done to the door frame."

"What about your side gate? Was that locked too?"

Abi blew out the breath she'd been holding. "No, but it was snibbed with a sliding bolt."

"So," Molly said, frowning at the road in front of her as though it was a sheet of paper with a list of crimes printed down the middle. "This dirty low-life walked into your backyard, quietly forced your back door open, enticed Fly outside, tied him to your clothes line, and then sauntered out through the side gate again?"

Abi nodded, her face tight, as though she'd already gone over that scenario repeatedly ever since she'd come across the chilling sight of Chi's beloved poodle with a rope around his throat, tied to the upright in the middle of her clothesline.

"It's okay, Abs," I said, carefully twisting around so I could catch her eye. "You, Chloe and Fly are safe in Nathan's apartment. Good idea to stay there until the bad guy's been caught."

"How are Chloe and Fly getting along with Mimi?" Molly asked.

"As happy as three frogs in a pond," said Abi with a grin. "Nath's worked wonders with that demon in dog's fur."

And Abi would know. When she'd first rescued Mimi, the little dog had spent most of her day, when not demanding food with bullying growls, yaps and snarls, hanging off Abi's ankle, teeth embedded deep into her skin. But with Nathan, it was love at first sight for both man and dog. Mimi, although still unpredictable with strangers, was now a loving, happy little dog, who adored her owner and anyone he insisted were his friends.

Once we hit the city limits, the traffic became even heavier. Abi and I held our breath as Molly weaved in and out of the traffic, ignoring the blast of horns that followed her and by the time we reached the parking bay at the rear of the Adelaide Remand Centre, I was ready to leap head-first from the car and kiss the polluted bitumen in relief.

After going through the usual security checks, we were escorted to the visitor's center where we found ourselves seated in the corner of the room at a table with four chairs.

While waiting for Chi to be brought in, I studied the simplistic wooden tables and chairs firmly bolted to the floor, the lack of cheer, the general institutionalism of the room. And had to remind myself that this was a jail, not an upscale hotel where people sat sipping cocktails under heavily ornate chandeliers. This was where bad guys were housed while awaiting their trial. But surely a few home comforts and colorful paintings on the walls wouldn't lead to a riot...

A few minutes later, Chi, a stern-faced officer at his side, shuffled into the room. I blinked, had to double check that it was the same man I'd spent time with at the shows over the last couple of years. The friendly guy who baked the best cookies in the state, the bright-eyed little man who'd smiled kindly at my jokes while continuing to brush and pamper whichever poodle he had up on the table at the time, had almost disappeared. Chi was never a big man, but now he was skeletal. As though life wasn't worth living so he'd given up on eating.

"Chi," I said, as he slipped into the vacant chair opposite me. "Thank you for seeing us."

He nodded, the dark rings under his eyes making him look even more gaunt. "Actually, it's me who should be thanking you. Other than my lawyer, you're my only visitors."

I could see Molly was feeling uncomfortable at the sight of Chi's changed state. She was fiddling with the gold bracelet on her arm, undoing the clasp and doing it up again.

"How are they treating you?"

"Made any friends yet?"

"Sorry we didn't bring a cake with a file in the middle."

We all spoke at once – the last a nervous attempt at humor from Abi – realized we sounded asinine and quickly looked away.

"It's fine," said Chi, his lips twitching slightly, which was an improvement on the resigned expression when he entered the room. "I know coming into a prison, with all its invasive security measures, must be awkward for you."

"Oh, Chi," I said, aching to give the poor guy a hug and knowing if I as much as lay one hand on him I'd have all the alarms in the room blaring. "We're so sorry about what happened to Stephen."

"Yes," said Molly and sniffed. "He might have been a bit, you know, um…difficult…" Molly flicked a panicked glance at me and I could see she was frantically trying to work out what to say without hurting Chi. "But we were all horrified at his death."

Chi inhaled deeply, seeming to set his expression into neutral before speaking. "I'd just like to say, in case there's any doubts, that even though Dana found me on my knees, beside Stephen's body, with the murder weapon in my hand, I did not kill him." He grabbed another breath, looked me in the eye. "I would *never* hurt Stephen. He was my soulmate."

"We know," I said and swallowed the dry lump in my throat. I was close to tears, which wasn't a good thing. If we were going to get any information out of Chi, it was time to get on with it. "I know this is going to be difficult for you, Chi, but how did you end up in the bus with Stephen's body? What happened?"

"I'd just come back from trying to find Stephen. I was upset with our quarreling and wanted us to make up before driving home. I know you mostly saw the bombastic side of my big boy, but there was also a sweet tender side he mostly hid from the outside world."

"And you couldn't find him?"

He shook his head. "So, I thought I'd text him to find out where he was and because I've lost a couple of phones in the past, I don't carry my mobile around with me at the shows any more, I leave it in the glovebox at the front of the bus." He paused as though steeling himself for the rest. "Anyway, when I opened the driver's side door and climbed in, I knew straight away something was wrong. I could smell the blood. And when I peered over the top of the seat, there he was. My Stephen. Sprawled on the floor with a knife in his chest." His voice caught in his throat and we had to lean closer to hear him. "He was just so still and white. And there was blood. Lots of blood. Everywhere."

"But you were found with the murder weapon in your hand. Why did you pull the knife out?" Abi huffed.

Chi looked down at the table and for a moment I didn't think he was going to answer. At last, he looked up. "I-I had to. My Stephen wouldn't want anyone to see him like that."

Time to channel his thoughts away from the back of the bus. "We do have some good news for you though," I said brightly. "It's about your dogs. They're being cared for by the RSPCA. I dropped in to see them a couple of days ago and they're all looking well-fed and comfortable."

"But what about Fly? Where is he? I've been so worried about him. If anything happens to our beautiful Fly, Stephen will…" He stopped, realized Stephen wouldn't be able to say or do anything anymore and covered his mouth with his hand.

Abi leaned across the table and took Chi's hand in hers. I held my breath, but no alarms screamed, no red lights flashed, no short-necked police officer came stomping across the room to lift Abi over his shoulder and toss her in a cell, so I let out a breath and decided it was time to fill Chi in on our present predicament. "As I said, your other dogs are at the dog rescue center but because Fly is so special, we thought it best if Abi took him home with her until you came out of prison."

Chi squeezed Abi's hand. "Thank you."

Abi gritted her teeth and told him of the latest development, of how we thought the murderer used Fly as a warning device in an attempt to stop us investigating. "By picking the lock on my back door and tying Fly up in my backyard, it was like they were thumbing their nose at us. A definite warning to butt out of the investigation." Her voice cracked. "So, I'm sorry, but we've decided Fly's not safe with any of us."

"Where is he now?"

"Don't worry, Fly's at my boyfriend's apartment, which is safer than Fort Knox," Abi assured Chi. "But the thing is, he can't stay there indefinitely. Nathan has to go into the office every day and we can't leave Fly on his own."

"That's why we need your help," I said. "Do you know anyone who would look after Fly? Somewhere safe? Somewhere right away from here?"

Chi ran a hand through his dark hair, blinked, a frown creasing his forehead as he contemplated the situation.

"I guess we could relocate him to the local dog-rescue kennels with your other *Windswept* dogs. He'd be safe there."

Three horrified faces turned towards me.

"Noooo!"

"Fly? At the rescue kennels? Never!"

"The shock would send him into cardiac arrest!"

I fake-reeled back in my chair. "Okay, okay. I'm sorry. I wasn't thinking."

The faces continued to scowl.

"But I know where he *would* be safe," I said, an idea slipping like a prize fish into my net.

The scowls instantly disappeared.

"We could hide him at another poodle-breeding establishment. A large professional one. A kennel where he wouldn't be spotted in amongst all the other dogs."

"And I know the perfect place," said Chi, eyes lighting up. "But it would mean getting Fly to the airport without being seen. Could you manage that?"

We all nodded like bobble-headed dogs.

"I have a cousin in Melbourne who also breeds poodles. If you could get Fly there, my cousin, Ho, could hide him in amongst his own dogs and he would be out of the killer's radar."

"When can you contact your cousin?"

"We are allowed one phone call a day, so I'll ring him, explain the problem and give him your phone number. If you can arrange the flight from this end, I'm sure Ho will do the rest." He took a breath and evidently thinking of his beloved poodle, his eyes softened. "Has Fly settled in okay with your friend, Abi?"

"Amazingly well," Abi said with a smile. "Although he doesn't know it, my Nathan is what you'd call a dog-whisperer."

"That's right," I added, ready to join Abi in boosting Chi's morale. "He and Fly even have the same taste in movies."

Chi's twitching lips crinkled into a full-blown smile. "And unsalted potato chips?"

"Of course."

With Fly's safety sorted, Chi shifted in the hard chair then leaned closer, his voice soft. "Are you any closer to finding the killer?"

"We thought we were and then our main suspect was murdered yesterday," said Molly.

Chi's eyes widened. "Murdered? Who?"

"Patricia Stamford. A woman Stephen had been blackmailing. Did you know her?"

"Never heard of her." Chi squished his nose in thought. "Had she ever bought a poodle from us?"

"Not as far as we know, but she was ticking a lot of boxes on the suspect list. Then yesterday, the police rang her husband to say she'd been murdered."

"Where?"

"Inside her home."

"Poor woman, I hope she didn't suffer." He let out a sigh, then a sudden spark of awareness lit his eyes. "But you know, this woman's murder, after Stephen's, could help my case. Being locked up in a 4 by 4 cell gives me a foolproof alibi for the second murder."

"It does," I agreed. "And we're not giving up on the investigation."

His smile, soft and almost-tearful, encompassed the three of us. "I can't thank you enough for what you've done already, but I don't want you putting yourselves in danger. There's a monster out there and I would rather spend the rest of my life behind bars than see one of you hurt."

"Poof!" said Abi with a flick of her wrist.

"We're fine," said Molly.

"Chi, we can't stop now," I told him. "While this killer is out there, we'll never be safe. Which means we have to catch whoever it is."

Chi leaned forward. "Promise me you'll take extra care."

"Scout's honor," I said, giving him a two-fingered salute. "But we need your help."

"Anything."

"There were a couple of sightings of a woman hanging around your dogs after the show. A large woman with long fair hair done in a single plait. We originally suspected it was Patricia, wearing a wig, but as it's turned out, we were barking up the wrong tree," I frowned at Chi. "Did you see anyone answering to that description hanging around after the show?"

He shook his head. "Sorry."

"Well, do you know who this mystery woman could be? Was there a woman in Stephen's life who hated him enough to kill him?"

"Only woman in Stephen's life was his stepsister, Julia. But I don't know what color hair she has or whether she's large or small. I've never met her. Julia and Stephen have been estranged for over four years. When Stephen's father died, he didn't include Julia in the will, left all his money to Stephen, who, she believes tricked their father into changing the will." He shifted in his chair. "All I know is Julia's a single mother and recently she started ringing Stephen, twice, sometimes three times a day, desperate for money because her five-year-old son needs an expensive operation to save his life." He let out another breath. "But Stephen refused to help her out."

He must have realized the silence that greeted this as condemnation for his beloved Stephen because he sniffed and continued. "It's the online gambling that changed him. Lost all his money, turned him into a blackmailer, desperate for his next fix." Chi shook his head. "My Stephen wasn't always arrogant and quarrelsome and nasty, you know. When we first met, he was happy, smiling, the life of the party. It was the blasted gambling. Online gambling ended up wrecking both our lives."

"And do you think this Julia could have come to the show, fought with Stephen over the money and killed him?"

Chi shrugged. "Maybe."

"Do you know her full name and where she lives?"

"Julia Channing. Same as my Stephen." He shook his head. "Don't know her address. All I know is she lives somewhere in Burra. Up north."

A discordant, ear-jarring buzzer assaulted the room, signaling the end of our visit. It was so loud, so strident, I gritted my teeth to stop my hands from covering my ears and showing vulnerability. "You know, the military should patent that and use it to deafen the enemy," I said to fill in the deadly silence that followed.

Chi's lips shifted into a tired smile. A smile so weak I had to look twice to find it. Like exhaustion hit him in the solar plexus and then lined up for a second punch.

We stood up, gathering our bags ready to leave.

"Don't worry, Chi," Abi said and leaned forward to give his hand a parting squeeze. "We'll find whoever did this."

I nodded in agreement. Chi couldn't survive in jail much longer, but at this stage of the investigation, we'd not only hit a brick wall but bounced off and face-planted in the dirt. What we really needed to move forward again was the answer to a few puzzling questions.

Like…who was this mystery woman?

Was it Julia? Had she come to the dog show to threaten her stepbrother into giving her money for her son's operation and when he laughed in her face, killed him?

Or what about Gemma? She'd become our friend, but thinking about the case rationally, Gemma had reason to kill both Stephen and Patricia. What if Stephen found out Chi had written the check out for her and he'd tried to take it back? Would that be enough to make her see red and kill him?

Only one way to find out.

We'd keep a closer eye on Gemma.

Plus, we'd pay Julia a visit – find out how many suspect boxes Stephen's stepsister ticked.

17

I set my phone to loudspeaker and placed it safely on top of the dryer before continuing to shove dirty clothes into my washing machine. "Any problems?" I asked Abi who was on the other end of the line.

She'd called to update me on Fly's clandestine removal from Nathan's apartment by one of Nathan's mates, a greengrocer friend from the Adelaide market. After transferring Fly from a comfortable couch into Matt's enclosed van via the units' underground carpark, Matt drove the poodle to the Adelaide airport, helped settle him in a crate and waited until the plane took off, on its way to Melbourne where Chi's cousin, Ho, would be waiting to collect him.

Chi must have been able to wangle his one-a-day phone call as soon as we left the Adelaide Remand Center because by the time Molly had driven us to Nathan's unit to drop Abi off, she'd received a phone call from Chi's cousin and arrangements were quickly made for Fly's overnight flight to Melbourne.

"There was only one hiccup," said Abi with a laugh which meant the hiccup wasn't major. "Mimi wouldn't let Fly leave the apartment without her. She'd fallen head over heels in love with the big guy. Hung off his leg so he couldn't get out the door without her."

"What a ditz!"

"Yeah. There's Nathan following the squirming, growling bundle of fur down the stairs to the underground carpark, still attached to Fly's leg. In the end he had to feed her treats to get her to let go and then cuddle and feed more treats to distract her while Matt shut Fly into the back of his grocery van."

"She okay, now?"

"Not really. She's refusing to allow anyone near the couch. Probably still has Fly's smell on it."

"Did Matt check that no one tailed him to the airport?"

"He said he purposely went a roundabout route and checked every time he turned off onto another road. No one followed."

Penelope, who'd sprawled out on top of the dirty clothes the moment I'd upended the second clothes basket, shot off to grab a toy when I shooed her away. She skittered back into the laundry, her plush caterpillar between her jaws, the long section of its body trailing behind her. Guessing she wanted me to play a game with *Cackypilla*, as Jake called the multi-colored dog-toy, I took it from her and tossed it out the door. She immediately pounced through the open doorway, retrieved the toy and dropped it at my feet with a cheeky you'll-get-tired-before-I-do grin. I rolled my eyes and after tossing the toy outside again, set the washing-machine on Cold Wash, killed the loudspeaker and returned the phone to my ear. "Thought maybe we could drop some groceries and fruit and veg around to the guys under the bridge before we leave for Burra tomorrow."

"Good idea. I have a couple a dozen really tasty pork sausages in my freezer that would go down well cooked over their open fire."

"While we were enjoying our meat and three veg for dinner tonight, I couldn't stop thinking about Corey and his friends eating leftovers from people's bins, so I raided our pantry and have everything boxed up ready to go. Which reminds me, was Nathan able to find Julia Channing's address?"

"10, Cassowary Lane, Burra." The smirk in Abi's voice made me grin. "Piece of cake."

"You can tell that oh-so-clever boyfriend of yours he has dibs on the biggest steak in our arsenal next time you two come over for a barbecue." I held a pair of Peter's smelly socks by the tips of two fingers before dropping them in the sink to soak. I'd let the disinfectant do its job before allowing the nose-crunchers anywhere near the rest of my laundry. "Don't suppose you've heard any news about Edward?"

"Gemma rang half an hour ago. Asked me to let you and Molly know the police released Edward with no charge. His alibi for the time of Patricia's murder checked out."

My mind pinged to our mystery woman. "And what about Gemma's alibi?"

"All clear. Gemma was at all her beauty appointments at the times stated."

I blew out a sigh. I really liked Gemma. She and Edward were made for each other and the thought that she could have been our mystery woman and murdered not only Patricia but Stephen too, had left me with an ugly taste in my mouth. "And what about Noble? Is he safe with Edward?"

"Gemma said the little guy's fine. She fed him pancakes for tea–"

"Pancakes?"

Abi laughed. "Yeah, with ice cream. She then gave him and his plastic ducky a bubble bath and Edward tucked him into bed and read him a Dr Seuss book."

At that moment, Penelope, over-excited from our game of 'Chase the Cackypilla', gave a high-pitched scream as she barreled into something unseen in the kitchen. "Sorry, Abi, gotta go. Sounds like Penelope might need a cuddle and a Band-Aid. She never looks where she's going when she's in full flight."

"Give her a kiss on the nose from her Aunty Abi."

"Will do. See you in the morning."

Penelope, eyes sad and droopy, expression that of the mortally wounded, met me at the kitchen door, caterpillar completely forgotten as she stood there, mournfully holding one leg off the ground.

Now, anyone who's ever owned a greyhound knows that 'look'. A 'look' that is often accompanied by what's called the G.S.D – The

Greyhound Scream of Death – a scream that sends their owner's heart leaping into their throat with fear of disaster. Thankfully however, even though the beloved long-tail is wailing, 'grievous bodily harm' – most times it's nothing more than a bump or a scratch.

Crooning nonsense, I dug my hand into the treat jar, pulled out a liver treat and a beef jerky and grinned when Penelope's supposedly broken shoulder miraculously disappeared.

While the treats were quickly eaten, I righted Penelope's attacker – a chair that lay upside down on the kitchen tiles – and distracted her further by snaffling her favorite dog- lead from the back of the kitchen door and holding it up for her to see.

"Walkies?"

One bound and she was beside me, dancing on the spot.

"I'm just taking Penelope for a walk," I told the comatose body stretched out on the sofa in the lounge watching some eye-drooping Science documentary on television.

The comatose body sat up and stretched his arms. "Want me to come with you?"

"Can't leave the kids on their own. I'm only taking her to the corner and back for a potty break."

After what happened to Fly, we'd been more protective of not only Penelope, but also our two munchkins.

"Okay, but switch the front light on. I'll poke my head out the door and check on you if you're not back in five."

"And do what?" I eyed the limp stick of celery holding his back with one hand as though selling cars all day was akin to eight hours of hefting 60 kilo bags of cement up a steep hill through waist-high mud.

Peter winked, strolled across the room, and with one arm loosely around my shoulders, kissed me on the lips. "If you're in trouble, my little Lois Lane, I'll slip into my Superman costume and fly to your rescue."

"Humph!" I said with a mock-scowl as I kissed him back. "And crash into the nearest lamp post and need rescuing yourself?"

"Just be careful." Peter's voice took on a serious note. "Okay?"

"Yes, Dad, I promise I won't fall in a hole or talk to any strangers while taking Penelope to the end of the street and back."

As I turned to walk out the door, Peter lightly slapped me on the butt. "Watch it Lois Lane, or Superman will whisk you into his magic telephone box. And the last thing on his mind will be making a phone call."

I let out a laugh. "Sorry, think I tossed your Superman cape in the wash with Jakey's Spiderman outfit. You'll have to wait until it's been put through the dryer before you can claim it."

By now, Penelope, painful shoulder a distant memory, was anxious to get going. She looked up at me, gave a little whine, then stared at the front door. No way would she pull me towards the door. Too polite. Too gentle. She'd rather cross her legs and dance on the spot than drag me outside onto our front lawn to relieve herself. Luckily, I could always read her body language.

The street lights splayed their shadowy beams across the footpath, illuminating the way. Most houses either had their porch lights on or lights shone through curtains or blinds in front rooms. I never felt afraid walking along our street, no matter what time of day or night. This was a family-friendly street and I knew most of the inhabitants of the three-bedroom, good-sized backyard, two-car homes, all with at least ten solar panels on the roof.

Degradable plastic poop bag in hand, I let Penelope sniff her way to the end of the street, first stopping under a tree, deciding no, that wasn't the perfect spot and sniffing out several other possible locations before finally settling on a patch of dirt that looked no different to the other five patches of dirt she'd rejected, before squatting and expelling a load.

I was about half-way back, load duly transferred to its little black doggy bag, when a small white van slowed down and drove slowly beside me. I frowned, my hand slipping down onto Penelope's head as I checked out the printing on the side of the van – 'Shape Up'.

"Hi there, Dana." A familiar voice came from inside the vehicle.

"You saved me the trouble of knocking on your front door."

I stopped and moved across to the van. Through the open window I could see a head of fair tousled hair, a cute nose and a wide-open grin. It was Rick Starling. Cute Beagle Guy. My one-on-one trainer from 'Shape Up' gym.

"Rick? You lost or something?"

"Nah, just wanted to let you know there's a cancellation next Friday so I can fit you in at 4 o'clock for another torture session." He lifted one of his manly eyebrows and his grin widened. "That's if you're up to a repeat, of course."

"You drove all the way here to tell me that?" I shook my head. "Why not a phone call?"

He let out a laugh. "Thought I'd be the Good Samaritan. You left your watch behind at the gym Friday, so, as I was coming this way to see a mate, thought you might be feeling naked without it."

He handed a Smartwatch, silver with a black band, through the open window.

I stared at the expensive piece of chrome and hi-tech that probably told its owner not only how many steps they'd taken for the day, but how many times they'd used the *f*-word, and shook my head. "This isn't mine."

"You sure?"

"Um…think I'd know if I owned something that cost two arms, a leg, and a serious bite out of my credit card. But thanks for trying to do the right thing." Reluctantly, I handed the watch back to him. "Hand it in at the desk and maybe they can find the rightful owner."

I looked toward our house and could see Peter, arms folded, standing under the porch light, eyes trained on me. Clearly wondering who I was talking to. So, before he could don his Superman outfit and make an exhibition of himself by flying too low and taking out several letter boxes, I thanked Rick and started to walk away.

He continued to follow me. "One other thing," he said as he came level. "I remembered something else from the show the day Stephen was murdered. Thought you might find it useful for your investigation."

Immediately the alert button kicked in. "You did?"

"Probably not important but when Stephen and I were talking, he mentioned the little guy with the scruffy black poodle."

"Corey?"

"That's right. Said he'd been teasing him and maybe taken it too far. The guy was so easy to get a rise out of he couldn't help himself. Anyway, like the worm that turned, the little guy had fought back that day and flashed a knife at him. Said he'd cut him if he ever bullied him again."

Corey owned a knife? Our sweet Corey threatened to 'cut' Stephen?

"Hey, I know I should have mentioned this before but Stephen was such a blow-all I dismissed it at the time as one of his usual attention-seeking fabrications."

While Rick pulled away from the curb and continued on to his mate's place, I stumbled back toward the safety of my waiting husband. The only man I could completely trust.

Had Corey tricked us? Shown us a sweet vulnerable side that didn't really exist? Had he lost control the last time Stephen bullied him and not merely 'cut' his tormenter, but driven the knife deep into Stephen's heart?

18

At 8.30 the following morning, I drove Abi's big white van slowly down Shipwreck Road, the bumpy dirt track that had long since lost its entitlement to being called a road, towards Nautical Bridge, the derelict footbridge and camp of the close-knit, 'under-the-bridge' homeless group.

After a dodgy drawing of straws, I'd been elected driver for the day, but it was more like Abi was tired, due to an all-nighter with Nathan, and Molly, well, Molly was always a little reluctant to get behind the wheel of Abi's over-sized van. After driving her own toy car, she likened Abi's van to an army tank.

The dogs were with us, all curled up at the back, Penelope snoring contentedly, but the munchkins were spending a day at the zoo with Peter and his Mum and Dad. That's what I love about my man, he might be forgetful and have stinky feet, but he was a good dad and a loving son – even if I knew he planned to opt out of zoo duties after lunch and spend the afternoon playing golf with his two best mates.

As I drew closer to the bridge, I could see our five homeless friends gathered around a camp fire, their shopping trollies parked within easy grabbing distance. There was an air of solidarity, of mate-ship, about the scene. And I remembered Furry Hat's motto for the group – 'All for one and one for all'. If I was going to question Corey about that knife, I'd need to watch my step, be extra vigilant. I didn't want the others closing ranks around me. Who knew how far they'd go to protect one of their own?

"Do you think they'll like my books?" Molly, wedged into the back seat of the van, amongst boxes of groceries and fridge bags containing Abi's pork sausages, had decided to contribute a dozen of her romance novels to the group as, in her words, 'reading happily-ever-after romances was the best antidote for unhappiness'.

"Molly, there's only one woman in the group." Abi, sitting beside me, rolled her eyes heavenward. "Can you really see those guys sitting down on their upturned boxes and tuning in to the antics of your star-crossed lovers? More likely they'll use the books as extra fuel for the fire."

"Or..." said Molly, now metaphorically standing on her soap-box, "my stories could transport these poor souls from their dismal everyday lives into richer happier times – even if it's only for a couple of hours."

"Works for me." I parked Abi's van as close to the bridge as I could and switched off the engine. Personally, I was hoping the bizarre gift of a dozen romance novels might prove a distraction while I isolated Corey and questioned him.

"Well, here goes nothing." Abi opened the car door and extracted two freezer bags of sausages from the back seat.

On the drive over, I'd filled the other two *Chicks* in on Rick Starling's latest revelation. That Corey Black had threatened to 'cut' Stephen. While I took Corey aside to question him, Molly and Abi planned to be my backup by distracting the others. Also, as a safety measure, Molly rang Hudson Driscoll, her boyfriend and filled him in on where we were and what was going down. Hudson, a policeman-slash-biker, who worried about Molly's involvement in the *Gumshoe Chicks* investigations but knew not to interfere, devised a plan. If she didn't ring him back within fifteen minutes of our arrival, to say all was well, he'd alert backup and charge to the rescue on his all-powerful Harley Davison.

I opened the car door and swiveled my legs around before stepping out. "Have you texted Hudson to tell him we've arrived?"

Molly nodded.

"Right. Let's go."

The three dogs, Penelope, Chloe and Busta jumped up, heads over the back of the seat, eyes pleading to come with us, but although I'd feel safer with Penelope at my side, I wasn't prepared to put her at risk. Molly and Abi felt the same way about their dogs.

"We won't be long," I told the three dogs and prayed that I knew what I was talking about. "Be good and there'll be a treat for each of you when we come back."

The box of groceries was too awkward for me to carry on my own, so Abi dumped her bags of sausages on top and helped me, while Molly scooped up her hot romances and followed.

"Hi," said Abi as we approached the group around the fire. "Thought you might like to sizzle some sausages for breakfast."

"There's a couple of loaves of bread inside," I added, placing the box of food on the ground. "In case, like me, you prefer your sausage in a sandwich."

We were greeted with silence. Corey's smile the only sign of welcome. Were they embarrassed that we'd brought them food? Angry at us intruding on their space again? Or was this just their normal reaction to visitors?

"And I have a really special surprise for you." Molly, evidently not twigging to the edginess in the silence, bustled forward, and with a smile that said how much she believed in her happily-ever-after books as an antidote for misery, proceeded to pass out her books to each person around the fire. "When you've finished reading, I'd love to know what you think."

The expression on the men's faces was priceless. And even, Matilda, the woman wearing multi-layers of pre-loved clothing, blinked at the book she held away from her, like it might explode at any moment. The cover portrayed a gorgeous hunk of a guy with muscles so enhanced they had to be photo-shopped, and a voluptuous female, both in a clinch so tight a cigarette paper would have trouble sliding between them.

"Hmm, can't say I'd say no to havin' his shoes under me bed," grunted Matilda at last, breaking the silence as she eyed the male hero on the cover of her book from all angles.

Bluey, Corey's protector from our last visit, sat staring at the almost-dress worn by the heroine on the cover of his book. Finally, he tugged at his beard and looked up, the puzzled frown on his face making me grin. "How does she keep her um...*thingies* inside the package?"

"Oh, that's Tabatha, the heroine in my latest book," said Molly, leaning over his shoulder and almost purring as she smiled fondly at the cover. "I'm so glad you like it."

While Molly was entertaining the troops and Abi unpacking the boxes, I tapped Corey on the shoulder. Time to get him aside so I could interrogate him about that knife. "Hey, Corey, be a dear and help me carry the other box of groceries from the car, will you?"

"Of course." As Corey scrambled to his feet, his smile, overflowing with sweetness, made me want to dive back in the car and drive away. Forget all about re-accusing him of murder. But I knew I had to go through with this. Killers could be very charming and they came in all shapes and sizes. Look at the central idea behind the movie, 'The Vanishing' – evil can lurk in the most ordinary and unremarkable of men – surely Corey fit that profile.

When we arrived at the van, I didn't open the door to collect the last box, instead, I took a deep breath and turned to face the child-like guy following me. "Corey, I've heard something that really worries me."

"Oh, dear." Corey's eyes widened, he reached forward and touched me on the arm. "I'm sorry you're worried, Dana. If there's anything I can do, just ask."

"Um...it's about you."

"Oh."

I watched him deflate as though I'd stuck him with a pin. "Look, this is just as hard for me as it is for you, so I'll just come out and say it. Did you threaten Stephen with a knife at the show the day he was killed? Warn him that if he bullied you again, you'd 'cut' him?"

If I thought he looked deflated before, now he resembled roadkill I'd run over and over and squashed on the highway. He gave an almost imperceptible nod.

"You *did* have a knife at the show the day Stephen was stabbed to death?"

"I carry my knife with me everywhere I go."

"Why didn't you tell me this before?'

He licked his lips, opened his mouth to answer, then evidently decided against it. Instead, he shook his head.

"You realize that if the police knew you'd threatened Stephen with a knife, you'd be in jail now instead of Chi."

"That's why I couldn't tell them." His voice was so small and shaky I had to lean closer to hear him. "I still have the knife. I carry it for protection."

He still had the knife?

As he began fumbling in the pockets of his heavy overcoat, I took a long step backwards, prepared to scream, head-butt him in the stomach, or run. The last one on top of the list. And when a six-inch knife appeared in his hand, I took another, even longer step away from him.

Then, before I had a chance to act, out of nowhere, I felt a sudden hot menacing breath tickle the skin on the back of my neck, making me yelp. I brushed at it wildly, leaping to the side, almost going down on both knees in my panic to face the new threat.

What the...

Heart thumping like a brass band in full performance, I spun around to find Bluey, Corey's protector, looming behind me, one quizzical eyebrow hitting his hairline at my unexpected dance routine.

He shook his head as though dismissing my antics as 'weirdly girly' and turned to Corey. "Huh! Call that a knife!" he growled and dug into the firewood inside his shopping trolley that he'd trundled along behind him. After moving one of his old rusty bicycle wheels to the side, he drew out something shiny, something sharp, something big enough to star in *The Texas Chainsaw Massacre*. He aimed a grin, spoilt a little by the remains of breakfast not only in his beard but between his teeth, at both of us, as though besting Corey in a public show-and-tell. "Now, *this* is what *I* call a knife!"

Corey nodded, then, knuckles white as he strangled the thick rubber handle, he lifted the knife in the air, the blade gleaming in the early morning sunlight.

Oh my God. I'd pushed him too far. He was going to stab me. With a lurch, my stomach plummeted and smashed around my boots while my legs tangled in an attempt to move out of his reach.

Then, like an actor in a Shakespearian play, Corey plunged the knife deep, up to the hilt, into his own chest.

19

I know I screamed, my mouth opened as wide as the Birkenhead bridge and dry broken stuff clunked around inside my voice box, but no sound came out.

My legs were overcooked spaghetti sliding around on a slippery china plate.

My heart stopped, ran up a tattered white flag.

Corey Black, the man I'd come to interrogate, had just committed suicide.

And I'd pushed him into doing it.

Wide eyed, I stared at him, waiting for the blood to spurt from his chest and for his body to crumple in a twisted heap at my feet, life oozing away at every faltering heartbeat.

But nothing happened. Corey was still standing there with the knife plunged through his heart. And he was grinning at me. Grinning like he thought killing himself was the best joke since the first goofy caveman grunted a comical one-liner and set his clan laughing over their Stegosaurus sandwich. I blinked. Felt my breath catching in my throat.

"See," said Corey, pulling the knife out of his chest, his grin widening. "It's a trick knife. The blade concertinas inside the handle when you press it against anything solid." He shrugged. "But bad people who scare me don't know that. So, I use it for protection."

Behind me, I could hear wheezing laughter and a honk of a nose. Bluey, owner of the gigantic wood-chopping blade had been bested. "Good one, Corey," he said, hocking up a spitball and depositing it in the dust at my feet. "Your secret's safe with me, mate."

With that, Bluey stashed his outsized blade back under the firewood, wiped his nose with his beard and trundled back toward the fire, leaving Corey and me standing alone.

Although I'd managed to force my face into a mask of calm after witnessing Corey's fake knife demonstration, I could still feel my heart banging against my chest, screaming at me to stop with the life-scares or it would quit, go out on stress leave. I reached for the van's door handle, hung on, took a shaky breath to center myself. "Sorry about that, Corey, but I had to ask you about the knife threat."

"It's all true. I did threaten Stephen – but with my trick knife there was no way I could actually hurt him." Corey, shoulders slumped, kicked at a stone with his dusty boots. Face drawn, body hunched, hair that hadn't seen a comb in a week, he looked like he'd aged ten years in the short time he'd been living under the bridge. "See, what happened, Stephen kicked my Pablo, said he'd accidently stumbled over him, but the smirk on his face said differently. I could take what Stephen did to me, but when he kicked my little dog, I-I guess I lost it. I pulled my knife out of my pocket and waved it at him. Told him I'd 'cut' him if he ever touched Pablo again." He paused, eyes never leaving mine. "But I didn't kill him."

"It's okay, Corey, I believe you." I reached out and squeezed his shoulder." Now, let's get this last box of food out of the car so you and your friends can eat hearty for the next few days. We're in a bit of a hurry, 'cos Abi, Molly, and I have a long drive ahead of us. We're off to check out Stephen's stepsister."

"His stepsister? Why?"

"Well, according to Chi, she had good reason to use a *real* knife on Mr. Not-So-Nice. He'd likely stolen her inheritance and then refused to help pay for a life-saving operation on her son. Julia Channing lives up north, in Burra."

"Burra?" Corey's eyes lit up. "I have an uncle who lives in Burra. Haven't seen him for about six or seven years." He grabbed my hand and gave me one of his best puppy-dog eyes. "Don't suppose I could hitch a ride with you to see my Uncle Stan?"

I eyed the man clutching my hand as though it was a floatie in a rough sea. He was wearing the same clothes he'd had on when we first found him under the bridge, his hair hadn't seen a comb for at least a week and I really didn't have to imagine what his socks smelt like.

"Um…not much room in the van. As you can see through those fogged up windows, we have our dogs with us."

"That's okay," said Corey, giving me more puppy-dog eyes. "Pablo can sit on my lap."

"Um…Pablo?" Who'd probably been rolling in mud and the remains of dead rabbits while enjoying life 'under-the-bridge'.

Corey let out a whistle, and his little dog came racing toward us followed by Molly and Abi, evidently thinking it was time to leave.

"We'll ask Abi. Okay? It's her van."

But as soon as I saw Abi's huge smile when Corey approached her, I knew we had two extra passengers.

"Of course," said Abi. "Always room for one – or two – more."

"And your Uncle might be able to help us with our investigations," added Molly, with a nod of her head. "Burra's a small country town where everyone knows everyone. Your Uncle can probably tell us more about Stephen's stepsister. And if not, he'll know someone who can."

I was so proud of Molly. She may be inclined to drift off into the world of whichever book she was currently writing, but she'd also become a valuable member of the *Chicks*. If we could get a picture of this mysterious Julia through the eyes of people who knew her in Burra, it might give us a better idea of whether the woman was capable of ramming a knife through a man's heart.

Corey, after insisting he only needed ten minutes to get ready, scurried across to his over-sized cardboard box, pulled down the blanket-door and disappeared inside. Pablo following.

We watched the other four happily cooking their sausages around the camp fire, slices of bread at the ready. Or should I say, three. The fourth, Musketeer Guy, had his head buried in one of Molly's romance books and by the expression on his face, was thoroughly invested in its contents.

When Corey reappeared, his hair was smoothed down, his face clean, and he'd changed into a pair of black jeans, a black tee and a navy-blue hoodie.

But the six-million-dollar question was – had he also changed his socks?

*****

Driving into the small country town of Burra was like entering a 1940's time-warp. We were greeted by stately old stone buildings built to last centuries alongside small local shops roofed with galvanized iron and toting full-length verandahs that shaded the footpaths. A thing our early settlers did to beat Australia's blistering summer heat but had been lost in the big cities where cement blocks one on top of the other decorated our landscape.

Corey's Uncle Stan owned a fodder store in the middle of the main-street of Burra. A fodder store, so authentic and rustic, it could have been pictured on the cover of a cozy mystery book.

I pulled up outside and switched off the engine. Bags of kibble and bales of hay spilled onto the footpath each side of the doorway and the shop window was decorated with colorful decals of cuddly dogs, cats, horses, chooks and cows. Just inside the open doorway, a large white, Sulphur-crested cockatoo paraded up and down its perch, informing anyone who'd listen that they were, 'mangy maggots', and when that brought no response, he reverted to screeching loudly, displaying his yellow crest and declaring, 'Polly wanna joint? Polly wanna j-bomb?'

Along the side of the shop, a bitumen driveway led to a large tin shed at the rear, where, according to a prominent sign out front, all fodder could be picked up and loaded once it was paid for inside the shop.

Abi was the first out of the car, her nose pressed to the store's shop window as she clucked over the adorability of six playful kittens displayed for 'Give Away'. A notice in the window advised the kittens had been left on the doorstep and all applicants for rehoming would be thoroughly scrutinized and the lucky new owners provided with a free bag of kitty litter, five tins of cat food and a booklet on the Care of Cats.

"Ooh, look at the calico baby. She's so adorable. And the black fluffy girl with the big yellow eyes. I love her," cooed Abi touching the window with her finger to entice the kittens to play. "Do you think Chloe would like a baby sister?"

"And what about that sleek gray kitten with the cute ears? Look! Look! He's climbing into the cardboard box," said Molly whose nose had joined Abi's against the glass.

I sighed as I locked the van and joined them on the footpath. What chance did I have of getting any sense out of those two while kittens were on the agenda?

"No! No! And not a hope in Hades!" I told them, marching through the open doorway of the shop, head firmly fixed to the front, refusing to let my eyes wander to the antics of the kittens at play. *Did Abi say there was a calico kitten in there? Oh my! I always dreamed of having a calico cat!* "We're here in Burra to investigate – not start World War Three by introducing a kitten to a car full of dogs on our three-hour journey home."

"Mangy maggot!" screeched the white cockatoo, ruffling her feathers and dancing up and down on her perch as I passed.

"And good morning to you."

"Polly wanna joint?"

"Polly's outta luck," I told her and laughed when she threw herself down and pretended to be dead. "What about a cracker instead?"

The cockatoo immediately jumped up and began dancing again, nodding enthusiastically with each beat.

"Hey, there's my Uncle Stan!" Corey let out a yell and stampeded past me across the shop towards a tall well-built man in his late-fifties, early sixties, emerging from the back room.

Dressed in khaki overalls over a checked shirt, a non-descript cap covering most of his bushy fair hair, the man stopped, opened his mouth and let out a roar. "Stone the bleedin' crows! Is that you, Corey?" He lumbered forward, wrapped both arms around his nephew in a bear hug, then stepped back, looked him up and down. "Ya lookin' a bit rough there, lad, and what in blue blazes have ya done to ya hair since I saw ya last? Cut it with a lawnmower?"

Corey, too excited to take the jibe to heart, turned to me and his grin widened. "Dana, this is my Uncle Stan. He's my *best* Uncle."

"You mean your *only* Uncle." His head to one side he studied his nephew more closely. "You still got yaself a job, Corey?"

"Um…not at the moment." Corey chewed on his bottom lip, eyes on the ground. "Long story. Got myself in a bit of trouble and lost everything, including my job."

"Well, you can tell me the story later," said Uncle Stan, putting one arm around Corey's shoulder. "But I could always do with some help with the books and another pair of strong arms around here. That's if ya interested of course. And there's the empty flat on top of the shop to doss down in if you want it. Hasn't been used since your cousin shifted to the city a year ago."

"Do you mean that, Uncle Stan?" Corey drew in a deep breath, bit down on his lip and threw himself at his Uncle for another hug. "Thank you, thank you. As I said before, you're my *best* Uncle."

"And you're my *best* nephew."

Aww…I swallowed the lump in my throat and sniffed. Looked like our friend Corey had a fresh start here in Burra. And he deserved it.

After the hug finished, Corey continued with the introductions. "And Uncle, the other two ladies checking out the kittens are Molly and Abi. They're all friends of mine and want to ask you some questions about a woman who lives around here. Her name's Julia Channing and we think she might be a murderer, but thought we'd ask you first."

Well, that took care of my well-thought-out lead-up speech to introduce the reason we were in Burra. I rubbed my neck and watched Uncle Stan's reaction to Corey's verbal vomit.

"Julia Channing? A murderer?" His thoughtful frown appeared to be tossing up between the two images and coming up with a 'maybe'. Finally, he shook his head and picked up the packet of bird seed on the shop counter, opened the flap. "Nah. She might be crazy as a cockeyed bandicoot and inclined to send unwanted guests off with a flea in their ear, but I can't see 'er actually doin' someone in. Although, as I said, Julia Channing's a bit odd."

By now both Molly and Abi were standing beside me, hanging off the big man's every word. Abi, on my right, leaned closer. "Odd? In what way?"

He raised both hedgehog-like eyebrows and stared down at her. "Julia's deep into that weird mumbo-jumbo mystical garbage."

"But is she dangerous?"

"Wouldn't say that…but just be wary. Single woman, on 'er own with a sick kid, she doesn't like to be messed with. One of my customers reckons she totes a shotgun."

Molly let out a squeak. "W-Why haven't the police arrested her?"

He shrugged. "Well, she's never actually shot anyone…yet. And hey, if I was a single woman and this guy knocked on my door, I'd be inclined to reach for my Winchester too."

"So, she doesn't do that with everyone?" Molly's voice sounded strangled as though she'd swallowed a prickly pear and it was still stuck in her throat.

"Nah." Stan smiled down at Molly. "And hey, you three might be lucky, Julia could be sittin' cross-legged on the ground, eyes closed, meditating."

"H-Hope so."

He gave another shrug. "Problem is ya won't get a word out of her if she is."

"What about her son?" I asked, trying to bring some normality into the conversation before Abi and Molly dived back in the van and drove out of Burra in a cloud of dust. "Do you know anything about her son?"

"Danny? Yeah, poor little begga's always sick and needs a big op to save him. Julia dotes on that kid. Spends a lot of time with 'im at the hospital in Adelaide." He upended the packet of bird seed and filled a couple of plastic bird feeders on the counter. Before he finished pouring, two colorful parrots, squawking loudly, flew down from wherever they'd been perched, watching us, and buried their beaks in the seed. Stan carefully placed the box in a cupboard under the counter before turning back to me. "Julia Channing might be two planks short of an outhouse," he told me, expression dead-serious. "But she's a brilliant mother. Ferocious and protective as a Komodo Dragon when it comes to Danny."

I drew in a deep breath before stating the words we were all thinking. "So, are you saying Julia Channing would be capable of murder if it involved saving her chronically ill son?"

Uncle Stan lifted his cap and ruffled a hand through his already bushy hair. He tilted his head to the side before answering. "Guess that's somethin' you'll have to ask her."

Crazy, murderous, or deep in meditation – that's exactly what I planned to do.

20

After saying goodbye to Corey's Uncle Stan, we bundled back into Abi's van and I set her GPS to take us to Julia's address, 10 Cassowary Lane, which was on the outskirts of town. As Corey had decided to return with us to sort out his belongings before starting work at the fodder store, he climbed into the van too.

I drove out of the town, past the old Telegraph and Post office which had been turned into an Art gallery, past Burra Town Hall its wide stone steps leading up to the heavy front door, past the Royal Exchange hotel – all beautifully preserved historic buildings constructed of stone and built to last a thousand years.

Both Molly and Abi were quiet, deep in thought – not sure if they had kittens or Julia's shotgun on their minds – but Corey bubbled over like a boiling kettle just out of my reach. He couldn't stop talking about his Uncle Stan, his Aunty Di, how much he loved the town of Burra and the new job that awaited him. Not that I could blame the guy. This was an amazing opportunity for him to start again in new surroundings with family close by. But did he have to lean forward against the back of my seat, his mouth so close I could feel his spit hitting the back of my neck? Pablo, perched on his lap, paws on the back of my seat, showed his enthusiasm by happily licking and chewing on my right ear.

About half a mile out of town, the van's GPS informed me, in its usual strident-female, nail-scratching voice, that Cassowary Lane was the next turn-off. Wooly sheep grazed contentedly in paddocks on each side of the road and stone farm houses with their large galvanized iron rainwater tanks dotted the landscape. Just waiting for an artist to capture the rustic scene on their canvas.

After making the turn, I wound down my window and breathed in a lungful of real country air. Aaaahh…if I bottled that air to sell in the city, I could probably charge $50 a snort.

"What if she shoots at us?" Molly, her voice scratchy, broke into my thoughts.

"Why would she?" I flicked a quick glance across at her pale face. "We're not dirty old men, Molly. Hey, if I lived out here alone, I'd probably do what I could to protect myself too."

"I guess." She drew the last word out, evidently not convinced. "But after what Corey's Uncle Stan said about her being a bit weird, shouldn't we just – I don't know – contact her by phone instead?"

"And say what? No, the only way to get Stephen's stepsister to talk, is face to face." I peered out the window at the ivy-clad stone cottage set back off the road. There was a bright red splash of geraniums near the front door, a long-eared donkey picking at a bale of hay in the paddock, a lazy plume of smoke wending its way upward from the stone chimney. Number 10 Cassowary Road reminded me of a storybook cottage. Yes, said my inner voice – exactly like the witch's house in *Hansel and Gretel*. I licked my dry lips and switched off the engine. "Anyway, we'll soon find out. Here we are."

"We need to get these dogs out and stretch their legs first," said Abi, not looking any keener on meeting the mad mystic who lived in that storybook cottage than Molly.

"Here's what we'll do, "I said opening the car door and stepping out onto the dry grass verge. "You and Molly give the dogs a short walk while I go knock on the door, test the waters. Give me ten minutes. If I'm not back by then, come and check on me." I turned to Corey who'd leapt out of the car, stretched his arms and looked ready to accompany me. "You. Stay here."

"But why?" The voice was whiney.

"If she sees a male she mightn't talk."

"But–"

"And we've driven all the way here to get information."

"I could get information. I could smile at her, and like, talk nice and…"

Leaving Corey to continue his argument on how, if I took him along, he could flatter Julia into talking to us, I opened the front gate, heavy and in need of oiling, and picked my way up the graveled path toward the cottage. This was a new Corey. Somewhere between 'under the bridge' and learning he was going to settle in Burra, he'd found a new confidence in himself. We had Uncle Stan to thank for that.

Eyes on full alert for the shine of a rifle barrel peeping through the trees, a scarred sacrificial altar displaying a gutted dead rabbit, or a bone-breaking booby trap set up for uninvited guests, I finally reached the front door in one piece – even if I had to bend over and re-air my gasping lungs before I could knock on the front door.

A sign on the door, written in red Magic Marker – or was that blood – stopped me with my hand half-way up.

!!!!!DO NOT KNOCK!!!!!

!!!!!DANNY ASLEEP!!!!!

I'M IN THE CONSERVATORY.

Right. I dropped my hand to my side and looked around. A conservatory, as far as I knew, was a garden room. That didn't sound so scary. Flowers were peaceful and beautiful – unless of course Julia was into cultivating a new, more aggressive type of Venus fly trap, or a crop of marihuana, although on second thoughts, they usually brought on peace and beauty to the user.

Giving my jeans a hitch, I set off to check the grounds at the rear of the cottage. I found a stable, probably for the donkey on cold nights, a padlocked shed, a ramshackle barn that looked like it hadn't been used this century, an extensive herb garden, but nothing that resembled a conservatory.

As I passed the back door of the cottage the second time around, I noticed an old wooden ladder leaning up against the building and heard a low *hmmm* sound which seemed to be coming from the flat roof of an added room, a large kitchen or sunroom maybe, attached to the rear of the cottage.

Surely Julia wasn't up on the roof…

Only one way to find out. With another hitch of my jeans, I tackled the ladder, which was not for the faint hearted. Timeworn and splintery, the middle rung of the ladder was missing, which meant a large precarious step between rungs seven and nine.

But oh, when I reached the top, the view was worth every precarious step. Large ceramic pot plants sprouting greenery of every shade in the spectrum lined three sides of the roof and colorful flowers smiled back at me or peeped out from under slatted wooden tables, or from behind comfortable outdoor chairs. On one side, was a partly sheltered cave-like structure covered in ivy. And in the middle of all this beauty, sitting cross-legged on a yoga mat, eyes closed, was a gypsy woman in her early thirties. Long dark hair threaded with colorful beads, nose ring, bright purple top and a long multicolored skirt.

Julia Channing.

While I was checking her out, the woman's long feathered lashes fluttered open, revealing dark, almost-black eyes, that seemed to see right through me.

"Sorry to trouble you…" I began, her unflinching stare reminding me of a wild dog, a dingo, I'd once surprised in the Australian bush. Like the dingo, her stare made the hairs on the back of my neck rise.

"What do you want?" Her voice was neither challenging nor welcoming.

"I'm Dana Fox," I said, still hanging grimly onto the sides of the ladder. "And I was wondering if I could ask you a few questions about your stepbrother, Stephen."

When there was no answer, just a continuing stare, I went on. "He was murdered at the dog show a week ago and I was the one who found him."

"Lucky you."

I frowned. "He *was* your stepbrother."

"And?"

"Look…Julia…I'm not what you'd call comfortable balanced on top of this crappy ladder. Okay if I join you?"

Then, without waiting for her answer I clambered up onto the roof and stood there, surveying the flowers, inhaling the flood of fragrances in the air. "Oh, my God, this is totally awesome." I said and waved my arms at the surroundings. "Did you do all this by yourself?"

Julia stood up in one fluid movement, stretched both arms in the air and, closing her eyes again, returned to her annoyingly incessant om'ing.

Totally ignoring me…

Humph. Madam's snarky attitude was getting old and I had a king-size aversion to being ignored. Eyeing the half-full watering can on the table nearby, I imagined myself upending the contents over Julia's oh-so-pretty hair, but instead, after enjoying the mental picture for a moment, much like Julia was doing, I drew in a deep calming breath, proud of my restraint. "My mother taught me that rudeness should only be tolerated in very small children and grumpy old men."

She opened her eyes and let out a sigh. "Look, if you're here to embarrass me into organizing Stephen's funeral, you may as well climb back down that 'crappy' ladder now." She tossed her hair off her shoulders and narrowed her eyes at me. "In fact, I'd rather organize a funeral for the roadkill I found on the highway yesterday."

I blinked. Okay…

"Look, Julia, the only reason I'm here is because I'm investigating Stephen's death."

"And you think I killed him?"

"I didn't say that. I just want to ask you some questions."

"Well, I don't want to answer any of your questions so you may as well go back to wherever you came from."

A head popped up at the top of the ladder. A head attached to a skinny male body wearing a black tee and a huge grin.

"Corey? I told you to stay in the car."

His grin, aimed at the woman in the glaringly bright purple top, widened. "Wow! Where have you been all my life? You're beautiful."

"Corey!" This is exactly why I didn't want a man in the mix. Julia's shotgun was probably loaded and hidden in the potted Kangaroo Paw in reaching distance from where she stood.

"And who are you?" Was that a flirty eye-lift from Julia? A hip crunch? A distinctly seductive pout.

"I'm Corey. And I think I'm in love with you."

Oh, my freakin' heck! I rolled my eyes to the Heavens and took a step back scraping my ankle against a stone wombat that squatted silently between a large wooden planter-box overflowing with healthy looking cucumber plants and a black plastic pot plant containing a solitary orange flower.

What was happening here?

Like a moth to a flame Corey stepped off the ladder and seemed to float toward Julia, his eyes never leaving her face. No more than six inches away, he stopped. She leaned toward him, licked her lips. And I swear sparks crackled between them like New Year's Eve fireworks.

"I have a new job in Burra," he told her. "I'm going to be living here, near you."

"Cool," she whispered staring at his mouth like she wanted to dive inside and lose herself in Corey's sweetness.

"And I love kids so there's no need to worry about Danny."

"Cool," she said again, the needle on her record player seemingly stuck as she leaned even closer.

I coughed. Cleared my throat so loudly I almost blew a tonsil.

Nothing…

"Can we um…finish discussing Stephen first?"

More nothing…

"Corey! Julia! This isn't the time for–"

Another head appeared at the top of the ladder. "Everything okay up here?" It was Abi. She climbed onto the roof followed by a pale-faced shaky-looking Molly who clearly wasn't in the habit of climbing tall wonky ladders. "You said to come and check if you hadn't returned in ten minutes. It's close to fifteen."

Suddenly Abi clocked the two lovebirds, no more than a whisper apart, devouring each other with eyes so hot, so scorching, it's a wonder they hadn't started a summer bushfire. Her eyebrows sky-rocketed. "Am I hallucinating? Or is that our shy introverted Corey and the shotgun lady acting like they need a room?"

I punched Corey on the shoulder. "Earth to Corey! We have a job to do here. You can get back to whatever it is you're doing with Julia once we've finished asking her some questions about Stephen. Okay?"

His breathing ragged, Corey slowly stepped away from Julia and blinked. Confusion, bewilderment and what looked a lot like he'd swallowed a love potion spread across his face. "That was…that was…"

"Weird?" Julia said, equally as bewildered.

He shook his head. "No…more like…amazing!"

"Excuse me," I put in feeling like a fifth wheel on a newly fitted-out car. "But can you *please* continue this-this-whatever it is, later? What I want to know, Julia, is if you were at the dog show last Saturday, the day Stephen was killed?"

The scowl she sent my way wasn't encouraging. "I told you before, I'm not answering any of your questions. You're not the police and its none of your business where I was the day my weasel of a stepbrother was murdered."

I whooshed out a sigh. She was right, of course. No matter how much we called ourselves the *Gumshoe Chicks* and investigated wrongdoings, we had no authority to demand answers to any of our questions.

"Okay, Julia, you win. I'm sorry we invaded your privacy today, but I thought, if we came here, asked you about Stephen, you might help us. Evidently not. So, I guess it's time we left."

Corey shook himself, appeared to snap out of his hormone-induced daze and frowned. "Julia," he said, taking one of her hands in his, carefully, gently, like it was a fragile baby bird. "These three lovely ladies are friends of mine. They've driven all the way here because Stephen's partner, Chi, a sweet man who is totally innocent, is in jail for his murder. The *Gumshoe Chicks* are good people. Regardless of how dangerous it might be, they're determined to find the *real* killer so Chi can be set free. That's why you should talk to them."

She moved closer to Corey and he put his arm around her protectively, drawing her closer to his side. "You want to know about my stepbrother, Stephen," she said and let out a shudder. "Firstly, even though he was adopted and I was my father's biological child, he somehow bullied, or tricked my sick father into changing his will, unbeknown to me, which cut me off from my inheritance. Secondly, he laughed when I pleaded with him to lend me money for a life-saving operation for my son. And finally, although I hated his guts and in my prayers at night repeatedly begged God to make sure he went to Hell...no, I didn't kill him." She sniffed and looked to be battling tears. "Not that it didn't cross my mind the last time I spoke to that ice-cold blowhard on the phone. Two weeks ago, when he told me my son's operation would be a waste of money, that Danny had a defective heart and would never be whole." She closed her eyes and a ragged breath sent her chest vibrating. "He called my little boy damaged goods, worthless, a drain on society."

"Oh, Julia, I'm so sorry," I said, swallowing a giant lump in my throat as I diligently studied the moss growing through the tiles at my feet and wished Stephen was still alive so I could kick him where it hurt.

By now both Molly and Abi had joined Corey in cuddling Julia and patting her on the back.

"I wasn't at the show the day Stephen was murdered, but maybe I can still help," she said at last, pulling away from us and striding across the tiles to the covered area, the cave-like structure set up between two potted apple trees. She flung open the black and silver beaded curtain leading into the cavern. "Let's bring out the dice, the tarot cards and Geneviève, my crystal ball, named after my Great Grandmother, from whom I inherited the gift of second sight. Maybe Geneviève can tell us more about Stephen's murderer."

A crystal ball named Geneviève? I shook my head slowly. Was this woman for real? She might be dressed like a gypsy but to profess to be a clairvoyant, to have inherited 'the sight'? Come on…

Still, once again we'd hit a brick wall in our investigation, so who was I to knock back the *woo-woo* words of a fortune teller? Maybe Julia's great-grandmother's ghost had spotted Stephen on his way down to the fires of Hell and he'd yelled out the name of his murderer as they passed.

The inside of Julia's ivy-clad cave was set up like a fortune teller's tent at a fun fair. A small round table covered by a black cloth interspersed with lightning-shaped motifs, tarot cards stacked on one side, incense spiking the air, and what looked like a large round ball, draped with a silver-starred cloth, in pride of place on the center of the table.

Julia pulled on a long black satin cape with gold stars, slipped a chunky gold necklace with an exquisite Celtic heart-shaped knot around her neck and sat on a stool behind the table. Her face motionless, she removed the cloth, revealing a crystal ball set on an antique wooden stand embossed with gold lettering. She pulled the mystic orb towards her, spread her fingers over the surface, and, eyes closed, fingers moving rhythmically, she began humming, chanting words that I couldn't understand…

Squashed between Corey and Molly, and with Abi peering over my shoulder, I leaned forward. From the depths of the orb, a fine white mist had begun to form, sending smoky tendrils inching outwards and upwards.

What was happening? A shiver sent goosebumps galloping across my bare arms making me wish I hadn't left my jacket on the front seat of the car. Reluctantly, I dragged my eyes back to the cause of the shiver and shook my head. Seemed like crystal balls had a lot more bells and whistles than the Magic 8-Ball I'd played with as a kid.

"Cooool…" breathed Corey into my left ear.

"Far out," agreed Abi in my right ear as she stretched on tiptoe to see over my shoulder.

"I-I don't like this," whispered Molly, her body language and the expression on her face telling me she'd bolt back to the car if I didn't anchor my arm in hers.

Julia stroked the crystal ball, the surface glowing a soft ethereal green under her persistent fingers. Her muttering grew louder, more insistent. "Geneviève! Geneviève! Show me the truth!"

Eyes glued to the crystal ball, my grip on Molly's arm tightened as the green mist slowly faded, ebbed away. And was replaced by what? I leaned closer. Was that a shadow? A darkness? A ghostly shape?

"Geneviève!" she called out again, her eyelids fluttering. "Show me who took the life of my stepbrother, Stephen. Show me the murderer…"

The inside of the globe clouded over and a form began to take shape.

"Holy witchcraft…" croaked Abi from behind me.

"Beware! Beware!" cried Julia, her voice otherworldly, that of a much older woman now. "You are all in danger!" Her voice rose in agitation and her piercing eyes sought mine, pinning me with their intensity. "Beware of a man. A man with evil in his heart. A man wearing a long fake plait…"

21

It was the day after our round trip to Burra and our mystical encounter with Stephen's wacky stepsister, Julia. My day so far had been full-on. After dropping the munchkins off at day-care, I'd shopped for decorations and other party stuff – Kayla's 4th birthday party on the weekend – plus hydro-bathed and turned seven shaggy dogs into fashion plates. Now it was time to meet Molly and Abi at Two Wells for lunch, before spending the afternoon hydro-bathing six of Rick Starling's beagles in readiness for their mid-week show.

As I said…a busy day.

Evidently Rick's hydro-bath was on the blink. I'd been surprised when he'd telephoned me early this morning, asking if I could drop in and wash his dogs. No worries, I'd said. Your hydro-bath's demise adds to my ever-needy bank account. He wouldn't be home as he had several clients booked in for one-on-one training at the Fitness Center so the key to the kennel house would be under a rock, shaped like a beagle, just inside the front gate.

The first thing Molly said when I pulled up in the carpark opposite the little cafeteria in Two Wells' main street was – 'Can't stop thinking about Julia's warning. *A man with a fake plait*…that doesn't make sense.'

No, 'Hi Dana', or 'Been a busy morning, Dana?' – just straight into it as though we were still on our trip home from Burra.

"Let's order first," I said, dragging a hand through my untidy hair as I climbed out of the car. I probably looked a bit rough after my morning's work but that was the down side of being employed as a mobile dog washer. There was more than likely slobber on my cheek and I could feel my hair sticking to my neck from where the last dog I washed – an exuberant collie – had transferred all excess water from his coat to me before I could wrap him in a towel to dry before blow drying his magnificent coat.

Neither Abi nor Molly commented on my appearance, so I brushed the dog hair from the front of my tee shirt and jeans, tucked a stray damp clump of hair behind my right ear and followed the other two *Chicks* into the shop to order an egg and lettuce sandwich and a much-needed coffee. Seemed hours since I'd swallowed a quick coffee and a cold slice of toast at home before rounding up Jake and Kayla to secure them in the back of the car and drop them off at *Baby Buntings*.

After collecting our orders, we found an empty table in the corner of the shop, as far from the open doorway as possible, and settled down, using the fourth chair to store our bags.

We'd scheduled this meeting at the Two Wells Café the day before, when, on arriving home from Burra, I'd been swamped by my two over-excited munchkins who'd stampeded out of the front door, shouting over each other in an effort to tell me all about their zoo adventures. A good night's sleep before debating the warnings and predictions of a crystal ball called Geneviève had seemed a good idea at the time.

"I've been thinking," declared Abi settling noisily into her chair and selecting three brown sugar sachets from the square plastic bowl in the middle of the table. "Some things in life just can't be explained rationally."

I lifted my eyebrows at her. "And this deep and meaningful applies to...?"

"Well...Julia and her crystal ball, of course." She ripped the corner off one of the sugar sachets and stared at it before upending the contents into her coffee. "So, while there was a lull at the shop this morning, I researched scryers, crystal balls and fortune-tellers and you know, it's spooky how acceptable, how on-target some of these fortune-tellers' predictions can be."

"Acceptable? On-target?" scoffed Molly, frowning at Abi. "How 'acceptable' is an unknown man with a long fake plait?"

"Well, the poor girl was in no condition to explain herself further, was she? Scrying evidently takes a lot out of a person, especially when she's dealing with the ghost of her grandmother as well. She was just lucky Corey was close enough to catch her when she stood up from behind the table."

When Julia had finished her predictions, or warnings, or utter baloney – take your pick – her crystal ball had gone totally blank. And when she'd attempted to stand up, her legs had given away and she'd fainted straight into Corey's waiting arms. As though the whole thing had been choreographed by a higher being. Corey immediately decided to stay with Julia, saying he couldn't leave her looking so pale and drained and shaky. Until she recovered, she needed his help. He could always borrow his Uncle's car and go pick up his stuff from under the bridge another day.

I'd rolled my eyes, gathered the *Chicks* and left the two New Age lovebirds to their blossoming romance.

"Maybe it wasn't a man she saw in her crystal ball," said Abi stirring the last of the three sugar sachets into her coffee. "After all, the image wouldn't have been very clear inside all that spooky mist. What if she actually saw our mystery woman? The one with the long blonde plait."

"But how would she *know* there was a mystery woman if she wasn't at the dog show herself that day?" said Molly scrunching her nose to emphasize her point. "What if Julia's performance was all a hoax and she *was* at the show? What if she fought with Stephen over money for Danny's operation and in a fit of anger, stabbed him?"

As I chewed on my egg and lettuce sandwich, I listened to the other two Chicks opposing viewpoints and was actually favoring Molly's skepticism when I suddenly remembered the intensity on Julia's face when she looked up from her grandmother's crystal ball and stared straight at me. I shivered as her words leapfrogged around in my brain. 'Beware of a man! A man with evil in his heart! A man wearing a fake plait...'

If that was a performance, Julia Channing should be up on the stage on Broadway. A highly paid thespian instead of a small-time fortune teller living on the breadline in Burra, South Australia. "Anything else to report since yesterday?"

Abi looked up from her salad sandwich, eyes twinkling. "Chi's cousin rang to say Fly settled in well. In fact, he immediately took over the kennels." Her grin widened and she shook her head. "That dog thinks he's such a superstar. Anyway, Ho said he put Fly in with several other poodles of similar coloring and breeding. A potential kidnapper would have no chance of picking him out of the pack."

"That's great news." A warm feeling of relief swept through me, making my grin even wider than Abi's at the thought of that gorgeous dog, happy and safe again. "Any other news?"

Molly nodded. "Well, Gemma and Eddy dropped in this morning while I was deep into writing the first love scene between Isabelle and Oliver, my two latest protagonists. Oliver had just coaxed Isabelle out of her knickers when the two real-life lovers knocked on my front door. I was a little disorientated at first. Called Gemma Isabelle a couple of times. She must have thought I'd been drinking."

"Did they find out how Patricia died?"

"She was strangled. Fought back evidently as several of her nails were broken."

"Oh God." Abi shuddered. "But at least she's left scratch marks on the killer. Also, the police can identify the DNA from under her nails."

"He or she would need to be on the police data base to do that," said Molly. "Edward said the first thing the police did was check him for scratch marks and then when his DNA came up negative and his alibi proved he was nowhere near the murder scene at the time of Patricia's death, they let him go."

I frowned. There was something about scratches and Patricia's nails being broken that woke something up in my mind. Something I should have remembered. But it wouldn't come.

"Have you finished work for the day, Dana?" asked Abi rousing me out of my thoughts.

"Would have been but I had a last-minute booking. Rick Starling's hydro bath is on the blink so I've got six of his beagles to shampoo, blow dry and make beautiful for a show they've been nominated for tomorrow. Rick's busy at work and can't get home to help, so I have to handle the dogs myself." I glanced down at the time on my phone and ran a hand through my already messed up hair. I was running late. Again. "I'll be pushing to finish by four thirty to pick up Kayla and Jake from day-care. And I can't afford to be late again. Can't give that snobby-nosed Patricia Stamford another chance to gloat and call me…"

An icy lump the size of a potato caught in my throat, choking me to a stop. Ohmygod. Patricia wouldn't be there to give me a mouthful of snark. No more would she be waiting for me, nose in the air, ready to smirk when I charged into Baby Bunting ten minutes late for pick-up. My stomach swirled, the coffee conflicting with the egg and lettuce. I'd never got along with Patricia Stamford but she was always a force to be reckoned with, a larger-than-life personality – and now she was gone.

"I can help with the dogs." Molly, quick to the rescue, squeezed my hand. "I've already completed a five-hour stint of writing today and I've hit a brick wall, so a break from the computer might get the next scene flowing."

"I can help too," said Abi grabbing my other hand. "No need for me to go back to work. Veronique and I decided we needed more of a work-life balance, so we're trialing a new scheme. When the shop's a bit quiet one of us has an afternoon off. My turn today."

"That's a good idea," said Molly.

"Anyway, all I had lined up for my afternoon off was a bit of shopping and I've already bought two tins of white paint to freshen up our front fence. The rest can wait."

"Thanks guys." I swallowed the lump and stood up, took a deep breath. Even with the help of my friends this was going to be a rush job, so it was time to get moving. "You finish your lunch while I just whip down to *Dress Up*, the costume shop at the end of the street. Kayla's party on Saturday is strictly fancy dress only and I need to hire costumes for Pete and me." I picked up my bag, slinging it over my shoulder. "I bought Kayla this gorgeous new fairy costume, all satin and bling. Can't wait to see the expression on her face when she sees it. So, to go with the theme, I was thinking I could dress up as a Fairy Godmother and Pete could go as Harry Potter. Whaddaya think?"

"Harry Potter?" Abi burst out laughing. "How old did you say your husband was?"

"Kayla will love it and it's *her* birthday."

"Well, I'm going as a pirate," said Abi adding another sachet of sugar to her remaining half-cup of coffee. "That's easy. Patch over one eye, a pair of bright-colored pants, plastic sword in my belt and a colored vest. *Heave ho me maties!*" She gave a pathetic imitation of a pirate that would have her enemies laughing themselves silly instead of retreating in fear. "What about you, Molly?"

"Princess," she said and smiled. "White dress, sparkly jewelry, silver high-heels and a cardboard crown."

"Cardboard? I have a real tiara you can wear," said Abi. "Only paste diamonds, but hey, it's Kayla's birthday party not an invite to see the Queen."

"And there's a toy parrot at the bottom of Busta's toy cupboard you can sew on the shoulder of your pirate costume. I can easily wash it and spruce it up a bit."

"Ooh, thanks Abi. Sounds perfect."

I could see Abi and Molly were ready to dive into an all-out discussion of their make-shift outfits for the party, so I lifted my bag from the fourth chair and took off for the costume-shop. A busy afternoon awaited me and even with Molly and Abi's help I had a lot to get through before collecting the munchkins from day-care at 4.30p.m.

Dress Up, originally a second-hand shop which had recently been converted into a costume hire shop with very little change of décor, was the only stage shop within miles.

I pushed open the door, smiled at the tinkly sound of the bell overhead and quickly found what I was looking for – no time to browse. As I was returning to the counter to pay and fill out the hire book for the two costumes, I passed a corner displaying several wigs. Should I add a wig to my Godmother costume? Not much to choose from. Lots of black Goth-type wigs, a couple of bald pates, a wild witch's wig, and half-hidden under a stringy ginger mop of hair was a blonde wig. I stopped. Stared. The blonde wig was done up in a long fair plait.

Oh my God…

Could that be the wig worn by the mystery woman? The fake plait Julia had warned us about? Had the murderer hired the wig from *Dress Up*, affixed it to his or her head after dressing in a bright green dress – according to several witnesses including my husband, Pete – and then returned the wig to the shop once he or she had carried out their dastardly plan?

Maybe I could find out who had it out on hire the day of the dog show. The day Stephen was murdered.

Or maybe this wasn't the mystery wig with the long plait and there were dozens just like it in all the other Costume hire shops in South Australia.

But this was as good a place to start as any…

Adjusting the two costumes over my arm so I could tuck the wig under the other arm, I hurried to the front of the shop to pay for them.

The lady behind the counter, a five-foot bundle of snark was dressed in what looked like clothes she'd chosen from her own costume shop. Kim? Kourtney? One of the Kardashians? Complete with long fake fur coat, form-hugging dress, hair piled untidily on top of her head and an expression on her face that seemed to be saying,' If you're not into what I'm wearing, don't look'.

She tugged a thick leather-bound ledger type book toward her and began writing down each of my items. "Looks like you have a party planned?"

I nodded and returned her smile, all the while trying to work out how to question her about who'd hired the wig the day of the show, without sounding like I was some sort of a stalker.

"That's fifty-five dollars all up," she said pushing the heavy book across to me. "And can you please sign your name on each of these items to say that if they're not returned by the due date, you'll pay a ten-dollar late fee for every day over?" Her smile appeared forced as though she'd had a few unsavory comments in the past in regard to this late fee. Before I could add to the comments, she shrugged. "Blame it on those who think due dates are only for others."

The smile I sent back at her was far from forced. In fact, it was jubilant. Here in front of me were the names of everyone who'd hired costumes from *Dress Up*. As I signed for the two costumes and the wig I glanced up at the other entries. Damn. Saturday before last wasn't on this page. I'd have to turn back a couple of pages to find who'd taken out the wig and that would look suspicious.

"Um…I don't suppose you have a wand to go with this Harry Potter costume, do you?" I asked, looking up from my signing.

"Oh, I have just the thing," she said flapping her hands like an excited schoolgirl. "It even has the lightning bolt, you know, the mark on Harry Potter's forehead on the handle of the wand. Hold on, I'll go find it for you."

As soon as the woman tottered off toward the back of the shop to unearth her special Harry Potter wand, I flicked the pages over, scanned the entries until I came to the correct date, ran my finger over the items listed on that day until I came across the wording: 'Wig 4: fair hair long plait', and a heart-stopping iciness spasmed in my chest as I stared down at the name beside the entry.

Rick Starling…

22

After floating out of *Dress Up*, thoughts in a spin, I stumbled back to the cafeteria on legs that threatened to dump me on the pavement at every step. Once inside, I ordered an extra-large coffee – strong, no milk, six heaped teaspoons of sugar – and after several sips, decided what I really needed was a large dash of something one-hundred-percent alcoholic added to the brew. The caffeine in the coffee was doing absolutely nothing to settle my shock waves.

In fact, it took several more sips and half-a-dozen deep breaths before I was ready to fill Abi and Molly in on my latest find.

"Rick Starling?" Abi's mouth resembled a fish out of water. "Are you sure?"

I nodded and drained my cup.

"So that gym bag he was carrying when he spoke to us at the dog show – it-it was packed with women's clothes." Abi's frown deepened. It must have been harder for her to accept that Rick Starling wasn't the man we thought he was. She'd known Rick when he was a younger, partying version of the Rick we were now accusing of murder.

Molly licked her lips and swallowed. When she spoke, her voice came out low, wobbly. "But was that before or after?" She pulled her jacket more closely around her body and shifted in her chair. "If Rick had already stabbed Stephen before coming over to have a laugh with us, the clothes in his gym bag were p-probably covered in blood."

There was silence for a moment while we all digested this fact. Abi was the first to speak. "And we treated him like he was God's gift to women."

"Dana even likened him to Thor, her favorite superhero."

I nodded, fiddled with the spoon on my saucer. "I did. Plus, a few days later I purposely placed myself alone in a room with the man." I gave an involuntary shudder. "Just think...he could have dropped a hundred-pound weight on my head, made sure I was dead, and then called it an unfortunate accident."

"So...what now?" asked Abi. "*We* know Rick, dressed as a woman, killed Stephen, but a wig he'd hired from a costume shop is not enough evidence to take to the police, is it?"

"Detective Lightfoot would laugh us out of the police station." Molly straightened her shoulders and dragged in a deep breath. "We need more."

"We do," agreed Abi looking equally determined.

I flipped them both a grin. "And I know how to get it."

The two *Chicks* leaned forward – eager to hear more.

"Remember I said that Rick's working at the gym today?"

They both nodded.

"Well, he gave me permission to be on his property and left the keys to the kennel-house under a rock shaped like a beagle. So..."

Abi's grin matched mine. "We forget the kennels and check out his house?"

"We look for evidence in both."

Molly frowned. "But he's only left the key for the kennels. How do we...oh no, no, no, I'm not using my lockpicks to break into his house. That's illegal."

"Come on, Molly, you can work wonders with your two trusty lockpicks. And if anyone asks, the back door was left open so I could go inside and help myself to a drink from Rick's refrigerator when I needed it."

Abi pushed back from the table and stood up. "Okay, that's all settled. Let's get this show on the road."

Leaving my mobile dog-wash parked safely in the Community Center car park, I led the way toward Abi's van which was parked three shops down from the coffee shop. Molly tapped me on the shoulder. "Aren't you were going to hydro-bath Rick's beagles?"

"Why waste my time preparing his beagles for a dog show that he won't be attending? With any luck, Rick will be cooling his heels in a 4 x 4 cell by tomorrow." I shrugged. "Anyway, once he discovers who was responsible for putting him in the cell – there's no way he's going to pay me, is he?"

"Hope Agatha knows where to go, 'cos I don't." Abi entered Rick's address into her GPS, named after the World's famous mystery writer, and turned the key in the ignition.

"Don't look at me." I shook my head. "This is the first time I've been hired to wash Rick's dogs and he only hired me today because his own hydro-bath broke down."

"Knowing what we know now," put in Molly slipping her hand into mine and squeezing. "Are you sure that's the only reason he wanted to get you out to his property?"

"Hmm…hadn't thought of that." I frowned. Just how gullible was I? And here was me thinking I was the most astute member of the team.

"Well, isn't it lucky you have your two best friends with you."

After leaving Two Wells, Abi got onto the main Mallalla Road and headed in the direction of Korunya – an indigenous word meaning 'rainbow' – an even smaller country town.

Following the directions of her GPS, about five miles along we turned off onto a little used dirt road that led through bushy scrubland with very few houses in sight.

Fifteen minutes later, as Abi pulled up in front of *Starling Beagles Lodge* a cacophony of barking, mournful baying and howling started up from inside the two kennel houses situated at the rear of the property. "At least there's no one to worry about the noise out here," Abi observed switching off the motor.

"And more importantly, Rick's not here. His car's not in the driveway. But we have to stay alert in case he comes back."

"Okay, so where do we start?" In the seat beside me, Molly visibly straightened her shoulders and turned her head towards me.

"Kennels first, but bring your lockpicks with you. Once we've searched the kennels for evidence we need to get inside Rick's house."

As the covert operator of the *Chicks*, Molly's instructions were to always carry her lockpicks, lovingly named Harry and Meghan, wherever she went as we never knew when we'd need her expertise.

Once Harry and Meghan had been successfully transferred to Molly's pocket, we climbed out of the van – no need to lock it as the only thieves likely to hang around here were stray cats and magpies – and made our way through the decorative front gate. And there, as Rick promised, next to the side fence, a large rock shaped and painted in the colors of a tri-color beagle, sat smiling up at us. Waiting for me to uncover the key hidden beneath his heavy rear end.

After a hurried search of both kennel-houses, we found nothing of interest except twenty-five eager-faced beagles who, if their wagging tails and bright eyes were anything to go by, were ecstatically excited to see us. There were tri-color, lemon and white, chocolate tris and a solitary white and tan. All asking for attention on top note and all at the same time.

However, with the dogs' nonstop racket, I kept peering over my shoulder, half-expecting Rick to come bursting through the kennel-house door to see who was disturbing his valuable canines. And of course, in my heightened imagination, he was brandishing an axe over one shoulder and a machine gun over the other.

Rick Sparling is at work, I kept telling myself, but my nerves refused to listen.

"What are we looking for anyway?" asked Abi swirling her hands around in a large orange plastic bin half-full of kibble before replacing the lid. "Nothing but kibble in here. No blood-stained green dress or written confession buried in the dog food."

"The blood-stained dress would be long gone. Burned and buried, most likely," I told her. "If we'd known Rick was the mystery woman earlier, we might have had a chance of finding the dress, but there's no way that juicy piece of evidence would still exist now."

"What about Rick's computer?" Molly pulled her head out of the freezer she'd been checking for who-knew-what, and closed the lid. "Maybe there's something incriminating on that."

"Good idea, Molly. So…out with your lockpicks and let's get inside Rick's house."

"Dana, didn't the woman your Peter spotted sidling out of the showgrounds drive a car like that?" asked Abi, pointing to an old white Holden sedan abandoned under a large pepper tree at the rear of Rick's property.

"Mmm…looking more and more like Rick is our mystery woman," I replied frowning at the car before hurrying toward the house. Like the wig, the car was hearsay and we needed positive proof of Rick's involvement before going to the police.

Molly, our sweet romance writer, was getting more proficient with her lockpicking skills and within two minutes we were through the back door of Rick's house and into a long passage with rooms leading off both sides.

"Let's split up. Molly you check the rooms on the left and I'll check the rooms on the right."

"What about me?"

"Abi, your sole job is to find Rick's computer. Check every room in the house until you find it then if there's anything on it to connect Rick with Stephen's death, attach it to an email and send it off your boyfriend. Nathan can take over from there."

I walked into the first room, an ultra-modern kitchen, and stood in the middle surveying the scene. Where to look? And what to look for? Rick's house was tidy for a man who lived on his own. Or did he? The three bottles of Black Cherry Vanilla vodka on the counter didn't scream single male, nor did the three rom-com videos stacked beside them. Although they could have been a setup for his next lovefest. A man as good looking as Rick Starling would have women sashaying out of the woodwork to attach themselves to him.

But no evidence linking him to Stephen's murder was helpful enough to jump up and wave at me. All I could find in the kitchen drawers were what you'd expect to find in every kitchen drawer in Australia. Cutlery, cook books, and all those little things you acquire over the years and have no other place to store them.

The lounge proved even less productive. Except for a lingering and strangely familiar perfume and a half-full box of caramel cremes on the coffee table, all I could see was a comfortable black leather lounge suite and a gargantuan television.

"Found anything yet?" I called out as I walked through the doorway into a room that looked like a guest bedroom.

"Two toothbrushes, six packets of condoms and several women's luxury toiletries," said Molly from inside the bathroom. "Whoever Rick's girlfriend is she spends more on one jar of face cream than I'd spend on my entire cosmetics in six months. Her perfume isn't for plebs either."

"What about you, Abi?"

"I found Rick's laptop buried inside a dirty clothes basket full of his laundry," Abi answered. "No wonder he hides it. I'm in the middle of forwarding some rather interesting emails to Nathan."

"Great, but make sure you delete anything you send from Rick's 'Sent' file," I warned. "Don't want him realizing someone's been into his computer."

"Will do."

"And we'll leave as soon as you've finished," I said lifting the corner of the mattress up to peer underneath. "Don't want to push our luck."

Finding nothing of interest in the guest bedroom I opened the last door on the right side of the passageway. Rick's bedroom. White walls, wall-length inbuilt wardrobe, the same lingering perfume, varnished wooden floor with a couple of tiger-print rugs, a King-sized bed with matching tiger-print quilt and a fat shiny black cat curled up in the middle of the bed.

That's when the memory of the scratches I'd seen on Rick's face when he rushed into the gym, late for my one-on-one training, flashed into my mind. Scratches supposedly from a wild black cat he'd rescued from the RSPCA. A cat no one else wanted. A cat that was so vicious it even scratched its rescuer.

I stepped toward the purring feline on the bed and stroked my hand slowly over his shiny black coat. He rubbed his head against my arm and a rough tongue licked the back of my hand.

Rick had lied to me. This fat domesticated feline looking up at me with a sweet expression and a contented purr wasn't the cause of the scratches on Rick's face.

My heart spluttered to a standstill as realization punched me in the gut.

One and one suddenly added up to a very frightening question. Were the scratches on Rick Starling's face caused by Patricia Stamford fighting back while his hands tightened around her neck, strangling the life out of her?

But why? How?

I shook my head. Of course. The familiar perfume I'd detected in Rick's bedroom and lounge? Chanel No. 5. Patricia's signature perfume. The tell-tale fragrance that had enabled me to dodge her on so many occasions when I was picking Kayla and Jake up from day-care. The perfume that heralded her arrival wherever she went.

But what was Patricia doing in Rick's house?

Was she cheating on Edward with Rick? In love with him? Or just after a little bit of rough? And had she come across some incriminating evidence, like blood-stained clothes, confronted Rick when he visited her at home and he strangled her to keep her quiet when she threatened to tell the police?

Abi, her face the color of cooking dough, suddenly appeared at the bedroom door, a laptop gripped tightly between both hands. I looked up, distracted from my thoughts.

"I found proof on Rick's computer that he was linked not only to Stephen but to Patricia," she said, jigging from one foot to the other.

"Um...that's good, isn't it?"

Abi shook her head. "Only if we live to report it. Rick's car is pulling into the driveway right now..."

23

For a long moment I stood staring down at the black cat who'd leaped off the bed and, still purring like a motor boat in full throttle, was now rubbing himself up against my legs.

Legs that were slow to move.

"Dana, we have to go!"

"Right." I forced my brain into action. "Out the front door and into the car. Rick will look in the kennels first so with any luck we'll be gone before he realizes we broke into his house."

I carefully stepped over the black cat who was busy trying to trip me up in an attempt to stop me from leaving, and sped along the passageway, heart thumping, toward the front door. Molly, first out, bolted for Abi's van like the favorite in a Group One race at Randwick. Opening the closest door – the driver's side – she threw herself inside, slammed the door behind her and turned the key to start the motor.

"No, no, let me drive!" yelled Abi hot on her heels, but before we could change positions to let Abi get behind the wheel, a steel-blue monster on four oversized tires shot out from the rear of the house.

"Ohmygod! It's Rick!"

Rick Starling, hunched over the steering wheel of his pick-up truck, looked as far from a gorgeous Thor look-alike as any man could be. His eyes were wild, his face, almost unrecognizable, was twisted in anger.

And his menacing vehicle, roaring and hissing toxic exhaust fumes, was aimed at an imaginary bullseye directly in the middle of Abi's van.

"Go!" I shouted at Molly, who was sitting hands on the wheel, eyes wide, mouth open, seemingly mesmerized by the approaching instrument of death.

She blinked. Screamed. And putting the car in gear, jammed her foot on the accelerator.

Aaaarrgggh!

The front of the van lifted in the air like a surfer's wave. Rough gravel scattered noisily in our wake. And Rick's deadly weapon missed the van by no more than a cat's whisker, ending up on the opposite side of the road and taking out a chain wire fence, causing a bleating herd of sheep to amble in protest to the other end of the paddock.

We had a head start…

"Ohmygod, ohmygod, ohmygod." Claw-like fingers clenched around the steering wheel, Molly leaned forward, her nose almost touching the windscreen. "I-I can't do this!"

"Of course, you can."

Abi, squashed into the front between Molly and me and evidently trying to forecast what Rick would do next, had her head turned around so she could see through the rear windows. "He's backed out of the fence. Oh no! And now he's following us." Her voice splintered like wood under an axe. "I-I don't believe this…I-I think he's out to kill us."

"You think?" I said bracing myself against the dashboard as the van veered off the road, lifting us off our seats when the two front wheels almost disappeared into a ditch and Molly, eyes closed, began reciting a string of Hail Mary's.

We were doomed.

If Rick didn't kill us with his oversized vehicle, Molly would with her abysmal driving.

"Molly, you're my dearest friend and I love you to bits," Abi yelled over the roar of the motor as it protested against Molly's rough handling. "But if you don't open your eyes and concentrate on the road, I'll personally put up a post on Facebook informing all your romance fans that you're still a virgin."

Molly's eyes shot open. "You'd do that?"

"In a heartbeat."

"Easy for you to say," Molly growled as she struggled to wrest the van back onto the dirt track. "You're not the one trying to dodge a killer truck."

As the van leapt in the air and crashed back onto the road, I tightened my grip on the dashboard. "Um…we have confidence in you, Molly."

Abi peeled herself from the ceiling. "We do?"

"Yes, we do. Now Molly, there's a house at the end of this road. If there's a car in the driveway, pull in. We'll be safe there. Rick won't want anyone to witness him murdering us."

"No one's home," shouted Molly shooting past the house with Rick so close behind us stones from under his monster tires were clattering against the back of the van. "What now?"

"Keep the car steady. I'm going to get my phone from my bag and ring the police."

"Keep the car steady?" Molly took her eyes off the road to glare at me. "You *do* know we're in the middle of a car chase?"

'Molly! The road!" I grabbed the dashboard again as the car swerved to the other side of the road while my bag, which had been on the back seat, hit the roof of the car spilling the contents in every direction.

"Damn. Can't see my phone anywhere," I said peering over the back of the seat. "Must have skidded into a corner somewhere. Abi, you ring the police. Tell them to get out here quick smart that we're being chased by a mad man intent on turning your car and us into spare parts."

"I can't." Abi's eyes were wide, anxious, as she stared back at me. "I left my bag in Rick's kennel house. And my phone with it."

Crash!

The bone-shaking jerk as Rick's pickup slammed into our van from behind sent us all pitching forward. Abi's head bounced off the windscreen and the only thing that kept my head from copying hers was the cement-like grip I had on the dashboard.

"Ohmygod, ohmygod, ohmygod!" Molly yanked the wheel to the right so sharply one of the van's wheels lifted off the road.

"If this was a movie," said Abi, massaging her head, "this is where one of us would lean out the window and start hurling baseballs at the evil guy's windscreen."

"If this was a movie," I reiterated, "there'd be a couple a dozen baseballs conveniently sitting in the back of your van to hurl at the evil guy's windscreen. Instead, all I can see is an old metal dog comb that's seen better days, a red leather dog's lead, an empty chip packet, and the two tins of paint you bought to freshen up your front fence."

Crash!

Rick's pick-up smashed relentlessly into the back of the van again. How much more could we take? Molly, although screaming obscenities with every crash, was doing a great job of keeping the van upright, but already the swelling on Abi's forehead was turning into a crater and a physio would be busy for weeks treating the whiplash in my neck.

As for Abi's van – even if we survived Rick's onslaught, her insurance company would take one look and write it off.

Crash!

The van leapt in the air and spun to the right heading for a paddock full of grazing cows.

"Ohmygod, ohmygod, ohmygod!" Molly clung onto the wheel like it was the last red M &M in the box, scraping the side of the van against the paddock fence as she turned the van away at the last minute. "I-I think I might have wet myself."

"I have an idea," I said squirming out from under Abi and massaging a lump caused when my forehead connected with the door handle. "The paint you bought for the fence. We'll throw it at Rick's car."

"How will that stop him? The tins will just bounce off and roll to the side of the road."

I hauled myself over the seat. "Not if we take the lids off first. The paint will splatter all over his windscreen and he'll be driving blind after that."

"Way to go!"

I half turned around. "Molly, no matter what happens, can you keep the car steady when I yell, *'Rick Starling's a scumbag'*?"

"You betcha!"

"Hang on, Dana. I'll hold onto you so you don't fly out the door with the paint," Abi heaved herself over the seat to join me. "We don't want *you* splattered all over Rick's windscreen."

Thanks so much for that grisly vision, Abi.

With the sound of the van's overtaxed engine screaming in my ears, I scrambled into the back of the van, fell on my knees, tried to stand up, couldn't, so crawled across to the cardboard box containing Abi's two paint tins and dug my fingers into the ridge around the lid of the first tin. It didn't move.

"Try this." Abi handed me the battered metal dog comb but before I could use it to prise off the lids, Rick rear-ended us again.

"Aaaargh!" I shot across to the other side of the van, clutching the paint tins and the comb to my chest.

This better work.

Grabbing a quick breath and while imagining evil Rick Starling dangling from the mouth of an African lion, I leaned back against the side of the van and using the metal comb, worked at loosening both lids.

"How's it going?" I looked up to see Abi, feet apart, one hand on the door handle. She rolled both shoulders. "'Cos if you're going to toss that paint, now would be a good time. He's close up and preparing another onslaught."

"*Rick Starling's a scumbag!*" I yelled as both lids came off and spun in the air.

Abi flung the back door of the van wide open.

Then, while she clung onto the dog-hitching rail inside the van with one hand and the back of my jeans with the other, I leant forward into the force of the wind and, with my hair in my eyes, the movement of the van threatening to dispatch me under the wheels of the pursuing vehicle, I squinted, took aim…

And let go.

Eyes watering, heart performing half-assed cartwheels with more flop than flair, I watched my two missiles hover in the air over their target for what felt like a long weekend. Until finally…

Both tins hit the jackpot.

Rick's face behind the glass registered surprise, but before he could react, paint exploded from the tins in a shower of whiteness and Rick's face disappeared from view.

'Whoohoo!"

While Abi roared her approval, I watched the monster pick-up swerve to the right and then to the left, smash through a road-side fence, go careering across a stubbled paddock, plough through the middle of a haystack…and come to a shuddering stop.

"Take that!" yelled Molly who'd slowed the van to a crawl so she could watch the proceedings.

"Keep going, Molly. We can't hang around and wait for Rick to get out of his car and join us," I said as I slumped to the floor of the van waiting for my legs to regain their strength. Wilting celery sticks aren't made to hold up a body. "Plus, we have to find my phone and ring the police."

As if my words had summoned them, the insistent wailing of police sirens broke through the air and what looked like three police cars rounded the far corner and headed towards us. "What the–?"

As Molly slowed the car to a stop, Abi jumped out, dancing on the spot, laughing and waving her arms. "Over here!" she yelled, pointing to the now forlorn-looking vehicle half-buried in hay.

"I didn't ring the police – couldn't find my phone," I said arching both eyebrows at Molly who was looking at me with a barely controlled smirk. "Molly? What did you do?"

"I rung Hudson before we left the cafeteria," she said with an I'm-a-real-badass grin spreading across her face. "Told him we had evidence against Rick Starling and we were going to his house to find more." She shrugged. "Guess he realized I wouldn't pass the message on when he said for us keep out of it and leave Rick to the police." A slight frown crossed her brow. "Don't know what kept him though."

A laugh bubbled in my chest and spilled over. "He's here now and it's good to see he's learning what it's like to be a Chick's other-half."

She lifted one hand in the air for a high five. "To getting the hell out of here as soon as the police have taken Rick into custody."

"And to stopping off at Abi's for a glass or three of wine to celebrate the end of another mystery."

Dear Readers

FOR THE LOVE OF DOGS is the second book in my new series, the *Gumshoe Chick Mysteries,* this time starring romance writer, Molly. There's three *Chicks* – Abigail Truelove, Molly Gibson and Dana Fox. All dog-show competitors. All 28-year-old Nancy-Drew-wannabees. All owners of pampered pooches. If you've enjoyed reading this why not go back to wherever you bought this book from and leave an honest review? Reviews are like dessert for us authors. In fact, they are part of what keeps me writing – knowing you've spent time with the characters I created, dressed up and injected with life. Especially for you.

If you'd like to catch up with me on Facebook, go to: https://facebook.com/JuneWhyteBooks.

Or to check out my website, go here: www.junewhytebooks.com

I'd also like to acknowledge and thank those who have helped me in my writing journey. My beta readers, Nancy, June K and Bev – couldn't do without you. My forever friends, Robyn and Wendy – I know I can always whip off an email with a question or ask for a second opinion and it will be answered with a smile. And Traci Andrighetti, USA bestselling author of the *Franki Amato mysteries,* whose suggestions and edits have seen me grow as an author.

And for those who haven't yet read, GONE TO THE DOGS, the first book in the *Gumshoe Chicks* Mysteries, I've included the first chapter, just for you.

Thank you,
June Whyte

GONE TO THE DOGS
CHAPTER 1

My name is Abigail Truelove and my life changed the day I discovered Petra Sullivan, my nemesis, was sleeping with the show judge.

The Ladies Kennel-Club was staging its Annual Championship dog show at the Royal Adelaide Showground and over the last four hours, two hundred or more competitors had stacked, primed, and shown off their dog's attributes to the presiding judges.

It was now down to the group finalists. Seven dogs, battling it out for the coveted Best in Show award. And as my smooth-haired dachshund, *Tempestuous Dawn* had won Best in Hound Group, I stood in the middle of the line-up, my dog stacked, alert, and ready.

An order from the judge sent the winner of the Gundog Group, the Honorable Lady Felicity Taylor, into instant action. She lifted her three chins high in the air and set off around the ring with her jet-black cocker spaniel in tow. God, that dog could move. Pity it didn't have a brain in its head. Not that it mattered. When it came to Best in Show material, surface beauty was all that counted.

Since joining the competitive show ranks, I'd learned that dog shows were akin to a battle ground. Like hard-fought wars, strategies to win that coveted Best in Show sash were planned with precision and dedication. Hours on the treadmill to keep up the dog's muscle-tone. Marathon do-overs with clippers, brushes and expensive beauty products. Secret diets passed down through generations of show families.

I'd inherited *Tempestuous Dawn* (aka Chloe, the most gorgeous and lovable dachshund on this earth) a year ago when my favorite relative, Aunt Tilly, died of a heart attack while kayaking in the North of Queensland. Not having children of her own, she also left me *Pampered Pooch,* an exclusive doggy boutique that sold designer-brand products on the High Street. At the time, my boyfriend, Luke, although happy with the money generated from the boutique, wasn't too keen on the canine edition to our family. He complained about the time I spent with the 'bloody dog' and pretended to be allergic to the minutest amount of dog hair left on the sofa. Right from the start, he'd advocated selling Chloe; said we'd get big bucks for the dog. But it wasn't going to happen. One – Aunt Tilly would rise up her from the grave if I dared put *Tempestuous Dawn* on the market. And two – I fell head over heels in love with the quirky little dog and decided I'd continue showing her. After all, this dog was a near-perfect specimen of the breed and under Aunt Tilly's expert handling had previously won Best in Show in every state of Australia.

Not that I'd enjoyed Aunt Tilly's success. At the first five shows I'd entered, Chloe had bombed. Dramatically. She hadn't even won her breed class.

But today, with the sound of crated dogs yapping from inside the pavilion and the overpowering scent of whichever new beauty product Lady Felicity had doused both herself and her cocker-spaniel, *Mein Freund Merry Widow*, I was determined to give it my best shot.

Lady Felicity, nose in the air, completed two laps of the ring and moved back into line with the other finalists. A total professional, she immediately presented her dog to the judge, head up, tail straight and four legs in perfect alignment. A twenty-year doyen of the game, the woman's show-ring skills and professional attire always went a long way towards collecting Best in Show ribbons.

While realigning Chloe's left ear so it sat in perfect placement to her right ear, I noticed my best friend Molly Gibson plucking nervously at the number tag pinned to her shirt. Molly had only joined the show dog ranks to keep me company. And although Busta, her smooth-coated Fox Terrier, absolutely loved to show off in the ring, Molly was happier in the background, helping to run the shows. This was the first time Busta had won Best Terrier in Group and by the way Molly was chewing on her fingernails, she wouldn't be opening any tricky butter-pats in the near future.

"Number twenty-six, lady with the smooth-haired dachshund, I'd like to see your dog's paces please." The judge, an older guy with a cowlick and shoes that were a little run down at the heels, nodded his head at me.

Again? God, this judge was taking more time to make up his mind than a group of politicians debating Climate Change.

I sucked in a quick steadying breath. "Okay, my love, let's show them what you can do." With a slight tug on Chloe's lead I stepped out of the line-up. Having already won Champion of Breed and Champion Hound, if I could keep Chloe's attention a little longer, she had a good chance of winning Best in Show.

Tempestuous Dawn floated across the ground with me powering along beside her, puffing like the little-engine-that-could. Understandable, considering I'd scarfed an entire block of Rocky Road chocolate, plus a large packet of M&Ms before entering the ring – show-nerves – so by the time we moved back into line, the sweat welling on my face was doing a pretty good job of removing my makeup.

But the moment we came to a halt, Chloe began to sag.

"No, no, no. Only a couple more minutes," I whispered, trying valiantly to keep her stumpy little legs from folding, while silently willing the judge to get his ass into gear and make a decision.

"Sorreee...I got held up in the Little Girls Room."

I blinked in surprise as the shark of the show-world, Petra Sullivan, bee-stung lips the color of old plasma, and hot pink jeans so tight you could define every delineation of her *hoo-ha*, sashayed into the show-ring, her overweight pug, the dubious winner of the Toy Group, dragging along behind her.

"Hey, you can't waltz in here now, you're too late!" I hissed through gritted teeth as Petra stopped in front of me to adjust one of her overflowing boobs.

How did she even get past the steward at the gate?

Petra's grin was so smarmy it would curdle yoghurt. She gave a tiny shoulder-shrug in response, then proceeded to push her way into first-cab-off-the-rank position at the top of the line-up. All the while ignoring the snorts of anger from the handlers of the other six Group winners.

Surely, Mr. Oliver Hutchins, who purported to have judged at big shows in both England and America, would order the gate-crasher out of the ring. This class had been in progress for half an hour. The judge was on the brink of announcing his winner. No way could a contestant enter the ring and be judged once a class was in action.

The rules were in black and white.

All eyes swiveled from Perky Petra to Mr. Procrastination. All waiting in anticipation for the interloper to be tossed out on her well-defined derriere. But nothing happened. Not a crumb of censure passed the esteemed judge's lips. No steward came to drag Petra out of the ring by her ultra-long false eyelashes. Instead, Oliver T. Hutchins grew an inch or two taller, sucked in his stomach and straightened his bow-tie. All the while beaming at the latest competitor as though she was a double decker chocolate-swirl ice-cream and he couldn't wait to lick her.

Had he been stalling? Waiting for Petra to enter the ring? Was that why he'd been taking so long to announce his winner?

At first, when the whispers skittered along the line-up that Petra was *doing* the judge, I couldn't believe it. That is, until Petra threw a little finger wave in the direction of Mr. Easily-Swayed and he answered with a suggestive lick of his lips and an almost imperceptible pelvic thrust. *A pelvic thrust?* At his age? I could feel the ire churning around in my chest, escalating with every spin and preparing to explode via my mouth with a few well-chosen, but completely unladylike words. Pitched at a very high volume. Hey, I'd been the bunny who'd spent hours on the phone with this guy as a representative of the Ladies Kennel Club. I'd been the one who'd pleaded and offered him more money than our club could afford to pay for his services.

Silly me...I'd got it wrong.

I'd stroked the guy's ego while Petra stroked his whatnot.

As I watched the judge swagger across the ring, his eyes lasering in on the pair of double D's escaping from the front of Petra's low-cut blouse, I knew we'd missed the boat.

Chloe must have sensed it too. Weary of all this standing around looking suave and beautiful, she decided it was way past her nap time. She dug several pivots out of the grass, turned three times on the spot, curled up in a ball and promptly fell sleep.

I didn't bother waking her. What was the point? Even considered the merits of joining her.

The judge, after sending Petra and *Princess Sauvignon of Glenville* for one measly lap of the ring, pulled the fat little pug out of the line-up and presented Petra with a trophy and the coveted multi-colored Best in Show sash.

Unbelievable.

The moment Petra exited the ring, the other six Group winners rounded on her. For a split second, I actually felt sorry for the woman. But only for a split second.

"You conniving little tart!" Stephen Channing, owner of the Non-Sporting Group winner, a beautifully trimmed-and-primped-to-within-an-inch-of-its-life apricot Standard Poodle, *Supreme Champion Windswept Fly By Me*, who'd won more Best in Show ribbons than most dogs had breakfasts, got right up into her face. His gold medallion, ear rings and matching necklace vibrating with his anger. "You bitch! You slept with him, didn't you?"

Petra wrinkled her nose. "Back up, Stevie. Your breath smells like you've been sucking on some guy's…dirty socks."

"Stone the flamin' crows!" snarled Wild Bill Hooter, the bearded winner of the Working Dog group. "Stephen's right. You're nothing but a tart!" He spat a lump of phlegm in Petra's direction, completely ignoring his Border Collie who was attempting to hump Petra's pug.

"*I'm* lodging a formal complaint to the committee." Lady Felicity snatched up her Cocker Spaniel who was also showing interest in Petra's pop-eyed pug and stormed off in the direction of the Secretary's office.

The accusations fell on deaf ears.

Petra, all smiles, shimmied a path through the angry contestants, all the while flapping her Best in Show ribbon in our faces, like a matador waving a red cape at a bull.

"What I don't understand is how you could *do* that, Petra? How you could climb into bed with a guy old enough to be your father, a guy you don't even know – just to win a ribbon?" That was Molly, my best friend. Of course, Molly's views on sex were a little out-dated. Like a marriage certificate in full view on the bed-side table and even then, nothing more erotic than the missionary position while lying back and *doing it for England.*

Over the years, I'd tried to drag my friend into the 21st Century, but it was a hard-uphill slog. Probably because Molly's parents died in a car crash when she was four and she'd been brought up by her strict Great-Granny Teresa, whose archaic ideas of carnality meant the actual word *sex* hadn't been invented yet.

There was a scuffle at my feet. I looked down and let out a laugh. Busta, Molly's exuberant Fox Terrier knew *exactly* what the word sex meant. He was going hammer-and-tongs on top of *Princess Sauvignon of Glenville* like it was Christmas morning and Santa had left the little pug under the tree, all boxed and gift-wrapped, just for him.

Petra's laugh was breathy, almost a snigger. "You're *so* naïve, Molly. It's almost as if you never left high school."

"But you didn't answer her question," I said, bending to help my friend extricate Busta from his carnal bliss before facing up to Petra.

"That's easy. I *adore* sex." Petra flicked her shoulder-length bottle-blonde hair over her shoulder as if that explained everything. "And if being horny gets me what I want in life, why not?"

I shoved Busta into Molly's arms and turned back to Petra. "Even if it means cheating?"

"Prove it."

"I intend to."

Petra barked out a laugh. "Oh, Abi, do you honestly believe Mr. Please-Pass-the-Viagra would admit to having sex in return for favours rendered. If so, you're as delusional as your weird friend." She eyed the accusing faces around her, all hanging on to her every word. "You know, if I divulged the names of all the guys I've slept with – just this month – at least *one* of you losers would be booting your other-half out of the cosy love-nest." As she spoke, her hard eyes, glinting with malice, zeroed in on me.

"What do you mean?" My voice came out strangled, as though a lump the size of a tennis ball had lodged in my throat. "What are you implying?"

Molly touched my arm. "Come on, Abi, she's just winding you up."

"I'm *implying* nothing." Petra stepped closer, a smirk thickening her cosmetically full-blown lips. "All I'm saying is *maybe* some men prefer to suck on juicy watermelons instead of–" she tipped her head forward and blatantly studied my chest. "–sour little lemons? And *maybe* some men look forward to fireworks in bed, instead of damp squibs."

I shrugged off Molly's restraining hand, a bitter taste of bile flooding my mouth. Was Luke really having it off with Petra? Was that why he seemed a little preoccupied, lately? Accusing me of not trusting him? Telling me I was too clingy?

Well, if this was a test – he'd failed miserably. It proved I was right all along not to trust him.

Or was Petra lying?

"If I find out you've been in bed with Luke," I growled, grabbing hold of Petra's arm and swinging her around, forcibly holding back from planting a fist into that smirking face. "I'll dice you into little pieces and feed you to the sea-gulls."

"Oh, dear, always so dramatic." Petra pulled away and laughed. "If it helps, *darling*, sex means nothing to me. It's just a bit of fun. Like scratching an itch."

My nails bit into my palms as my fists tightened.

"Come on, Abi, don't let her get to you," Molly broke in, dragging me away, her face pale. I took my eyes off Petra long enough to glance across at my best friend. Molly looked upset. Sick. She had that haunted expression on her face – the one that said, '*Oh, God, it looks like a fight... and I'm so not into fisticuffs or hair-pulling because I'll be the one who ends up in hospital or paying for a new hairstyle to cover the gaps in my hair.*'

"But Petra slept with Luke."

"She's winding you up. Can't you see that? No way would Luke cheat on you." Molly's grip on my arm tightened. "Especially with a woman who treats sex like an Extreme Olympic Sport. Luke loves you."

All the red-hot anger crashing around inside my chest suddenly abated and dribbled away. "Does he?" I could hear the wobble in my voice. "That's the problem, Molly. I'm not so sure he does."

24

If Batman and Supergirl didn't stop hurling handfuls of fairy bread at each other and screeching like fire-engines whenever the bread connected, I'd pick them both up by the scruffs of their superhero cloaks and drop them into time-out. I even considered removing the fairy bread from the table, but then realized there was an even larger, more tempting bowl of ripe peaches cozied up beside it.

Kayla, the birthday girl, looking oh-so-cute in her new fairy costume streaked past me closely followed by Kristoff from Frozen who appeared to be waving a live frog in the air. A frog? I couldn't remember inviting a frog to the party. Quickly stepping back, right into a wailing 4-year-old Casper, whose chocolate ice-cream ended up mashing into the back of my long glittery white Fairy Godmother costume, I peered wildly around the yard for Peter.

Help!!!

My husband, looking rather adorable in his Harry Potter outfit, was busy topping up the empty glasses of all our adult guests and laughing at something Corey had said.

I yanked my faux tiara off and scratched my head. Here I was knocking myself out supervising all the pintsized superheroes, cowboys and various Frozen characters, while over by the barbecue was an empty wine glass with my name on it.

My mother, bless her, was herding the kids to the bottom of our yard and instructing them to sit on the grass in front of a hired party entertainer, dressed as Bobo the Clown. He was juggling what looked like eyeballs but were probably only painted hard-boiled eggs.

I grabbed a fortifying breath – a definite requisite when in charge of a 4-year-old's birthday party – and headed over to the barbecue. And the wine.

What a week!

After Rick had been led away in handcuffs, Molly, Abi and I had spent several hours in the interview room at the police station rubbing noses with Lightfoot and his merry men. All rather narrow-eyed and intense. Like we'd screwed up by solving the mystery for them. And tell me this – why do policemen insist on asking the same question in five different ways? Why don't they write down the answer the first time so they don't forget?

Anyway, we found out Rick had not only killed Stephen, who'd been blackmailing him after snooping around and discovering a sophisticated meth lab in one of the property's outlying sheds, but also Edward's wife, Patricia. While Edward was involved with Gemma, Patricia had been making whoopee with Rick. She'd stayed over some nights – hence the girly stuff and the faint scent of her Chanel No. 5 in his house – and had evidently stumbled across evidence that her 'oh-so-hot-and-handsome lover' had dressed up as a woman after the dog show was over and eradicated his blackmailing problem by stabbing Stephen six times in the chest.

She'd threatened to go to the police with her evidence. He couldn't have that – so he'd strangled her.

Who can understand what turns a normal-seeming guy into a murderer? Rick Starling had looks, a well-paying job at the gym, inherited money to set up his beagle breeding and showing establishment...so why turn to illicit drugs and murder? Maybe he'd been affected by his own drugs? Mental problems? Revenge? The threat of being found out?

Anyway, Chi was quickly released from prison, his beloved poodle

Fly flown back home and he, along with Gemma, Edward, Corey and his new 'friend' Julia, had joined us *Chicks* and our partners to celebrate not only Kayla's birthday, but our third successful mystery.

And what wonderful new friends they were.

I grinned at *Lord* Edward, dashingly dressed as a buccaneer right down to the loose-fitting breeches, colored waistcoat and skull and crossbones emblazed boldly across his baggy cap. He was chasing Gemma around the yard, swishing his wooden cutlass and yelling, 'Heave ho me hearties!' and, 'Come here, wench! You're for the Cat O' Nine Tails!' Gemma lifted the bottom of her ball-length gown – think she was someone from one of the Jane Austen books but not sure who – and giggled as she dodged Samantha, her yapping, over-excited poodle and flopped back onto her chair, both hands up in the submissive position as Edward caught her up in a smacking kiss.

And there was Corey, happy in jeans, suede top and cowboy hat, chatting away to Julia who, wearing her normal colorful gypsy clothes, hadn't bothered with a fancy dress. Corey was now employed at his Uncle's fodder store, living in his cousin's unit over the shop, and he and Julia had listed themselves as *soulmates* on their recently merged *Facebook* page.

Sidling up behind *my own* soulmate, Peter, I wrapped both arms around his waist and pulled him to me. He turned his head and nuzzled my ear. "Hey, Magic-Boy," I said in my best Dolly Parton croaky voice, "Can you spare one of those mouth-watering steaks for this hungry Fairy Godmother?"

Swishing his cape, he spun around to face me, his Gryffindor tie flying over one shoulder, his Harry Potter glasses slipping down his nose. "Only if you grant me three wishes."

"*Three*?" I repeated. "Bit greedy, Magic-Boy."

"Hey, what's the point of having a fairy godmother for a wife if I can't ask for a million dollars, a trip around the world and my very own personal towel in the bathroom?"

I hit him over the head with my cardboard tiara and laughed when his glasses slid further down his nose. "Come on, Magic-Boy, pass me your best hunk of steak and I'll grant you your last wish. I'll even buy you a towel that has HIS embroidered on the front."

"Just watch out you don't change into a pumpkin at midnight," he said wrapping a slice of steak and a heap of caramelized onions that were making my stomach rumble, inside two slices of wholemeal bread.

"You need to read the Cinderella story again," I said, relieving him of the sandwich and thanking him with a kiss that tasted of wine, steak, onions and chocolate. My four favorite flavors. "It's Cinderella's coach that turns back into a pumpkin. Not her fairy godmother."

Collapsing onto a chair between Molly and Abi, I chewed on a bite of my steak sandwich and moaned. It was *so* good. "Where's your other-halves?" I asked them after taking the edge off of my hunger.

Abi nodded to where the entertainment was taking place at the bottom of the garden. Both Nathan and Hudson were helping out by setting up a horizontal box in the middle of the lawn and the clown, who'd previously been juggling eyeballs, was now telling the children how he was going to climb into the magic box and disappear.

The audience were all agog. I could see Jake sitting cross-legged next to Edward's son, Noble, and while Noble sucked his thumb, Jake was bouncing up and down, clapping his hands and giggling.

I smiled and relaxed in my chair. This is what I'd wish for if I had my very own fairy godmother. To be surrounded by love and laughter. I felt a polite nudge on my left knee and looked down into eyes that brimmed with love. Dark brown eyes that gazed adoringly up into mine.

It was Penelope – the sweetest greyhound in the world.

I smiled down at her.

Scratched her favorite spot – the indentation right behind her left ear.

And fed her my last bite of steak.

Dear Readers

DOGGONE IT is the third book in the *Gumshoe Chicks Mystery* series, this time starring Dana, owner of *Hydro Hound*, a mobile dog wash, mother of two adorable but energetic munchkins under 4, and the voice of reason. There are three *Chicks* – Abigail Truelove, Molly Gibson and Dana Fox. All dog-show competitors. All 28-year-old Nancy-Drew-wannabees. All owners of pampered pooches. If you enjoyed reading DOGGONE IT, the third book in the series, why not pop over to Amazon, or whichever online store you bought this book from and leave an honest review? Reviews are like dessert for authors – with a cherry on top. In fact, they are part of what keeps me writing, knowing you've spent time with the people I created, dressed, and injected with life. Especially for you.

If you'd like to catch up with me on Facebook, go to: https://facebook.com/JuneWhyteBooks.

Or to check out my website, go here: www.junewhytebooks.com

For those who haven't yet read, FOR THE LOVE OF DOGS, the second book in the *Gumshoe Chicks* Mysteries, I've included the first chapter, below, just for you.

Thank you,
June Whyte

1

"**B**ad dog, Busta!" I eyeballed the show-judge's suede, postbox red, ribbed, knee-high boots with the round toes and platform soles. The *ruined* knee-high boots with the round toes and platform soles. "I'm so sorry." Face hotter than a bushfire in summer, I tugged on Busta's lead to bring him to heel. But it was too late. The damage was already done. My show dog, *Sir Willoughby of Cornwall*, Busta to his friends, had cocked his leg on the judge's eye-catching red boots – and immediately drained the swamp.

And it was all my fault. Me, Molly Jayne Gibson – romance writer and perpetual day-dreamer.

Instead of concentrating on setting my fox terrier up for the judge's appraisal, my mind had wandered to my latest romance, my work-in-progress, *Three's A Crowd*. In it, the two love interests, Gray and Tabitha, weren't co-operating at all. You see, although Gray was all for hopping into bed and getting on with it, Tabitha, who'd been left at the altar by Gray's best friend, Ethan, wasn't so easily convinced. In fact, nothing I suggested was changing Tabitha's mind. Not that I could blame her. Three hours earlier, she'd been dumped by a man she thought was the love of her life and Gray, who'd rescued her, was now being an insensitive A-hole. Yep. And I needed to do something about that too.

Meanwhile, back in the real world, by allowing Busta to express his opinion of the fifty-something show-judge, also, the Mayor's wife, I had embarrassed myself, big time.

"My God, these boots cost me a bomb. They're Gucci, for Christ's sake." Dressed in a too-short-for-her-age red mini and makeup layered on with a paint roller, Lady Hamilton-Davies wobbled two steps backwards while pointing an accusatory finger at the now butter-wouldn't-melt-in-his-mouth, Busta. "Get that beast away from me!"

"I'm sorry, I don't know what came over him. Honestly. He's not normally like this." I dug in my pocket for some tissues to wipe the woman's boots, but all I could find was a packet of gum, a small notebook and a biro. "Would you like me to put your shoes under the tap? Give them a bit of a scrub? Maybe I can wash away the stains."

"Under. The. Tap?" The woman's mouth opened so wide I discovered she'd never had a tonsillectomy. "Are you insane? These boots cost me more than you'd earn in a month."

As I averaged around $2000 a week writing sizzling hot romance novels, I seriously doubted that statement. But said nothing. Instead, I let out a deep sigh. To say the judge was unhappy, was like saying spiders enjoyed being splattered to death with a sledge hammer. Naturally, I'd recompense the woman for the damaged footwear, buy her a new pair, but ohmygod, I'd never live this embarrassment down. The day Molly Gibson let her dog, Busta, pee on the judge's shoes, would be a permanent fixture on the show grape-vine. I only prayed some smart entrepreneur hadn't used their phone to video the event and already downloaded it onto Facebook where it would quickly go viral.

From the corner of my eye, I could see the smirk on my opponent's face. Busta was up against the winning female fox terrier for the Best in Breed sash. And by the smug expression on the dog's face, it was almost like *Miss Moppet* knew she'd won the award. She stood straighter, adjusted her head to present her good side and lifted her stumpy tail higher. However, the dog's owner, one hand covering her mouth, shoulders shaking in suppressed laughter, was demonstrating exactly how much ribbing I would need to endure before Busta's little party trick was forgotten.

"Here!" The judge snatched a wide blue satin sash from the table and tossed it in the direction of the posing *Miss Moppet*. "Competitor number 16 is Best of Breed." She then swiveled around to face me, her overblown lips parting to display pearly whites gritted in a snarl. "And if I ever see *that* dog again, I'll personally neuter him."

And with that, she stomped her foot and strode out of the ring.

*****

Half an hour later, the hysterical yapping of small dogs and the ear-splitting crackle of an overhead PA system – background noises to complement the clash of crockery and low chatter in the showground's cafeteria – barely made a bump in my concentration as my fingers flew over the keyboard on my laptop.

After Busta had bombed out of his class, I'd returned my unrepentant canine to his crate, and decided to take myself off to a corner of the cafeteria, to be alone. As you do, when you consistently put out three steamy contemporary romance novels a year and your deadline for the third for the year was fast approaching. I also needed to work on Gray's personality. Transform him from a domineering out-for-what-he-could-get A-hole into a warm caring hero so Tabitha could fall in love with him.

Eyes glued to my computer screen, I typed faster…

Gray's probing tongue sent Tabitha's panties crackling as his kiss deepened. This was the night she'd been dreaming about for months. Her wedding night. The night she'd express her total unconditional love for her new husband, Ethan, Sydney's most eligible and wealthy bachelor, the man she'd planned to spend the rest of her life with. The man who'd left her at the altar, walked away from her, saying he wasn't ready for a marriage commitment, he was already overcommitted to running his three companies. But instead, here she was ready to hop into bed with the wrong man – for the wrong reasons. Gray, Ethan's best man at the wedding. Gray, who'd found her after her embarrassing

3

rejection, hunched up behind a bush, crying, her wedding dress torn and dirty. He'd comforted her, taken her for a ride on the back of his Harley to the beach where she'd ended up in his arms.

But having sex with Gray, because she was angry with Ethan, was wrong on so many levels. Gray, a leather-clad biker with a conquest in every town, was only out for what he could get. Succumbing to his charms would only end in more heart-break. Or at the very least, a hot and steamy one-night stand with no meaning.

And that would make her feel cheap.

Resisting the inevitable pull his smoldering blue eyes, wild shoulder-length fair hair and strong tantalizing fingers were having on her libido, Tabitha pushed him away. "I'm sorry, Gray. I can't do this."

Gray's grip on her arms tightened. He yanked her closer. "Admit it. You want me!"

(No, no, he was still an A-hole... I chewed on one nail, deleted his words...replaced them.)

Gray instantly let her go and stepped back. "Are you sure, Tabitha?"

(Yes, that was better. Made Gray seem softer, more caring...)

Tabitha blinked up at him. "Think about it, Gray. You'd be cashing in on your best friend's wedding night, and I'd be getting back at him through you."

Eyes never leaving hers, he gently brushed a lock of hair from her face...

"Oof!" My chair clattered to the ground with a loud thump, as did my rear end, while my left elbow connected with an unyielding steel table leg.

"Oh dear, I'm so sorry. I wasn't looking where I was going."

The voice was deep, the plain brown shoes and cabbage green socks in my direct line of vision suggested male. A picture of Gray, with his aquiline nose, long shoulder length fair hair and sexy dimple drifted into my mind. Was this a re-enactment of a romantic 'cute meet' from one of my novels? Was this the man who would finally sweep me off my feet? If so, he'd certainly done a good job so far. I was sitting on the cafeteria floor.

Nursing my throbbing elbow, I peered up through a curtain of dark hair, and sighed. Nah. No romance hero here. It was only Harry Driscoll, a man in his late fifties. One of the many competitors who rocked up at a dog show week after week, hoping for a ribbon or trophy to take home.

Bottling my disappointment as merely a typical malfunction in my oh-so-predictable-and boring life, I gritted my teeth, ready to give the man leaning over me a piece of my mind. To tell him exactly what I thought of a guy who charged through a cafeteria like a bull in a china-shop, knocking inoffensive women off their chairs.

But something in the man's expression stopped me. Something that reminded me of a skinny ginger cat I'd found on death-row at an RSPCA facility two years ago when I'd been dropping off warm blankets for the animals. Panic? Fear? Dread? I'd taken the cat home with me, named him Flerken after Captain Marvel's feline friend, and he'd repaid my kindly act by shredding the sofa. *And* the lounge room curtains. *And* several important documents he took a dislike to on the kitchen table…

But Flerken was still around, still a little psycho, and spending most of his day on the desk in my office, either sleeping, destroying my papers, or stretched out across my keyboard preventing me from working.

"Here, let me help you up." The man sent a quick anxious glance over his shoulder before extending one hand and pulling me to my feet.

"Where's the fire?" I shook my head.

His returning smile, lips merely flattened, eyes everywhere but on me, said he didn't really get my poor joke.

"I'm sorry," he repeated, brushing what looked like dirt from the floor off my denim jacket. "Are you hurt?"

"I'll survive," I said. "But what about you? Harry, isn't it? I've seen you around the shows. Love your Giant Schnauzer, by the way. He's a real eye-catcher."

Harry's strained features softened momentarily and for the first time he actually looked at me. "Yes, Scout's as cute as a button. You should see him carrying his little toy ducky around the house. Such a gentle giant."

"You seem upset, Harry. Is there anything I can do to help?"

Harry's eyes connected with mine for a moment, as though he wanted to confide in me, and then he blinked, sent an anxious glance over his shoulder and his expression closed down. "No, no, I'm just running late to meet a-a…friend." He straightened his tie and sent another half-smile in my general direction. "Now, you have a good day."

And he was gone. Just like that.

I watched the man continue on through the cafeteria. He stumbled into another chair before reaching the door at the end and then disappeared through the opening.

Was he drunk? I hadn't picked up on the smell of alcohol, but I'd heard vodka was odorless. Maybe the poor guy had received bad news and drowned his sorrows in a bottle. And then I remembered the haunted look in his eyes. Was he in trouble? Was someone chasing him?

I straightened my chair and sat down again, tugging my laptop towards me ready to continue converting bad boy Gray into a realistic romance hero…but I'd lost the flow. The owner of the lovable Giant Schnauzer, had pushed both Gray and Tabitha's predicament out of my mind. Harry Driscoll was normally such a sweet little man. Who would he be running from?

"Aha! So, this is where you're hiding out. Heard on the grapevine that a certain evil fox terrier was kicked out of the showring for peeing on the judge's posh knee-high boots." My best friend, Abigail Truelove, grinning akin to the fictional Cheshire Cat, plonked herself down in the empty chair across from me and wiggled her eyebrows. "Now, that wouldn't be our saintly and oh-so-well-mannered *Sir Willowby of Cornwall*, would it?"

My other best friend, Dana Fox, her grin equally as large as Abi's, her hands overflowing with food – a sandwich, two chocolate biscuits and a jumbo-sized cream cake – carefully eased into the other empty chair and arranged her goodies on the table in front of her. While never putting on weight, Dana could eat her way through more food than both Abi and I put together. Probably needed the energy to keep up with her two over-active sprogs, both under four. If that was me, I'd need Valium to cope – not food. "And I also heard the poor judge had a fit of the vapors and had to go for a lie down." Dana shook her head in mock sorrow. "And to think Abi and I missed out on the entertainment because we were both competing for Best Hound in Group in another show ring. Unbelievable."

While Dana showed a stunning greyhound called Penelope, the gentlest dog in the universe, Abi's champion standard dachshund, Chloe, was also a regular contender for Best Hound in Group.

"Well, don't keep me in suspense. How'd you go?" I asked, purposely steering the discussion away from Busta's misdeeds.

"Judge barely gave us a second look. The Halliday's Afghan, *Butterwings Shillough,* performed like the star she is and swept all before her. And the judge gave runner-up to a basset hound." Dana tipped her head to one side and another grin wrinkled the corners of her lips. "But getting back to Busta's classy act today, did Lady Hamilton-Davies *really* threaten to neuter him if he ever came under her again?"

I decided the Busta story was getting old. Pretending I hadn't heard the question, I saved the latest *Three's A Crowd* document and shut down my laptop. Gray and Tabitha could stew in their own dramas for a while longer. Might sort themselves out and decide whether they wanted to get hot and personal. Or not. I wouldn't get any more work done with my friends here, and anyway, I was hungry. Trying to squeeze in some writing time before leaving for the dog show this morning, I'd ended up running too late to indulge in breakfast. It was now two in the afternoon. And that sandwich with the crisp lettuce, cheese, tomato, cucumber, avocado and what smelt like roast chicken sitting on the table in front of Dana looked tempting.

Then, without warning, Harry's frightened face popped into my head again. The more I thought about him, the more I believed he was running from someone when he knocked me over. I'd always thought of Harry as old-school. A gentleman. And to crash into me and then continue on with only a quick sorry, was not his style at all.

A chill came out of nowhere and scuttled in spiked boots up my spine. "Did either of you happen to see Harry Driscoll just before you entered the cafeteria?"

Abi frowned. "The guy with the Giant Schnauzer? No, but I did see him earlier in the day. He was talking to that oh-so-charming poodle breeder, Stephen Channing, over by the secretary's office." Abi's frown deepened. "Although, when I say, *talking,* I mean Stevie was being his usual bullying self, shouting at Harry and waving his arms, while poor Harry was huddled over, trying to shrink into a ball the size of a chocolate Jaffa. What Stevie's partner, Chi, sees in that man, I'll never know."

"Why do you want to know about Harry Driscoll?" asked Dana, biting into her cream cake with the delicacy of a mountain lion.

"It's probably nothing, but he blew through the cafeteria like a tornado on speed a few minutes before you arrived. Knocked me off my chair, sort of helped me to my feet, and then took off again. And by the expression on his face, plus his body language, I'd say the Monster from the Black Lagoon was after him with a well-sharpened pitchfork."

"Interesting." Abi had that glint in her eye. The one she gets when she smells a mystery. A month ago, she'd tripped over the dead body of the bimbo her ex-boyfriend was cheating on her with, which prompted the three of us to reinvent *The Gumshoe Chicks*, a sleuthing group formed way back in our high-school days, to solve the murder. I shivered. While Abi and Dana, my two gung-ho friends, relish taking on bad guys, me, I'm happy when I'm slap-bang in the world of my make-believe characters, channeling them into happy-ever-afters.

Getting involved with real life villains? Not so much.

Dana's tongue flicked out and she licked cream from the corner of her lips. When she spoke, her voice was matter-of-fact. "Did Harry say why he was in a hurry?"

"Something about running late to meet a friend."

Dana shrugged one shoulder as if the matter was closed. "Well, there you go. Mystery solved."

I screwed up my nose. Maybe Dana was right. Maybe I was dramatizing the whole affair. Still, Harry's behavior was odd and I couldn't get the image of his strained panicky face out of my head.

Chewing on a thumbnail which was already down to the quick, I felt around in my jacket pocket with the other hand. I was sure I'd dropped a packet of gum in there before I left home. Nothing helped settle my nerves like a packet of gum. And let's face it, gum tasted a hundred percent better than thumbnail. "Maybe you're right, Dana. But if he was meeting a friend – why did he look so terrified?"

"Might have had something to do with meeting a woman," put in Abi. "Perhaps Harry is having an affair?"

"In which case, Harry's love life is none of our business," said Dana.

"No, Harry's a gentleman. He's not like that. He wouldn't cheat on his wife."

"Molly, you are such a baby when it comes to relationships," said Abi, frowning. "I don't know how you manage to write all those steamy romance novels without learning something about the ways of men. You've barely said a dozen words to Harry Driscoll in the two years you've been showing Chloe. How would *you* know he's not like that?"

"Because he's a gentleman," I mumbled, my hand closing over the packet of gum in my pocket. "And gentlemen don't have affairs."

Abi gave a hoot while Dana chuckled into the last bite of her cream cake. She wiped her lips with the back of her hand and reached for her sandwich. Food was rarely eaten in regular order when Dana was hungry. What with a full-time job running her own mobile dog wash, *Hydro Hound*, plus two gorgeous but demanding kids and a husband who adored her, Dana had learned to grab food whenever a small block of time opened for her. The order of eating that food was the last of her concerns. "Did he say anything specific to make you think he was in trouble?"

Along with the gum, a crumpled piece of paper that hadn't been in my pocket before I entered the cafeteria, tumbled out.

"Where did that come from?" I said, attempting to flatten the paper out on the table. "It's not mine."

And then I remembered Harry brushing non-existent dust from my jacket after he'd helped me from the floor.

"It was Harry. He must have slipped this into my pocket while brushing me down."

We all stared at the three words scrawled in black text across the paper. The words that sent my heart into orbit and Abi and Dana's eyebrows somewhere up around their hairline.

YOU'RE DEAD HARRY.

"Right." Abi's chair made a scratching sound on the wooden floor as she bounced to her feet. "Looks like we have another mystery to solve."

"Hang on," said Dana, the voice of reason. "Why should *we* get involved? It's not like Harry Driscoll is our best friend. We only know him enough to say hello and nod our head when we pass him at a dog show."

"What? So, we're going to sit back, knowing Harry's been threatened, and do nothing about it?"

"Nooo." Dana rolled her eyes. "But we're only going to *find* Harry. Advise him to go to the police. Ask him if he knows who sent the note. That's all." She reached for the other half of her sandwich before hefting her family-sized bag over her shoulder. "'Cos you *do* realize this is a death threat? And that means there's a wannabe murderer out there who wrote it?"

A wannabe murderer…

I sat staring down at the three words on the crumpled sheet of paper. I knew 'terrified' when I saw it and Harry had been radiating all the signs.

And no wonder…

But did I really want to find out who sent that note?

www.ingramcontent.com/pod-product-compliance
Lightning Source LLC
Chambersburg PA
CBHW020640260626
47157CB00008B/2845